Angela and the Enchanted Bell

By

Sheilah Rogers

*This is the first of the series
I hope you enjoy it
Love Sheilah*

This book is a work of fiction. Places, events, and situations in this story are purely fictional. Any resemblance to actual persons, living or dead, is coincidental.

© 2003 by Sheilah Rogers. All rights reserved.

No part of this book may be reproduced, stored in a retrieval system, or transmitted by any means, electronic, mechanical, photocopying, recording, or otherwise, without written permission from the author.

ISBN: 1-4107-6935-6 (e-book)
ISBN: 1-4107-6934-8 (Paperback)
ISBN: 1-4107-9569-1 (Dust Jacket)

Library of Congress Control Number: 2003094299

This book is printed on acid free paper.

Printed in the United States of America
Bloomington, IN

1stBooks - rev. 10/28/03

CONTENTS

CHAPTER		PAGE
1	The Secret of the Bell Charm	1
2	The Kingdom of Trillan	12
3	Pets for Angela	26
4	The Quest	36
5	A Surprising Encounter	49
6	The Accident	56
7	The Report	62
8	The Meeting In The Stone House	70
9	An Uncertain Future	83
10	The Triumphant Return Of A Queen	87
11	The Magic Of Invisibility	98
12	A Playhouse At Last	104
13	Confessions	108
14	Dangerous Information	117
15	The Trap Is Sprung	129
16	Release From Captivity	141
17	Astonishing Revelations	150
18	Stavro's Dreams Fulfilled	167
19	News Of Annwynn At Last	181
20	Plans To Be Made	190
21	Annwynn's Ordeal	198
22	Escape From Ilsted	211
23	Azoria	220
24	The Capture of Bowdren	222
25	Stavro To The Rescue	226
26	The Healing Room	232
27	Stavro's Perilous Journey	239
28	The Grand Ball	249
29	Vanished from Sight	265
30	Darvith's Worst Nightmare	272
31	The Search	277
32	Griffin's Just Reward	284

AUTHOR'S NOTE

Everyone, I am sure, remembers as a child being able to see imaginary beings. These were magical creatures that were present during our daily activities that others could not see. Only our eyes viewed playmates with whom we experienced wonderful adventures; adventures that we could never share with adults. This story, and others to follow, describes such happenings.

Much of my early childhood was spent in solitude, but thanks to a vivid imagination, I was never lonely. To this day I can remember meeting with 'the little people' as an elderly Irish neighbor used to call them, who even at her great age, claimed to be able to see dancing in the tall grasses at dawn and dusk.

I am an archaeologist, a professional artist and a mother who has traveled extensively, living abroad for several years. One of my interests has always been ancient folklore.

Angela and the Enchanted Bell

This is the first of several stories about a bright, mischievous and very independent young girl.

Our heroine Angela, and her mother Sarah, a writer of historical novels, recently moved from a large city to a cottage situated in the outskirts of a small community.

Angela's adventures began when she found a tiny bell resting on the mossy bank of a stream, in the meadow near her new home. The bell allowed her access into mysterious realms, realms filled with intrigue and interesting inhabitants. The excitement builds from her first encounter with Darvith, a beautiful fairy-like creature from the land of Trillan, to her visits to other secret Kingdoms.

CHAPTER 1

The Secret of the Bell Charm

Angela was filled with expectation as she ran barefoot down the path that led from her new home to the surrounding forest and meadow. Rain had fallen the night before and puddles of water still lingered here and there. She deliberately splashed through each of them as she raced toward her first stop on this beautiful morning. The lovely brook on their property had been calling to her for days and she was anxious to see if there were any fish, or better still, frogs, in her stream.

The fragrance from the new growth of early spring was almost overpoweringly sweet. As she continued down the path a pleasant pungency added to the mix, drifting up from where the Skunk Cabbages grew in the boggy, lower section of the property. All of these wondrous new scents helped to rid her memory of the strong smell of the cleaning solution that she and her mother Sarah had been using all week. The cottage was finally ready; it fairly shone from top to bottom. They were able to move in yesterday. At last she was free to explore!

Angela smiled whenever she thought of their new home. From their first glimpse, Angela and Sarah felt that the cottage had somehow jumped from one of the pages of a book of fairytales. It was such an enchanting sight with its shingle roof, rose covered stonework, leaded windows and deep window seats. Adding to its charm were splashes of vivid colour in the surrounding gardens where Hollyhocks, Delphiniums and Larkspurs bloomed amongst the tangle of weeds. They had looked at each other that first day and made an instant unanimous decision.

The realtor, Mr. Porkwitt, a plump little man with a look of perpetual worry, mentioned that the former owners had actually built the cottage, and indeed lived in it for over thirty years. "A couple by the name of Hopton, Adrian and Diana." He confided in a hushed tone as he leant toward Sarah, "They kept pretty much to themselves; didn't have any youngins'. Strange set up...Odd them living out here all that time and not mixin' with the town folk." He tipped his head downward and looked up at Sarah and added solemnly, "Oh there was plenty of talk about them I can tell you...plenty of talk." Mr. Porkwitt scratched his bald little head and continued. "Then one day, out of the blue, Adrian walked into my office, handed me the keys and told me to sell the place. That was three years ago, and no one has seen or heard from them since. I don't know what I'll do with the money from the sale. I guess I'll just bank it in their name." He scratched his head again and added, "Funny business though, isn't it. Just thought I should tell you about the mysterious disappearance before you bought the place." His forehead was now deeply furrowed with worry and his small blue eyes blinked repeatedly. Tiny droplets of perspiration formed on his upper lip. He sniffed three short little sniffs and once again scratched his head.

Angela suppressed a giggle. He looked amazingly like one of the gentle little piglets in the nursery rhyme waiting for the wolf to blow down his straw house.

Sarah had the same thought and winked at her daughter. She then took Mr. Porkwitt's hand in hers and thanked him for being so kind, quickly adding, "We still want to purchase the house." His face shone with contentment and relief. He had finally sold the Hopton cottage.

That was days ago, and now here at last, the stream lay before her, glistening in the bright sunlight. The sheer pleasure of the moment filled her senses and she sighed deeply, and then murmured softly, for she often talked to herself, "I'm going to sit at the bank of the stream and put my feet into the water."

Making herself comfortable on a cushion of moss, she slowly eased her feet into the stream. The water felt blissfully cool and she watched contentedly as the water washed away the last of the mud that had clung to her toes. She was completely lost in the moment when all at once, something that resembled a toad, jumped off to her right only to quickly disappear into a deeper pool further along in the stream. Angela was momentarily startled and then began to laugh at herself.

At just that moment, a bright object on the moss beside her caught her attention. When she picked it up to examine it more closely, she discovered it to be a tiny golden bell. "Why how exquisite!" She exclaimed as she examined her newly found treasure. It was very beautiful and finely carved with what appeared to be a kind of writing. The sunlight caught the delicately traced pattern and the bell shone like the finest of gold; to her delight and amazement, it chimed when she tilted it and a wonderful sound rang forth. A melody so clear and true that Angela found it difficult to believe that such a tiny bell could have produced it. She examined it more closely and decided that it must be a piece of jewelry, perhaps a charm from a bracelet. "Yes! Of course, that would explain its beauty." Yet she couldn't help wondering how such a tiny object would have found its way to this remote place.

Unable to resist, she tilted the tiny bell and once again the lovely chime rang forth.

All at once, a beautiful, human-like, creature appeared. A tiny, perfectly formed female, no more than eleven inches tall, with waist length, tightly curled blond hair and very bright green eyes. She wore a long dress made from a sheer printed fabric in pale green. Angela thought she was the most beautiful...she paused in thought...the most beautiful what? For once in her life she was at a loss for words. All she could do was stare at her visitor with eyes wide with amazement.

The beautiful creature smiled up at her and said comfortingly. "Do not be afraid for I will not harm you." Her bright green eyes now danced with mischief as she continued with obvious amusement. "No, I am not a fairy."

Angela, more nervous than ever, asked with a slight tremor in her voice, "How...how did you know what I was thinking?"

The enchanting creature laughed again. "I can read your mind of course." She sighed mockingly. "Alas, it wasn't much of a challenge...quite a primitive specimen really."

Before Angela could respond to this insult, the tiny creature began to speak again. "I do hope that I haven't been too direct. I apologize if I've offended you." Then smiling kindly, she introduced herself. "My name is Darvith and I live in the land of Trillan. This lovely stream shields the entrance to that land." Darvith smiled again and her voice softened. She explained, "The bell you have found is one of our control devices. It has many different and important uses. The lovely sound initiates a variety of spells, depending on the number of times it chimes."

Angela whispered, her voice now filled with awe. "Then it's magical. Cool! Can I make wishes come true with it? I can think of a million wishes." She was filled with excitement!

Darvith lifted one eyebrow and commented dryly, "I'm sure you can...however it is only 'magical' if a Trillan uses it, and most certainly not for anything as trivial as wishes." She added somewhat derisively, "You, a mere Earthling, could ring it forever and nothing would happen."

Angela grinned at her mischievously and replied, "Well now that's not true, 'you' happened." Quickly adding, "And I only rang the bell twice."

Darvith smiled in spite of herself. She was beginning to like this Earthling child. She continued with a more serious tone to her voice. "I'm afraid that particular happening had more to do with the fact that you 'possessed' the bell, than the fact that you 'rang' it." You see we were curious to learn if you were in some way helping our enemy the Elgats, or just an Earthling who accidentally found the gateway to our land.

She continued gravely, a frown now visible on her lovely face. "Our country is being systematically raided by the Elgats, a cruel, toad-like, people, who live somewhere in the meadow behind you." She corrected her last statement. "To be truthful, we don't really know where their land lies. We feel it must be close because their raids are so frequent." She added thoughtfully, "The fact that they have discovered our shielded entrance seems to suggest that we have a traitor in Trillan."

Darvith paused for a moment. Three enormous Monarch butterflies were fluttering around them. One paused to rest on Angela's knee while the other two positioned themselves on a nearby rock.

"What exquisite creatures!" Darvith exclaimed with obvious wonderment in her voice. "I have never before seen them in flight! How beautiful they are!" Once again the butterflies circled the pair then flew off. In doing so a wing brushed gently against Darvith and showered her with a light dusting of iridescent powder. She laughed softly and murmured, "How wondrous the realm of the Earthlings is! I wonder if its inhabitants appreciate its great beauty." Quickly adding a barely audible, "I doubt it."

Darvith sighed deeply and continued with her explanation, "You see, we use the bells, like the one you are holding, when we enter the realm of the earthlings and earth creatures. Just one chime will put all the creatures in the meadow into a trance, and give us enough time to collect the flowers and roots we use in our medicines. Thus, even the butterflies sleep." Consequently no one is hurt. The animals remember nothing, and the earthlings attribute the loss of time to daydreaming."

Darvith laughed, somewhat derisively, and observed loudly, "You earthlings seem to do rather a lot of daydreaming. I believe that it's due to all that unused brain." Then she added with still more laughter, "I often wonder how you manage to accomplish the simplest of tasks, when you use such a teeny tiny piece; it is SO overworked and SO undernourished. One of the 'Great Mysteries' I suppose." Darvith was now bent over with laughter.

Angela was left with the distinct impression that Trillans felt Earthlings inferior creatures. She smiled, Something had just come to mind.

Darvith's eyes once again danced with mischief. She had been reading Angela's thoughts and said scornfully. "Ah yes, but what's the advantage of being a giant if you haven't got a giant brain to go with your size. You're not even using a quarter of what you have...most of it is still

Angela and the Enchanted Bell

sleeping and likely to continue to do so...and yes, I do think Earthlings are rather dim."

Angela glanced sharply at Darvith and frowned. Her thoughts had obviously been read again and she was annoyed.

Darvith smiled and offered an apology. "Please forgive me, I'm not known for my tact. Most of my fellow Trillans, think I'm impossibly blunt. I'm sure you'd agree, wouldn't you Angela? Please forgive my rudeness; stay with me a little longer."

In truth Angela had no intention of leaving. She wasn't ready to end this intriguing encounter; in fact she was still trying to convince herself that this rather obnoxious little creature actually existed.

Once again Darvith had read Angela's thoughts. She laughed merrily and answered. "I can assure you that this 'obnoxious little creature', your very thoughts, does exist and needs your help. Please say you will help us?"

Angela smiled but insisted that she would have to know more about Darvith's request before she would agree to help.

Darvith smiled and replied, "That seems reasonable. First tell me where you found the bell and if you noticed any other creatures in the area at the same time. Tell me everything you can remember no matter how insignificant it might seem."

Angela related all that had taken place by the stream and Darvith listened attentively. "Obviously the frog you saw was an Elgat and he or she dropped the bell they had just stolen from us when they saw you. This is certainly good news from our point of view." She added with a giggle, "Although it's hard to imagine why 'any' creature would be frightened of an Earthling."

Darvith quickly put her hand to her mouth in what seemed a mock gesture to Angela. "Oh dear! I've been rude again haven't I? Well you know one can't change one's personality overnight; it might take years...and years. I'm afraid my dear you are just going to have to get used to it. However, one thing I promise you Angela. I will never let any harm come to you." With that vow given, she gently touched Angela's arm. She spoke slowly and with great conviction, "I have a plan, it includes you and you must be very brave."

Angela began to feel very uneasy and wondered just what this tiny creature had in mind when she said 'very brave'. How could she possibly be of any use to the Trillans? Who were they? What were they? Angela experienced a brief sensation of panic but her curiosity soon overcame her fear. She inquired somewhat tentatively, "What is it you wish me to do?"

Darvith replied with great enthusiasm, "Why you must return to Trillan with me and meet with the Elders of course!" She continued confidently, "You will keep the bell you now hold for the time being, and I will give you the power to use it." She lifted an eyebrow and added, "However, the power will be limited. It will be a special magic for you alone and for one specific purpose. When you ring the bell 3 times, you will be for a time, the size of a Trillan child. In order to regain your normal size, you will again ring it 3 times." Darvith smiled and shrugged her diminutive shoulders, adding, "Very simple instructions you must admit, even for an Earthling."

Angela's already pink cheeks reddened with anger. She had almost reached the end of her patience with this pint-sized tyrant, but she managed to remain silent.

Darvith smiled winningly, completely unaffected by Angela's angry silence. She had no intention of pretending to be someone she wasn't. And it was common knowledge that Earthlings were densely stupid. Still, she had to admit to herself that this particular Earthling might yet be useful and she didn't appear to be all that dim. Perhaps she should make an effort to modify her behavior. She patted the child's arm in a manner that was meant to be comforting.

Angela was beginning to find the gesture very annoying and intended to comment on it, but first she decided to ask Darvith about something else that had been troubling her. She asked innocently, "Won't the bell be too heavy for me when I'm as tiny as you?"

Darvith had bristled at the word 'tiny' and scowled. "Don't be stupid! Really! You can't be that dense! Haven't you noticed that the bell is weightless?"

Angela stammered, "I...I thought it was light because it is so small."

An exasperated Darvith sighed deeply and remained silent for a long moment. Then quite suddenly, she smiled and explained, "It's your size. You're so large I tend to forget you are only a child after all." Then clapping her tiny hands, she commanded, "Ring the bell! Quickly now, we have no time to waste!"

Angela stared at Darvith in disbelief and replied, "I can't go with you now! You can't expect me to go with you...just like that! This is all too weird! I'm going back to the cottage. You can keep the bell. And if all Trillans are as rude as you are, I don't care to meet them, I have other things to do with my time."

Darvith stamped her foot and shouted, "Don't be so sensitive! I'm sorry Angela, but the truth is that many lives may soon be lost. The Elgats haven't harmed anyone yet, but there is bound to be some sort of confrontation soon. You wouldn't want that on your conscience now would you? Think of all those innocent little Trillan bodies lying about...once so full of life...gone forever."

Unexpectedly Darvith burst out laughing. "Why you little monster! You were picturing my lifeless body laid out stiff and cold. Have I really made you that angry?" Now Angela joined in the laughter.

Darvith used the moment to cast a spell. It was Trillan magic. Angela now willingly agreed to meet with Darvith tomorrow at 11AM. Darvith felt some pangs of guilt but reasoned that it had to be done. There was no other alternative. She would guard Angela while she was in Trillan...Indeed she would give her own life if necessary. She gazed up at the little earthling and smiled. "I must leave you now. Don't be late tomorrow! Your presence in Trillan is of the utmost importance. Just ring the bell and I'll appear. Don't be frightened; I will protect you."

Darvith then dove into the stream and disappeared from sight.

Angela was left with a strange uneasy feeling. What was happening to her? She held the tiny bell in her hand and wondered why it seemed so natural to her that she should have agreed to go with Darvith to Trillan. It seemed as normal to her as going to town. She wondered why she had no desire to tell her mother of today's events. Angela had always told her mother everything that happened during her day. She continued to sit on the mossy bank, gazing into the stream, allowing her thoughts to drift slowly with the current. The rippling sound was soothing and almost hypnotic. It seemed to be saying Trillan...Trillan...Trillan...come to Trillan.

While Angela was not a beautiful child, she did have a wonderful presence. She radiated a certain ethereal quality. Delicate China-Doll colouring played a large part in this impression. Added to this, her glistening silver-white curls darted around her face like tiny silver wings, giving her an angelic appearance. This was both misleading to the observer, and at times very useful to a child who was forever getting into some kind of mischief.

Angela's eyes were magnificent. Indeed, they were her best feature. Everyone noticed them. They were a deep azure blue, framed by thick black lashes. The unusual combination of dark brows and eyelashes with silver white hair always elicited a comment from the people that she met. Some had even accused Sarah of allowing her daughter to use mascara. Angela wisely ignored the questions and ceased trying to explain her colouring to everyone who asked. She no longer told people of the accident that killed her father and caused her jet-black hair to turn to silver. After all, even the doctors weren't sure why it happened. And besides it wasn't anyone else's business. She was certain of that! She, like Darvith, did not suffer fools gladly.

All at once Angela laughed out loud and turned away from the stream. "If Darvith had been watching me, she'd say 'isn't that just like an Earthling, daydreaming her life away.' I guess I've just proven her point." She laughed again and continued talking to herself as she ran up the path to the cottage, arriving just in time to help prepare supper and set the table. Soon Angela and Sarah were chatting happily while enjoying their delicious meal. They both felt completely at home in their new surroundings.

The cottage was more than just a shelter to them. It had a welcoming energy that somehow made them feel both comforted and safe, like the shelter of loving arms. Angela commented on this feeling when Sarah tucked her in that night. "This house likes us Mom."

Sarah nodded her head in agreement. "I feel it too darling. I know we are going to be very happy here." She kissed Angela gently and murmured, "Goodnight sweetheart. Sleep well." Then quietly left the room.

CHAPTER 2

The Kingdom of Trillan

Angela awoke at daybreak. The wonderful aroma of freshly brewed coffee, greeted her as she descended the stairs. When she checked the tiny warming oven in the stove she found a breakfast of bacon and eggs with toast awaiting her. Angela poured some fresh orange juice and happily began her breakfast.

Sarah was already at work. Angela could hear the tap, tap of the typewriter keys hitting paper. She smiled inwardly. Sarah refused to use a computer even though it would make her work easier, claiming that she was inspired by the sound of the typewriter keys hitting paper. It obviously worked, thought Angela. Sarah had written three very successful novels and was now working on her fourth.

Angela loved her mother very much and admired her courage. The decision to leave their wonderful apartment in the city had been a difficult one for both of them. The accident that had killed her father had changed their lives in so many ways. The big apartment seemed to amplify their loss.

Angela and the Enchanted Bell

After many long discussions, they both decided that a move to the country would be for the best. It was to be a new beginning for both of them. Angela would leave her overcrowded school in the city and instead attend a small country school. She knew she would miss all of her old friends, especially her best friend Mugsy, but she would make some new friends. All would not be lost for Mugsy would be spending all of next July with them. Angela could hardly wait.

There was something else to be excited about. Pets had not been allowed in their city apartment. Now she was going to have a cat and a dog. Sarah promised to check the newspaper this very day. Angela was very, very happy.

After finishing the dishes and tidying up, she called in to see her mother.

Sarah, as always, greeted her with a big hug. "Good morning sweetheart! Where are you off to now?"

Angela gave one of her sunniest smiles and replied, "I just thought I'd like to play in the meadow for awhile. Perhaps I'll visit with the Trillans. The tiny people who live there."

Sarah smiled warmly at her daughter, and after giving her another hug, and said; "Don't forget to return from your visit with the 'Trillans' in time for lunch. We're going to town this afternoon."

"Don't worry mom, I won't forget!" Angela called out merrily as she raced out the door. She was very excited as ran down the path to the stream. The tiny bell was held tightly in her hand. She still found it hard to believe that the events that took place yesterday were more than just a daydream...just another of what her mother called 'flights of fancy'. At last she reached the mossy bank. She immediately sat down cross-legged and waited.

Darvith appeared in an instant and peevishly began issuing orders. "Well! What are you waiting for, some kind of invitation! Ring the stupid bell! Don't tell me you've forgotten my instructions already!" She might just as well have added, you little moron.

Angela, who was not used to being addressed in this rude manner, hid her annoyance and hurt as best she could. Perhaps all tiny creatures are bad tempered. Perhaps it has something to do with their size. Her bottom lip trembled. But she forced a tiny smile. She wasn't going to let this little tyrant see her cry.

Darvith sighed deeply and with great impatience grudgingly offered an apology of sorts, quickly explaining to Angela that there wasn't a great deal of time to waste. The Elders were always busy and didn't like to be kept waiting.

Angela agreed to hurry, but she had just one question that she wanted to ask first.

Darvith was now tapping her foot. She snapped, "Well! Get on with it! What is it you wish to ask?" The sharp edge of her voice barely disguised.

Angela, undaunted by this rude behavior, continued with her question. "Will you assure me that I will be able to regain my normal size and return to my life as it is now?"

Darvith stared at Angela in utter disbelief. "Wool! It's like talking to wool!" She shouted angrily! "Of course you will return to your normal size! You can't imagine that you would be of any use to us if you were our size! You...You...Earthling! Ring the blasted bell! Now!!"

Angela took a deep breath and rang the bell three times. Her first sensation was one of exhilaration, followed by a shiver, and in seconds, she had shrunk to a height of about 6 inches. All at once the peaceful meadow seemed a dangerous place. A jungle filled with menacing creatures. Why she wasn't even as tall as the Forget Me Nots that covered the bank of the stream. The Stream! It was like a raging river now, it roared past at a frightening rate and was filled with menacing whirlpools and rapids.

Angela was suddenly very frightened and wanted desperately to return to her normal size and be safe once more. Darvith gave her what was meant to be a comforting hug, then held the child's hand, as a golden light appeared to be surfacing in the stream. Darvith explained to the uneasy child that the Elders must have observed her fright and decided to send the Royal Coach. She smiled and said, "Now you won't have to dive into the water with me Angela. That should make you happy. Yes?"

Angela was speechless. Had Darvith really believed that she would dive into that...that...torrent? Never in a million years would she have been so foolish. "Never!" She said aloud.

Darvith smiled knowingly at the little earthling then focused her attention on a golden capsule that appeared to be breaking the surface of the water just in front of where they were standing. It moved easily toward them and upon reaching the bank of the stream the top opened up, revealing a cushioned area where one would expect passengers to sit.

Because of its shape, Angela expected the conveyance to move back and forth, as a canoe would have, should one be foolish enough to step into a canoe. Angela didn't like boats of any kind. However, much to her relief, this craft remained perfectly still when she stepped into it. Once seated, she felt safe and surprisingly calm. Calm enough to ask another question of Darvith. "How could the Elders see that I was frightened?"

Darvith ignored the question by pretending not to hear it, while motioning to Angela that they were about to enter Trillan and not to be nervous. The stream vanished and they passed through a deep rose light to emerge in a lovely shimmering lake.

Angela turned to Darvith and asked somewhat dazedly, "What...what happened to the stream?" Once again Darvith ignored the question.

Angela scowled at her. She was becoming very annoyed. She was there as a favor to the Trillans, at least Darvith could have the courtesy to answer her questions. She sighed in exasperation. "Well, will you at least thank the Elders for me? It was very kind of them to send the Royal Coach. I really appreciated it."

Darvith smiled and replied, "In a moment you will be able to thank them for yourself. Be patient."

At just that moment the roof of the conveyance lifted and Angela gasped in surprise. Her wildest expectations had not prepared her for her first glimpse of Trillan. The land was bathed in a wonderful golden light. A light that made her feel very relaxed and calm. All of her fears quickly vanished.

Buildings, unlike any she had ever seen, were placed in a wide circle surrounding the lake. They appeared to be made from Crystal, Gold and a white marble-like stone and reflected the golden light in such a way that made them appear to glow, just as if each building had a halo.

The land itself, at least from where she was now standing, seemed to consist of rolling hills that were covered with grasses and flowering plants of every shape, size and colour.

The whole scene was one of perfection. This was how Angela imagined Heaven to be and expected to see Angels with harps of gold at any moment. She smiled inwardly. Well Darvith was no Angel so that pretty much ruled out Heaven.

Darvith grabbed Angela's hand and pulled her toward a great multi-storied building. She frowned at the awe-struck child and commanded peevishly, "Angela! Do hurry! We are late enough as it is!"

The sheer magnificence of Trillan's Capital City had robbed Angela of all thoughts until Darvith broke the spell. Now, suddenly she was full of questions. "Tell me more about the Elgats?" She asked, while looking up at Darvith, and at the same time thinking how strange it felt to be so tiny. 'It's all relative.' Mr. Chisholm, her 4th grade teacher in the city would have said...or would he have said irrelevant?' She smiled to herself and decided that he would have said both.

Darvith scowled at the youngster and exclaimed in exasperation, "What a scrambled brain you have! It has absolutely no power of organization! How do you manage to get through the day without some serious kind of accident?"

Angela laughed out loud, in spite of the insult, then, pleaded, somewhat breathlessly, "Can we walk a little slower? I'm not able to keep up with you."

Darvith looked down at the little girl and felt some pity for her. "Oh all right! Why not? There's only one among them I'd give the time of day to, and he won't care if we're a little late."

She then began to relate some of what she knew of the Elgats. "According to the Elders, the Elgats were once very friendly towards us and we traded freely with them for over a thousand of your years. At that time they were still, as we are, Earthling-like in appearance." She quickly added, while raising an eyebrow, "Alike in appearance only...we are 'far' superior in intelligence. In fact we have many gifts that Earthlings would love to possess."

Angela grinned up at Darvith and agreed. "I'm sure you're right. Please tell me more about the Elgats?"

Darvith gazed into the child's eyes. Satisfied that the interest was genuine, she continued with her history lesson as they walked. "Well, as I was saying, we traded with them. They were said to be an honest, handsome people, with intelligence equal to that of Trillans. There were even some Oathings between our people."

Angela looked up at Darvith questioningly. "Oathings?"

Darvith shuddered involuntarily and replied, "It's an Oath made legal by a special Ceremony that couples two people together. I will never take an Oath with another!

Never!" She continued, "Our Oathings are forever. Can you imagine being tied to another forever? I can't imagine a fate more terrible!" She continued, "I should add, that while the Oathings were tolerated, they were not encouraged, by either community, our cultures were, and probably still are, too incompatible. Their temperament is by nature very violent, whereas ours is peace loving. Certainly not a good set-up for a happy existence under the same roof."

Darvith added with a smile, "Their appearance is striking. While all Trillans have blond, usually tightly curled hair, green eyes and light skin...Elgats have beautiful, wavy black hair and brilliant blue eyes. I must admit it is a very attractive combination."

Angela smiled up at Darvith. "I had long black hair not so long ago."

Darvith's eyes suddenly reflected great sadness. She had not bothered to do a reading of Angela's past and just now learned of the tragedy the lovely little child who was gazing up at her so earnestly, had endured. She was angry with herself for not being more patient, and resolved then and there to be more understanding. She replied, "Yes, I know Angela. You have suffered great sadness for one so young. I'm truly sorry." Darvith smiled down at the child enchantingly. "You would have been a lovely little Elgat."

Angela beamed. Somehow it was important to have won some approval from Darvith. She said softly, "Thank you for the compliment. Please tell me more about the Elgats?"

Darvith continued with a hint of pride in her voice, "First I will tell you more about Trillan. Since Trillan history began, recorded history that is, we have lived in peace. Any problem that might arise, and cannot be settled by simple debate, is taken to the elders. They are an appointed group of men and women who will then gather all of the information and discuss the problem.

When this process had been carried out, they give all the data to the great crystal. It is responsible for the final decision. None of the judgments have ever been questioned because they are always fair and unbiased."

Darvith lifted an eyebrow and stated, "And now you want to learn of Elgat justice. Am I right?"

Angela nodded. "Oh yes. I want to hear all that you will tell me of your people and their enemies. I find it very interesting."

Darvith continued the history lesson. A more serious tone was now evident in her voice. "According to our Texts on Elgat customs, the Elgats settle all of their disputes in a much more violent and forceful way by hand-to-hand, combat, and both men and women settle their disputes in this manner. All men and women are trained to be warriors from a very early age."

Darvith smiled a little ruefully and continued. "I must say that this is one aspect of their society that I find very appealing. I would love to be a warrior and be able to come and go as I please." She added sadly, "Women in Trillan really have very little opportunity to make a life for themselves. There are only two choices, either to Oath with another or serve as an elder. The professions are all closed to us."

Darvith smiled down at Angela. "Ah! But I have strayed from our topic haven't I! "Well as I was saying, they are all warriors and serve in a sort of 'Military' for a time. Their weapons consist of a sword, a dagger, and a net. According to the text, when they fight to end a dispute, they fight to the death of one of the combatants. In their eyes it is the guilty one who dies. You can see how incompatible their system is with ours." Darvith smiled and added with a wink, "Although I must admit I can think of several people in Trillan I would slay if I were a warrior. You will meet one of them soon."

Darvith continued solemnly, "As far as their appearance goes, no one knows why their bodies have changed so drastically, or if the disfigurement is a permanent affliction that they must endure. Our master healers believe that it might have something to do with their diet. We would gladly help them if we could, but it is unlikely that we will be given the opportunity."

Darvith smiled down at Angela. "And that brings me to the reason you were brought to Trillan. We have decided that you will become our protector, at least for the time being. The fact that you, 'The Giant Earthling', are a friend to Trillan and its inhabitants, coupled with the fact that the Elgats are for some unknown reason frightened of you, should be enough to deter them from future raids."

Angela, once again, had an uneasy feeling and inquired, "How many Elgats are there? Do you have any idea Darvith?"

Darvith shook her head and answered, "I've no idea. Then, suddenly aware of Angela's misgivings, she added chidingly, "My goodness! Don't tell me you're frightened! It is 'they' who will be frightened of you! Why the very sight of you, striding through the meadow, will strike terror in their hearts!" Darvith laughed.

"After all, they will have no way of knowing that you are harmless, and alas, not very bright."

Angela scowled. She was about to respond to this latest insult, when Darvith took her hand. Their destination stood before them, the Great Hall of Trillan.

They ascended a broad staircase and entered a golden room with an enormous vaulted ceiling. A beautiful spiral staircase was positioned at one end. Angela thought it was the most graceful structure she had ever seen. At the other end of the room she observed what appeared to be several television sets attached to comfortable looking, high-backed chairs.

Darvith, who had been reading the child's mind, shook her head and said softly, "No. They are not television sets. They are the crystals that hold all of Trillan history.

Angela and the Enchanted Bell

Any citizen can enter the hall at any time and check the various records, mainly births." She went on to explain, "You see, we are forbidden by law to use a name twice. I realize it seems an odd law, but it is a law that is vigorously enforced, and there is severe punishment to anyone who breaks it, 'death', as a matter of fact." She continued, "No one seems to know why it is in place, and many have tried to have it changed, all to no avail. Only one of the Elders voted to keep it, but one vote was all that was needed. The Elder's name is Griffin, and the fact that he wants the law in place must means that it is of some benefit to him. I, personally, believe that he uses the records in some way and he doesn't want them to be cluttered with excessive numbers of the same name. However, as a consequence, our birth records department is very busy all the year round."

Angela was about to ask a question when Darvith raised her finger to her lips in a request for silence. A soft chime sounded as she led Angela to a bench in the center of the room. The Elders were ready for the audience with the little Earthling they had heard so much about.

Angela studied them as they entered the room. They were dressed as she had expected, in long white robes, but the rest of their appearance was a complete surprise to her. Instead of the stern, older faces, she had expected to see, she was greeted by smiling, young-looking beings.

An Elder, who introduced himself as Planus, stepped forward and took her hand in his. In a kind voice he said, "Well Angela, you are quite a sight for us to see. We've never entertained an Earthling before, and indeed have never seen one who resembles 'you' in any way."

Now all of the Elders approached her with great interest, admiring her silver hair and her brilliant blue eyes. These seemed enormous at the moment, as she was experiencing a certain amount of anxiety. This unexpected attention was more than a little unnerving.

Planus was the first to sense her discomfort and said, with a kindly smile, "Now we must all step back and allow Angela to ask any questions she might have of us."

Thus comforted, Angela took a deep breath and smiled at them. She was about to speak when a very handsome young man, who had just joined the group, stepped forward. Scowling, he shook his head and commented angrily, "How can this Earthling child be of any use to us? How dare you disobey my orders and allow Darvith to bring this creature to Trillan!"

Darvith instantly moved to stand in front of the group. She glared at the Elder who had just spoken and stated contemptuously, "Elder Griffin! Had we been able to reach you today, you would have been consulted! You have been absent from the Great Hall from yesterday afternoon until a few minutes ago! We were unable to contact you at your home! Perhaps you will be good enough to leave a message as to where you can be reached the next time you decide to disappear from our capital!" Darvith lifted her chin in defiance.

Angela was very frightened for she could see the rage in Elder Griffin's eyes, and feared that he might strike Darvith. When, much to her astonishment, he smiled and said, "Of course...of course...I am at fault. The next time I leave the capital I will certainly leave notice as to where I can be reached. You are absolutely right Darvith my dear." He moved toward Darvith to take her hand but she cleverly knelt down as if to pick something up from the floor and avoided his outstretched hand.

Thus thwarted, Griffin approached Angela. Again he smiled. It was a smile that in no way engaged his eyes. "Tell me little Earthling, do you honestly think that you can be of any help to us?"

An icy chill ran through Angela's body. This handsome, smiling young man, for some strange reason, terrified her. As if for comfort she reached for the hand of Darvith who now stood by her side, and answered, "I can only try, I don't know if I'll be successful."

Darvith raised her chin again and added with great conviction, "Angela is brave and a friend to Trillan. The Elgats are frightened of her; indeed, frightened enough to drop the 'Trance Bell' they were attempting to steal. It would have been very valuable to them. Out of the goodness of her heart she has agreed to help us. She knows that she doesn't have to, and I believe we are very fortunate to have such an ally. She has nothing to gain from our friendship. She has 'my' complete trust."

The Elders agreed with Darvith and asked if Angela would visit with them at the same time tomorrow when they would have a plan of action to present to her.

Angela wondered if she was the only one who noticed that Griffin remained silent. She agreed to return the next day. Now she was anxious to escape from Elder Griffin's presence and suggested to Darvith that they 'run' back to the shimmering lake where the royal coach sat waiting for them. It was agreed. They raced back, entered the coach and within seconds rested in the stream by the mossy bank.

They jumped out together and Angela immediately rang the bell three times. Nothing happened! She was filled with panic! What could be wrong! Then she glanced over at Darvith and saw that she was bent over, laughing uncontrollably.

Darvith confessed, amid gales of laughter, "Oh! I am sorry Angela. I just 'couldn't' resist the impulse. If you could only see the expression on your face! Forgive me, I can be so wicked. Please ring the bell again, I promise not to interfere."

Again Angela rang the bell three times, this time with the desired result. She glared down at the beautiful little Trillan. "I don't think that was very funny! You'd better promise not to do that again or you can find another 'giant' to help you! I mean what I say!"

Darvith nodded her head sheepishly, "I promise." Then she added thoughtfully, "I'm afraid that you might mislay the bell. I'll add it to a chain and make a pretty necklace for you. Would you like that?"

Angela nodded and in an instant the bell hung from a beautiful golden chain around her neck. She admired the chain for a moment and remarked on its beauty, then asked, "But how will I explain it to my mother?"

Darvith smiled and replied, "Oh that's easy. I shall make it visible only to you." With that she announced offhandedly, "I must leave now. Goodbye! I'll see you tomorrow." Then jumped into the Royal Coach and vanished into the stream.

Angela sighed deeply and sat down on the mossy bank. What was going on? Was she only imagining all of this? She felt for the bell that now hung around her neck. It was still there hanging on the chain Darvith had materialized from out of nowhere. She gazed down at the tiny Forget-Me-Nots that had towered above her only minutes ago. The meadow behind her was once again beautiful and benign. Well, she mused, if Trillans did exist, they would certainly need a Magic Bell or two just to keep the predators who lived in the meadow, at bay.

All at once her reverie was broken by the sound of someone calling her name. She turned and glimpsed her mother Sarah running down the path. Her long hair, like glistening strands of gold in the bright sunlight.

Angela, like most children, thought that her mother was the most beautiful mother in the whole world. But there was something else. Now as she watched her run to the stream bank, laughing and barefoot, she became instantly aware of the 'something else'. It was that, in many ways Sarah was just like another child, a grown-up playmate with the heart of a child. She wasn't a childish woman. She was just a woman who was very in touch with her own inner-child self. There was a difference.

Angela and the Enchanted Bell

    Sarah was out of breath by the time she reached the bank where Angela sat waiting. She immediately collapsed on the moss beside her daughter and began to catch her breath. Raising an eyebrow slightly, she chided, "I was worried about you honey. Where were you half an hour ago? I called and called."

    "Sorry mom I didn't hear you." Angela sighed. "I've been meeting with the Trillans." At just that moment what looked like a frog caught their attention as it jumped into the stream. An excited Angela exclaimed, "I'll bet that was one of those thieving, Elgats."

    Sarah laughed and inquired, "A what? I thought you were visiting with the Trillans."

    Angela hesitated for a moment and then replied, "Just one of the creatures that lives in the meadow."

    Sara smiled. "I see. They live here 'with' the Trillans."

    Angela shook her head. "No! They are enemies! In fact the Elgats have been raiding Trillan and stealing important and valuable treasures."

    "It sounds pretty complicated." Sarah lifted her feet out of the water and said, "Well I don't know about you sweetheart, but I'm starving! "I'll race you to our front door. The last one there has to make me a cup of tea."

    Angela quickly overtook her mother and sat playfully on the doorstep eating an apple, just as if she'd been there for hours. Sarah laughed when she saw her and stated, "I'm just going to have to get more exercise."

    It was decided that after finishing their lunch, they would drive to Goldenrod; the nearby town where Angela would soon be attending school, for this was the day they were to see about the promised pets.

CHAPTER 3

Pets for Angela

Earlier that week, Sarah noticed an ad in the local newspaper mentioning that free kittens were available immediately and would be given to good homes. What better home than their cottage?

There was grocery shopping to attend to as well, but Angela succeeded in coaxing her mother into picking up her kitten first. She hoped and prayed that the kittens would still be available. Therefore their first stop would be at the home of a Mr. Ivan Strom.

They drove to the address given and knocked on the door of a very well kept home. A boy, who was about the same age as Angela, greeted them. He had tightly curled blond hair and the most impish, bright green eyes Angela had ever seen.

The boy was suddenly serious. "You're here about the kittens...Right? Sorry, they're all gone. We gave the last one away not more than five minutes ago. You're just too late...sad but true."

The expression on Angela's face mirrored her disappointment. She was crushed.

The boy immediately laughed and said, "Hey! Can't you take a joke? I was just kidding!" The boy grinned at them again then turned and yelled, "Dad! There are some people here to see the kittens!"

"Okay!" Boomed a deep masculine voice from somewhere in the house. "Just bring them downstairs Eric."

Angela and Sarah followed the boy into the upstairs hall and then down some basement stairs. They entered a huge area, well lit and obviously, by the stacks of wood shavings about, a workshop. The smell of wood shavings reminded Angela of her father's workshop, which was really just one of the spare rooms in their apartment in the city. It was nothing like this! How her dad would have loved all this space! She wondered if her mother had the same memory, but she could read nothing in her eyes.

The man who greeted them was tall and heavy-set, but not fat. There was an amused, kindly expression in his eyes, which were a clear, bright blue. His nose was largish; his mouth was firm, and chin, bold. He had a good strong face and his friendly manner put Angela completely at ease. She decided that she liked him.

He strode over to where they were standing, extended a huge hand toward Sarah, and announced heartily, "My name is Ivan Strom." And then motioning to Eric, said, "And this is my son Eric." He continued, "You're the first to see the kittens. Their mother adopted us more than a month ago and we just didn't have the heart to do anything but keep her. She was pretty wild at first but seems to be quite happy and settled now." He continued with a kindly smile, "We've grown very fond of her and have decided to keep her. Of course we can't keep all of the kittens and that's why we put an ad in the paper."

Mr. Strom wasn't talking to Angela. He was looking straight at her mother Sarah. That is to say he was looking down at Sarah...way down. Sarah was only a few inches taller than Angela, and at this moment, dwarfed by this giant of a man, she looked like nothing more than a child herself. Sarah would not have appreciated the comparison. She was quite sensitive about her lack of height and by the way some people treated her because of it.

All the while, Angela had been studying Mr. Strom's face and decided that he'd be a perfect Nordic Chieftain, or a follower of Eric the Red, charting the vast North Atlantic in a tiny Viking craft. Yes, Mr. Strom would be a perfect Viking.

Angela now turned her attention to her mother, and noted that she seemed oblivious to the effect she was having on this latest captive. She smiled inwardly. Her mother had cast yet another spell.

When Angela was very young, about four, Sarah had read the fairytale, "The Enchantress of Antrim', to her, and ever since that day, the golden-haired fairy Maeve and her mother Sarah melded and became as one. Angela had never mentioned this melding to her mother. Nevertheless, to Angela, her mother would always be an Enchantress who could cast spells. She had seen it happen time and time again.

Angela decided to listen to the conversation that was now taking place between the smitten Mr. Strom and the Enchantress. "It's kind of you to keep the mother, I'm sure there are many who wouldn't have done so." Sarah commented approvingly, adding, "She was very fortunate to have found the Stroms. This is a fine comfortable home for her and her kittens." Sarah smiled as she turned to her daughter. "Now I think its time for you to make your decision."

Mr. Strom led the pair to a large box that had been built for the birthing, and there a beautiful Ginger cat rested with six adorable kittens. Most of which were fast asleep. One very alert looking kitten with a black and white face, was standing on the others in order to see out over the top edge of the box. He was getting ready to make a leap to freedom, when Angela caught him. She held him close and within seconds he began to purr.

Mr. Strom laughed and said, "That one is a real character! I never know where I'm going to find him next." He added, "By the way, the kittens are already litter trained, they're such smart, clean little animals." He reached into the box and scooped up the tiniest kitten and placed it in the palm of his huge hand. The tiny bundle was completely unafraid and curled up, closed its eyes and went back to sleep, just as if this was where he always slept. Mr. Strom smiled broadly. "This one we will keep. He's what farmers call the 'runt' of the litter and his mother seems to be especially attached to him. We call him Samson." He knelt down and allowed Angela to stroke the tiny kitten, then continued, "We've handled the kittens a lot, right from the time they were born, very gently of course." He went on to explain, "Our veterinarian, Mr. Patrick, claims that it's important to handle kittens early on or they won't bond with humans."

Angela was having a very difficult time trying to decide on which kitten to choose, they were all adorable. She finally narrowed it down. There were two, the adventurous black and white one and a ginger one with a perfect 'M' on its forehead. Try as she may she simply could not make a decision.

Sarah, sensing her daughter's dilemma, suggested an alternative. "You can have both kittens if you forget about having a dog for the time being. They will be good company for each other and it will be great to have two good 'mousers' around the house."

Sarah turned to Mr. Strom and confessed, "At the moment our new home could use some adult cats. We've just moved into a cottage a few miles from town, and by the state it was in, I think that most of the creatures in the forest have lived in it some time or other, including some very wiley, mice."

Mr. Strom smiled and nodded knowingly. "So you've bought the Hopton Cottage. I'd heard that it had been sold. I'm glad to hear that it will be lived in once again. I hated to watch it fall into ruin."

He added somewhat sadly, "I thought of buying it once myself, but it wouldn't have been practical. I do love to have land around me though. In fact I used to own a farm ten miles west of here, but I just couldn't make a go of it." A note of pride could be heard in his voice when he added, "I was the last of the eight farmers in this district to sell."

He smiled warmly and said, "There is an 'upside' to this story. I now have much more time to spend with my son Eric." He mussed his son's hair and continued, "We've had some great times in this woodshop. Some of his woodcut designs are so good they have been winning ribbons at our Local and Provincial Fairs. He inherits his artistic talent from his mother, Gathel."

Mr. Strom was about to add something but stopped himself. Instead he asked, "Is the cottage in good enough shape to live in? I'm a good carpenter and would be happy to help you with any repairs. I seem to remember that the pantry needed some shelving."

Sarah smiled and nodded in agreement. "Yes it does, but I'm sure you're very busy, and next week will be soon enough to begin repairs. Angela and I have spent the last week cleaning and tidying up. We both feel that it's cozy and comfortable now. We love our new home and can't believe our luck in finding it."

Sarah continued enthusiastically, "The flower gardens need a lot of weeding and thinning, but I'm really looking forward to the task. I have always wanted climbing roses and flower gardens, and now I have both!"

Again she smiled at Mr. Strom and asked, "By the way, do you know anything about the former owners, the Hoptons? The cottage is so beautifully designed. We would love to know more about the builders."

Mr. Strom rubbed his chin and replied, "I've lived in this district for all of my life and only saw them once. As far as I know they didn't visit much, they sort of kept to themselves." He added, "I think they were friendly with Gwynneth Jones. She owns a shop in town where she sells Metaphysical stuff, Crystals, New-Age Music, scented candles and the like."

Sarah could tell from the tone of his voice that Mr. Strom didn't quite approve of Miss Jones, 'or' her shop.

Mr. Strom scratched his head as he recalled the Hopton's sudden and unexpected departure. "Their disappearance caused a lot of discussion at the time. Our local police sergeant checked into it but decided that everything was in order. The Hoptons were just another eccentric couple." He smiled at Sarah and said half jestingly, "Their disappearance isn't going to worry you is it?"

Sarah returned his smile, and shook her head. "Heavens no! If anything it makes the cottage even more interesting." Quickly adding, "By the way, my name is Sarah Flynn and my daughter's name is, Angela.

At just that moment, Angela called out to her mother. "I've made my decision!" She held up both the ginger kitten and the black kitten with white face and paws.

Sarah was secretly delighted that this choice had been made. A dog would have been a good deal more trouble. Cats were delightfully quirky and independent. She adored cats.

Sarah continued to talk with Mr. Strom while Angela and Eric carried the kittens upstairs and carefully placed them in the deep cardboard box Angela had lined with one of her old baby blankets. These were her very first pets and she was filled with happiness. She glanced over at her companion and decided that she liked Eric after all and asked him what grade he was in. "Grade four." Was his quick reply.

"Why so am I!" Exclaimed Angela brightly. "Great! Now I will at least know one person in my class!"

Eric grinned at her and added, "Mrs. Dickson teaches our class and she's very good. She is a little scary though. She always seems to know what we're going to do just before we do it, like she can read our minds or something. Dad says that it's because she's been teaching for such a long time." He added, while shaking his head, "Can you imagine doing anything for thirty years? She even taught my mom and dad! All of us kids like her though. She's strict, but fair, and takes us on really cool day trips."

Angela was very interested in all that Eric could tell her about the school she would soon be attending, and asked, "How many students are in your class?"

"Nineteen." Eric replied with a grin, adding, "Twenty now with you added. It's possible that you might go to another school, there are three, but I imagine it will be mine. The Hopton cottage should be in our district.

Angela was amazed at the class size and exclaimed, "There were thirty students in my class in the city! Our teacher, Mr. Chisholm, didn't have a chance to get to know any of us, or what we were thinking, for that matter!" She shook her head slowly and sighed deeply, "Poor Mr. Chisholm. I'm afraid I was responsible for most of his gray hair. Things just seem to happen when I'm around."

Eric grinned and nodded. "I have that same problem. I always seem to be in the wrong spot at the wrong time." He added with a little laugh, "Mrs. Dickson often calls me 'Ivan' instead of Eric when she's making out my punishment, so I guess I must behave a lot like my dad when he was my age." Both children laughed.

Angela felt very comfortable with Eric now and changed the subject to one more personal. She inquired, "Where's your mom, out visiting the neighbors?"

The question was innocent enough, but the expression on Eric's face made her wish she hadn't asked it. He was quiet for a moment and then replied, "Mom doesn't live with us anymore. She and my sister Berta live in Norway." He quickly added, "Mom and dad are still friends and all that, they just couldn't seem to live together without fighting all the time." He added ruefully, "Mom has a terrible temper. I mean terrible! Our family must have gone through hundreds of sets of dishes. She gave new meaning to "Flying Saucers".

Once again both children laughed, and it felt good to relieve some of the tension.

Eric continued, "Berta spends a month with us in the summer, then I return with her to Norway for the other month." He added, "It's not so bad really, dad is great and lots of fun. I miss mom and Berta though, and wish they were still with us."

Angela felt a rush of great sympathy and told Eric of her father's death. The two children were comforted by the fact that at least there was someone else who really understood. Even though the circumstances were very different, the result was basically the same. They both missed the parent that they had lost.

It was Eric who decided to change the subject. Once again his eyes danced as he blurted, "It must have been cool to live in a big city! Didn't you hate the idea of moving to a small town in the middle of nowhere?" Quickly adding, "Oh not that it's not a nice town...it's just that there are so many things to do in the city. Where was your favorite place to hang out?"

Angela grinned at Eric and replied, "Oh I will probably miss a few things all right, but most of all, I'll miss Mugsy."

Eric tilted his head and asked, "Who or what is a 'Mugsy'?"

Angela laughed as she replied. "The 'Who' is Mary, Ursula, Gillian, Sheila, Young, she's my best friend. You'll probably meet her this summer." Angela's smiling face reflected her many happy memories of Mugsy. "She's going to stay with us in July, then I'm to go to the city for August and stay with her family." She smiled at Eric and continued, "You'll like her! Everyone likes Mugsy! She's a model. You've probably seen her picture in magazines." Then as an afterthought she added, "She has a twin, a brother named Rocky. He's a pest like most boys."

Eric responded to the insult with a mock punch, then, asked, "What is Rocky short for...another long set of names? Poor guy!"

Angela laughed and replied, "I'm afraid he was named after a character in a movie. His dad named him."

Sarah and Mr. Strom, had reached the top of the stairs, it was time to leave. Once again they shook hands, and Sarah and Angela both thanked the Strom's for the kittens.

Angela placed the box with its precious cargo, on the back seat of their car. She made certain that it was secure by sitting next to it during their drive to the city center, where they planned to do their shopping.

Goldenrod was a charming little town of about 3,000, and although small, it had a reasonably large shopping area.

The streets were all lined with huge shade trees. A lovely Park nestled snugly at its center, where still more beautiful trees shaded benches where weary shoppers or visitors to the Community could sit and relax. There were flowers of every variety blooming in the well-tended beds. Still more flowers surrounded a lovely pond, where a family of swans now glided gracefully among the lily pads.

"It's all quite beautiful." Angela murmured in a soft voice.

Sarah Squeezed Angela's shoulder affectionately and remarked, "I'll bet that pond freezes over in the winter and the townspeople skate on it. I haven't skated on a pond in years, not since I was your age!" She added happily, "I love it here! You do too don't you honey!"

Angela nodded in agreement. She was very happy, very happy indeed.

Now it was time to begin their shopping. All of the stores they visited had gaily-colored awnings and each window seemed to display items that were of interest to one or both of them.

"This is fun!" Exclaimed an excited Angela as she and Sarah journeyed from store to store. Everyone was helpful and soon they were making many new friends.

Angela continued to make frequent trips back to their car to make sure that her kittens were comfortable. Each time she would pet them until they purred with contentment.

Sarah decided to visit the Metaphysical shop owned by Miss Jones. Unfortunately the shop, titled, 'Unique Sightings', was apparently closed for the day. Sarah peeked through the front window and could see a myriad of interesting things. She murmured softly, "I'll definitely have to come back soon."

CHAPTER 4

The Quest

Weary but happy they returned to their cottage. It had been a very eventful day and Angela was looking forward to spending the rest of it playing with her kittens.

She gave them names. This had taken some very serious thought and study, but the decision had finally been made. They were to be Cedric and Boris.

Cedric, the black and white one, was very neat and tidy even to the way he ate his food and slept in his bed. She watched when she first put them in their new box how he packed down a nice little circle where he intended to sleep and curled up in it in a little ball. The name Cedric suited him perfectly. He was also the smarter of the two and very curious.

Boris on the other hand was a bit of a slob. He had an enormous appetite and in his haste to eat as much as possible, much of his food clung to his whiskers and fur where it quickly dried, thus making a later clean up much more difficult. In fact his side of the sleeping box had already gathered bits of scraps, mementos from his first meal. Unlike Cedric's carefully made little circle, Boris's blanket was pushed up into a mound of folds, which he sprawled across while sleeping on his well-rounded stomach.

Sarah had been studying Angela while pretending to read a magazine. She smiled to herself. Angela's temperament was so very like that of her father Rory. She resembled him in many ways. Until the car accident, Angela and her father shared the same coloring. Rory had often told his daughter that she looked just like 'Snow White' in the popular fairy tale, with hair as black as ebony, skin as white as snow and her eyes as blue as the sky above. He always made Angela feel very special and very loved. Their combined laughter reminded Sarah of blue skies and sunshine. She missed Rory still but she knew he'd be proud of the way she was handling things and would want her to get on with her life.

However, Sarah did at times worry about Angela's vivid imagination and her flights of fantasy. There were times when Angela lived in another world completely foreign to Sarah. It was beyond mere pretending.

Once Rory, who had also been an only child, explained to her that children who are raised without siblings frequently have very rich fantasy lives, which develops into real creativity when they reach adulthood. He added that many famous writers and other gifted artists were without brothers and sisters. Sarah smiled inwardly when she remembered how she had pointed out that she, the writer, had been one of nine siblings, while he, the building contractor, was the only child. They had both laughed.

Sarah's parents were Italian farmers and her maiden name was Serafina, Sophia Vitti. Her first name was shortened and the spelling changed, when she entered public school, but at home she was still Serafina to all but her father, who called her Dusty. She smiled as she remembered with love, her family gathered around the kitchen table, everyone talking and laughing at once.

Angela was named after Sarah's mother Angelina, who had died the year before Angela was born. The first day of kindergarten, Sarah had overheard the teacher Miss Plum, shorten Angelina to 'Lena' and because she didn't like the sound of Lena, asked her to use Angela instead. From that day onward, she called her little girl Angela.

Rory always used to call his little girl 'Angel'. How appropriate his name for her was now. The silver of her hair gave her appearance a delicate quality when her face was in repose that could certainly be described as angelic.

Sarah smiled. She believed that someday Angela would become a writer and make good use of her imagination. Perhaps she would tell tales of her adventures with the Trillans, Elgats and their treasure. What was to be next she wondered with a smile?

It was time for their nightly cup of cocoa in front of the fire. This event was becoming a ritual.

It began the first night they stayed in their new home. The heat and electricity hadn't been hooked up yet and it was a very cold night. Sarah lit a fire in their enormous fireplace and after drinking a mug of hot cocoa they slept in sleeping bags near the hearth in order to keep warm.

Angela loved the experience and before long imagined that they were in deepest Africa sleeping near a blazing fire, in order to protect themselves from the wild animals they could hear calling out in the night. The dancing flames of the fire added to this image; the spell was cast. Angela decided then and there that she would someday visit Africa and sleep near a campfire under the stars. She had wonderful adventures in her dreams that night.

But now the whole cottage had warmth to it and this was just a very nice way to end the day. They sat in front of the fire, gazing into the flames while sipping hot cocoa, each momentarily lost in their own private thoughts. Sarah was re-working a plot line for her new book, while Angela was wondering just what was going to take place in Trillan in the morning.

At last it was time for bed. The kittens were to sleep in their box in Angela's room. Sarah entered her daughter's room to tuck her in as she always did each evening.

Angela teased, "I think Mr. Strom likes you. He's a nice man don't you think?"

Sarah smiled lovingly at her daughter and replied, "Don't be silly. He was just being friendly...and yes, I do think he's nice."

Angela then related all that Eric had told her about his mother and sister.

Sarah sighed and murmured softly, "That is so sad. She must have felt that leaving Eric with his father was for the best. I don't think I could ever have done that. Not for any reason." quickly adding, "However, I mustn't judge her. After all, I don't know anything about life at the Stroms." Then as she bent down to kiss Angela on the forehead, she whispered, "I don't want you to worry about them. Eric and his father seem to be very happy together. Now go to sleep you little Drogen!"

This was Sarah's pet name for Angela. When Angela was very young she had several imaginary friends. One of whom was a Drogen, not to be confused with an ordinary Dragon that breathes fire. Drogens, as Angela had explained when her speech became clearer, breathed astonishing stories from magical lands and were wonderful companions.

That night Angela fell asleep smiling, as she remembered her friend, the Drogen and all of their adventures together.

It was dawn when she awoke to find two little visitors playing in the great masses of her silver curls. Actually it was the rather raspy purring of her tiny guests that had awakened her.

After carefully disentangling them, which was not an easy task, she decided to discover just how they had managed to get out of their box. As she gazed down at where it was positioned near her bed it was easy to see how kittens with nice, new, sharp little claws could have pulled themselves up to where she was sleeping. Angela felt certain, had she been awake to witness the event, that it would have been Cedric to appear first, followed by a somewhat reluctant Boris. Whatever the route, their early morning visit had been a delightful wake-up call, and she was able to spend an hour playing with them before she heard her mother preparing breakfast downstairs.

Angela felt as if a million butterflies were playing in the pit of her stomach whenever she thought of her visit to Trillan in a few hours. She would not have been as nervous if she thought Elder Griffin might be absent from the meeting. She was filled with doubts and fears. However, she had promised Darvith, and Angela always kept her word.

After a hearty breakfast, she did the dishes and then called in to see her mother who was already busy at work. "I've finished my chores and taken care of the kittens. They are sleeping now." Angela reported, and then asked, "Is it all right if I go down to the meadow for a hour or two? I promise to return in time for lunch." Sarah agreed and Angela ran off down the path with the tiny bell now safely held on the chain around her neck.

Before she sat down on the mossy bank, she looked around very carefully. Darvith had promised that the bell would offer protection while in her diminutive state, but Darvith was full of mischief and Angela didn't quite trust her yet. She was just about to ring the bell when she noticed the beautiful golden light in the stream.

When the Royal Coach emerged, Darvith was waiting for her inside. Angela quickly rang the bell three times and jumped into the boat. In doing so she landed on Darvith's lap. Darvith scowled disapprovingly and Angela

Angela and the Enchanted Bell

immediately moved to the opposite side of the coach. It was then that she noticed how beautifully Darvith was dressed. She sighed deeply and looked down at her simple cotton dress.

Darvith had read her mind, smiled at her and said comfortingly, "Don't worry about your dress. You look just fine and I'm sure you feel a lot more comfortable than I do at the moment. I hate dressing up in this tight clothing."

The Royal Coach quickly emerged in the shimmering lake. A huge crowd of cheering and clapping Trillans greeted them. Angela was delighted and frightened at the same time.

The elders appeared before her with what appeared to be the Royal Family of Trillan. The great throng of Trillan citizens retreated and became silent.

Elder griffin stepped forward and extended the introductions. "Angela, I'd like to present you to our Royal Family." She curtsied and they all smiled at her welcomingly. Darvith stood with them. What a surprise to learn that she had been speaking to a Princess. Darvith didn't behave like a princess, that's for certain!

Griffin continued, "Our King, Tallis, and his Queen, Ilga." Then turning to Darvith, "And Princess Darvith, whom you have already met, Princess Annwynn, and of course not to forget, Princess Tova, our youngest."

Angela was speechless. Princess Tova was blond and green-eyed as were her parents the King and Queen and Darvith, but Annwynn was completely different. Her hair was long and black and formed deep waves that swept down to the ground. Tiny tendrils of tight curls framed her beautiful pale face. She was breathtaking! Annwynn's bright blue eyes were magnificent, and her thick black lashes were so long they reminded Angela of butterflies whenever she opened and closed her eyes. Why she must be an Elgat, decided Angela to herself, forgetting that the Trillans could read all of her thoughts.

Annwynn smiled at her kindly and replied, "Yes Angela, I am an Elgat." She continued, "I was found in the Earthling's meadow when I was still a baby, abandoned by my own people. As I was completely alone, I was taken back to Trillan before I could become some wild creature's meal." She turned and smiled at the Royal Family. "I was then fortunate enough to have been adopted by the Royal Family. It was a generous act and I am exceedingly grateful to have been accepted as a citizen of Trillan."

Annwynn looked troubled as she continued, "It is my wish to help you in any way that I can. Perhaps the fact that I am an Elgat by birth will be useful in some way, I sincerely hope so."

Elder Griffin once again began to speak, and once again Angela was struck by the strange cold fear that his mere presence evoked. What was it about him that brought forth this response? He had a wonderfully handsome face and an enchanting smile. Of course! It was his eyes! They were the cold, ruthless eyes of a predator. Angela shivered involuntarily.

Griffin had been reading Angela's thoughts and knew of her feelings toward him. He didn't care if the Earthling brat liked him or not. But he decided that he should try to thwart any unnecessary conjecture on her part as to Annwynn's presence in the meadow when a baby.

Griffin began the tale of her discovery in his melodious voice. "We found the baby Annwynn over a thousand of your years ago. 'I' noticed that she wore an unusual pendant containing three golden discs, indeed she wears it to this day, and 'I' insisted that we must save her because she obviously was an important member of her community." Griffin smiled, and continued, "The others with me that day wanted to leave her behind, but 'I' insisted that we bring her back with us and placed her in the care of the Royal household. And that is why we have dear little Annwynn with us today."

Angela and the Enchanted Bell

At this moment the tall, regal looking, Elder Planus stepped forward. "Don't you think that it's time we began to discuss a plan for Angela. That 'is' the reason we brought her here today isn't it? Not to say that Princess Annwynn isn't a wonderful topic."

Annwynn walked over and put her hand on his shoulder. He immediately covered it with his own. They were obviously dear friends. Annwynn smiled up at him then down at Angela as she explained, "Planus, Darvith and I grew up together. We were inseparable, in fact we spent our whole childhood getting into and out of the trouble Darvith was forever landing us in. Oh! But those were golden days!"

Planus agreed and was about to recount something when Griffin tried to interrupt by raising his hand, "All right, I'll change the subject Griffin."

Planus then took Angela's hand and asked, "Have you told your mother about us?" Adding kindly, "It doesn't matter if you have. We were just curious. We saw you sitting on the bank of the stream together and could see that you were having a long discussion." He added appreciatively, "Your mother is very beautiful. She looks like a Trillan."

Angela thanked him graciously for the somewhat immodest compliment and replied, "I guess she does at that." Then frowning slightly, she asked, "Where were you? I thought we were alone."

The elders all laughed.

Angela scowled. She did not like to be laughed at. "I fail to see what's so funny!"

Planus immediately took her hand and squeezed in gently. "We were very rude to laugh at you. To answer your question, we knew you were sitting on the bank of the stream because we could see you through our great crystal. We see everything that takes place in that area. We can watch but we can't hear, and we can only watch during the day." He added, "Unfortunately, in spite of this surveillance we have been unable to catch the Elgats entering Trillan. They must have an entrance we know nothing about."

Angela was silent for a moment and then said, "Well, as a matter of fact I did mention your names to my mother, but she didn't really take me too seriously; I have what my mother calls, a very vivid imagination." She continued, "She thinks I'm going to be a writer some day and that I'm sharpening my creative thinking skills by inventing fanciful tales." The she added, "I must admit that there are times lately when 'I' think that I'm imagining all of this, but then when I'm here with you it all seems so very real. It must be happening."

Planus smiled at her kindly and said, "I'm sure that the existence of a realm so very different from your own is very difficult for you to accept. Please believe that we are all very grateful that you have agreed to help us." Planus continued, "When you return to the meadow today, we would like you to give it a thorough search and see if you can find any sign of the Elgats. As you more or less know what they look like, it might be a good plan just to sit quietly in an inconspicuous area in the trees that border the meadow, and wait."

This seemed to be a very good idea. Angela knew of the very spot she would use as her hiding place.

Darvith walked toward her and took her hand, suggesting it was time to leave. Angela once again curtsied to the Royal Family and then waved goodbye to the Elders and to the crowds of Trillans who remained.

The crowd responded with a great cheer as Angela followed Darvith into the Royal Coach. Within seconds they arrived at the bank of the stream where Angela quickly disembarked and regained her normal height. There were no Trillan tricks today. Darvith had kept her promise.

Angela was filled with curiosity, and asked if Darvith would stay for a few minutes; she wanted to ask her about something.

Darvith reluctantly agreed, but cautioned that it would just be for a few minutes for she had a very busy day ahead of her in Trillan.

Angela nodded her head in agreement and began carefully, not wishing to sound too curious about something that was perhaps none of her business. Then she decided that she might just as well get to the point, Darvith could read her mind anyway. Angela blurted out in excitement, "Please tell me more about Annwynn? Does she have any traits that differ from the Trillans? Does she hope to eventually rejoin her own people? What do the Trillans really think of her? Had their attitude toward her changed since the raiding began? Has anyone ever accused her of being a traitor or spy?" Angela stopped to catch breath and was about to continue with still more questions when she noticed that Darvith was red with rage.

Angela's last question was the final straw as far as Darvith was concerned. She glared up at the child who now towered over her and stamped her tiny foot in a fit of temper. After kicking Angela's now 'enormous' shoe, she yelled, "How dare you suggest that she might be a traitor? How dare you say something like that out loud where others can hear."

Angela was momentarily caught off guard by this unexpected display, and stammered, "But...but...there is no one here and the Great Crystal only allows the Elders to 'watch' us." Quickly adding, "They had to ask 'me' about my conversation with my mother." Then Angela added with a broad grin, "All they will have seen was a very angry Trillan, hopping about and looking very silly."

Darvith laughed out loud. She had been behaving in a ridiculous manner. Angela was now sitting beside her with her feet in the water. Darvith patted her hand and said, "You are absolutely right. I should learn to check my temper. It's just that Annwynn is very important to me. She is such a gentle creature, both Planus and I have always felt that we must protect her." She smiled at Angela and said, "Now, if there is nothing else, I really must be going."

Angela caught the back of Darvith's dress as she turned to leave. "Not so fast! You're very good at avoiding questions aren't you Darvith. You haven't answered any of mine and yet you plan to leave anyway."

Again Darvith laughed. "You know Angela, I'm beginning to like you. You have spirit and intelligence. As a reward, I will tell you a few things about Annwynn." Darvith continued, "You may have wondered why we can't use the Great Crystal at night. The reason is a simple one. Trillans can't see in the dark. Night vision has never been a necessity for us because our land has always been bathed in the golden light, except for 3 brief hours in the early morning when everyone is resting. Annwynn has night-sight. I have never told anyone else so you must keep it a secret."

Angela nodded her head in agreement, then asked, "But how have you managed to keep this gift a secret?" Quickly adding, "Do you think that her night-sight is the result of being an Elgat? How would the Trillans react if they learned of it?"

Darvith was silent for a moment and then replied, "I'm not sure, but I don't think it would be favorably. There is little room for uniqueness' in Trillan society. There are many who resent her presence now."

Darvith sighed deeply and was silent for a moment. She confided somewhat sadly, "Annwynn is to become a life-mate soon. Vorden, a young Prince from one of our outer kingdoms, the Velds, is in love with her and has asked my father the King, for permission to court her." Darvith added, "Ordinarily, the fact that she is a Princess would allow her to choose her mate without interference.

However, as a Prince is involved, my father must make the decision for her." She patted Angela's hand and added, "If Vorden had chosen me I would have run away...perhaps to make a life for myself in the Earthling meadow. I will never Oath! Never!"

Angela was very interested to learn all she could from Darvith about the customs and kingdoms of Trillan. She inquired with great excitement, "Please tell me more about the Velds? You've never mentioned them before."

Darvith sighed in exasperation. "Really Angela! How could I possibly tell you all about our lands in the brief time I have spent with you! Do you actually believe that our land is any less great than your own? I suppose you think we live under the ground, under this very stream!" She began to laugh.

Darvith's expression quickly changed to one of remorse, as Angela turned away in embarrassment. She sighed sadly and explained, "Oh Angela, if I've insulted you, I'm sorry. I just can't seem to help myself. I'm impossible! Annwynn and Pianus are my only friends in all of Trillan. No one else will tolerate my outbursts." She smiled disarmingly. "Because I value your friendship, I once again ask you to forgive and forget." She continued, "Please believe me, I would explain the existence of our land to you if I could, but I think you're far too young to grasp the concept which allows us to live in another dimension that now and then touches your own." She added brightly, "Perhaps when you are older and if we are still communicating, I will be able to explain it to you."

Angela smiled forgivingly. She liked Darvith and was proud that she was thought of as a friend. She asked, "Does Annwynn care for Prince Vorden? What is he like?"

Darvith tilted her head slightly as she replied, "She likes him more than any of the other young men who follow her around, but she could certainly live without him, if that's what you mean. However, even if she hated him, she must become his life-mate if the King commands it" She added kindly, "You mustn't worry about Annwynn. Prince Vorden absolutely adores her and will see to it that they have a very happy life together. He is a kind, handsome young man, and a very rich one. His Kingdom produces all of our gold and precious gems."

Angela was about to ask another question when the Royal Coach began to glow and Darvith quickly jumped in. "I must return to Trillan now Angela...be clever and gather as much information as you can. I will meet you here at the same time tomorrow! Good luck!" Within seconds the Royal Coach had vanished.

Angela stared intently at the stream, trying to imagine what Darvith had meant when she said 'another dimension'. She said aloud, "Well, where are they going when they enter the stream if they aren't going into the water?" Darvith was right. She didn't understand.

CHAPTER 5

A Surprising Encounter

Angela decided that she should return to the cottage for lunch and eagerly ran up the path, for suddenly she was very hungry. The delicious aroma of freshly baked bread greeted her as she approached the open door to the kitchen.

Angela was surprised, and not altogether pleased to see Mr. Strom and Eric seated at the kitchen table.

"Oh good!" Sarah said with a welcoming smile, "I wondered where you had gone. Eric spent an hour looking for some sign of you, but I suppose you were off on your bike."

Oh dear, thought Angela, I can't have Eric prowling all over the meadow. How am I going to complete my mission for the Trillans with him around?

Sarah continued without waiting for an explanation from Angela. "They came out to see if there was any heavy work that they could help us with. Wasn't that kind of them?"

Angela smiled sweetly and nodded in agreement while thinking just the opposite. It was a good thing that 'they' weren't Trillans and able to read her mind. She was very annoyed. However, luck was with her. The Stroms were going to leave immediately after lunch. Now that she knew they would be leaving soon, Angela began to relax and enjoy their company.

Mr. Strom, with Eric's help, took all the necessary measurements for the new cupboards and also for the shelves in the pantry. At last they would have enough room for all of their dishes and supplies and thankfully the Stroms were soon on their way.

Angela helped her mother with the dishes. During their conversation, she asked Sarah if she could leave the kittens downstairs, just until she returned from the meadow. She was afraid they might get lonely, upstairs all by themselves.

Sarah agreed and then looked at Angela a little oddly, with one eyebrow slightly raised.

Angela gazed back at her mother and asked, "What? Is there something you want me to do this afternoon?"

Sarah smiled warmly at her daughter. "No. There is nothing that I want you to do. Away you go! But this time try not to vanish from sight!"

Angela was startled and glanced quickly at her mother. Mischief danced in Sarah's eyes; she had just been teasing. After giving and receiving a hug and kiss, Angela was out the door and racing down the path to the meadow.

She decided that she would just sit quietly for a while and made herself comfortable on a stump near to the stream. She sat and waited...and waited. Finally, just as she was about to shift her position to an old log, she noticed some movement in the grass. Her heart began to pound. Was she about to see an Elgat? The excitement she felt was difficult to contain. At last she could see what had been moving so stealthily through the grass. Angela suppressed a giggle. Why it was just a tiny mouse! But not an ordinary mouse to be sure. This mouse had a type of harness on its body and a collar around its neck.

She decided that it must be a pet mouse that had somehow escaped...but escaped from where? The cottage had been empty for several years. She supposed that it could have survived that long in the wild but it seemed most unlikely. Intrigued, she decided to watch its progress through the meadow and silently followed the tiny creature. She grinned, for in her mind, she became a huge silver cat preparing to pounce on its unsuspecting prey.

The mouse continued to move slowly and carefully away from the stream and she would often momentarily lose sight of it in the tall grasses. Now and then it would stop and remain perfectly still for minutes at a time. Every hair on its body seemed to be on alert. Angela guessed that it sensed her presence and stood absolutely still each time it stopped.

Again, she stood waiting for it to continue its journey, when all at once, another animal, one that she had been completely unaware of, pounced at the mouse. The frightened rodent jumped out of the way just in time, and darted into a small hole in an old tree. Mercifully, the enraged weasel was far too large to fit through the hole. After viciously scratching at the tree and growling ferociously, it gave up its quarry and disappeared into the tall grasses in search of easier prey.

Angela shivered involuntarily when she remembered how tiny she had been just a few hours ago. She had been just as small as the poor little mouse that was now carefully inching its way out of its hiding place. Soon it was once again on its way and made slow but steady progress toward a part of the meadow unfamiliar to Angela. She followed stealthily.

A beautiful and unexpected sight greeted her. The meadow, until now, had sloped very slightly upward. It was just enough of a slope to shield what lay beyond from the stream below. Now, a short distance before her, a large oval, pool, glistened in the sunlight. Tiny bubbles were rising to the surface at the end nearest to where she now stood.

"Why it must be a natural spring!" Angela exclaimed with delight. A small stone building bordered on one edge of the pool; large, flat stones, which formed a sort of walkway, covered the remaining edges. These stones had obviously been put in place by human hands. It was not a natural formation.

One of the stones near the far end of the pool had a medium-sized gap where the excess water could escape and make its way to the lower part of the meadow. This was the section of the property that the Realtor Mr. Porkwitt had referred to as swampy and unusable land.

Angela believed it would be a paradise for exotic creatures like Garter Snakes and Bullfrogs; and contain lots of interesting plants like Skunk Cabbages and Catkins. There might even be a pond with Lily Pads. She had deliberately saved the low swampy land, so full of delights, as the last to be explored. She frowned and murmured, "I wonder why Mr. Porkwitt didn't tell us about this wonderful pool? Strange."

Angela moved toward the stone building. It wasn't a large structure, only about the size of a child's playhouse. Most of its stonework was meshed with a tangle of morning Glory.

Upon closer inspection she discovered some rose vines, soon to bloom for they were covered with an abundance of tiny pink buds. Angela cleared away some of the weeds that had been choking the plant's growth and then placed the well budded vines carefully around one of the window casings. She stood back to admire her work and exclaimed, "Yes! That's much better!" She added happily, "I'm going to have a playhouse at last, and in such a perfect spot! This is wonderful! I can't wait to show mom!"

In spite of all this pleasure, Angela had an inexplicable feeling of uneasiness, a feeling that hostile eyes were

Angela and the Enchanted Bell

watching her. She quickly looked about, but there was no one in sight.

Unexpectedly the well-dressed little mouse ran over her foot and disappeared into the stone building. "So there you are!" She smiled and said softly, "Well, I might as well have a look inside while I'm here."

When she stepped through the doorway she was surprised and a little disappointed to discover that her playhouse was open to the sky. As her gaze followed the upper edge of the wall, she was startled by a small, human-like creature and immediately jumped back. Could it be an Elgat? Was she being watched by an army of Elgats waiting to attack?"

All at once ironic laughter filled the air and a very handsome creature stepped out from behind a stone on the upper edge of the wall to her left. He scowled and shouted, "An army of Elgats indeed! It wouldn't take an army of Elgats to eliminate one little Earthling!" Again he laughed. "So you've come to spy on us for the Trillans." He raised his sword to her and shouted, "You've come to spy, admit it! I can guess what they have told you about us! Lies! All lies! Trillans are exceptionally good liars!"

Angela did not like his manner and decided to answer in the same tone. She was after all, a giant and therefore to be feared! She replied quickly and stated firmly she was told that the Elgats have been raiding Trillan and stealing important artifacts.

The Elgat was quiet for a long moment and Angela studied him closely. He was perfectly formed and looked enough like a miniature of her father Rory, to be his twin. He had the same white skin and astonishingly blue eyes as both her father and Princess Annwynn. His wavy black hair was pulled back from his handsome face and held in place by a long braid down his back. He looked every inch a warrior and Angela could see that he carried the traditional dagger and net as well as the sword.

All at once the Elgat cried out in great pain. A burn blister was beginning to form where a ray of sun had touched his skin. He quickly retreated to the shaded area behind the stone. Angela moved to where she could watch, and observed that he covered the burnt area with a type of white liquid. It seemed to heal immediately.

The Elgat glared at Angela and declared angrily, "Now you know of the affliction that has cursed our people for a thousand years. Our skin cannot tolerate the direct rays of the Earthling's Sun. You are very fortunate to have such a wondrous light source and suffer no ill effects from it!"

Angela nodded in agreement and then innocently asked, "Do you live in darkness under the ground?"

Again he glared at her angrily, "Don't be stupid!
We're Elgats not moles!"

Angela was becoming increasingly annoyed with his belligerent attitude. However, she managed to hold her temper in check, and continued as politely as she could, "Well what do you use for your light source, wherever it is that you live?"

The Elgat was silent for another long moment and then answered stonily, "We used to use the Great Crystal before the Trillans blocked our access and took the Golden light for themselves." And then he added rudely, in a voice filled with contempt, "What we use now is none of your business!"

Angela could see that he was about to leave and quickly decided to use a different approach and offered, hopefully, "Perhaps the Trillans don't realize that they have blocked your access to the light...perhaps it is just some terrible misunderstanding."

The handsome Elgat laughed as he shook his head in reply, "Oh no, there was no mistake, the Trillans knew exactly what they were doing."

All at once his expression softened. He had been reading the child's mind. She was an innocent. He smiled at her and said kindly, "I think you mean well Angela, but I can assure you that the Trillans always plan their actions well in advance, whether for good or evil. If I were you I would watch my back at all times."

His voice had lost most of its harshness and Angela felt that he was telling her the truth and not trying to trick her with his responses. He could obviously read her mind; he called her by her name, and probably decided that she was just a 'dim' Earthling child, led astray by the Trillans.

He smiled again, and it was a wonderful smile that engaged his eyes in an impish way. He said, "I have an idea Angela. Why don't you ask them why they kidnapped our Royal Princess? Why they have kept her a prisoner all of these hundreds of years? Why they force her to work in the meadow like a commoner? I've seen her there with another slave with frizzy blond hair." He laughed. "I would love to see the expression on their faces when you ask them!"

This was the opening that Angela was hoping for and she immediately jumped at it. She explained that the Elders were hoping that she could make contact with the Elgats and try to arrange a meeting. She would be happy to ask his questions of the Trillan Elders and report back to him with their answers.

The plan was agreed upon by both of them. He raised his sword as he spoke, as if he were making an oath. "I will meet with you tomorrow but this had better not be a Trillan trick, for if it is, I promise, this time the Trillans will pay dearly for it! Our Princess must be returned to us!" In an instant he had disappeared.

CHAPTER 6

The Accident

Angela suddenly felt very tired. Peacemaking was demanding work. She glanced at her watch and decided that she should return to the cottage. She didn't want her mother to worry, and anyway she wanted to show her the playhouse and pool.

She entered the kitchen door and called out, "I'm home mom! I've found a wonderful place in the meadow that I want you to see!" She stood behind her mother's chair and putting her arms around her coaxed, "Please come now? Please? Please? Please?"

Sarah smiled at her daughter and said, "Don't get carried away now!" She rose to her feet and slowly stretched. "It's time I took a break anyway...let's go to that wonderful place you've found!"

They ran down the path and up through the meadow. Angela led her mother to the stone house. Just as they approached, a shaft of light filtered down through the trees and illuminated the pool. It sparkled and shimmered in the sunlight.

Sarah was appreciatively silent for a long moment and then murmured softly, "What an enchanting place. I wonder if the Hoptons were responsible for fashioning it or if it existed long before they built the cottage?" She added with a smile, "How I love a mystery."

Angela smiled happily, "I knew you'd like it mom. Will you help me fix the stone house so I can use it for play?" Then without waiting for a reply, She ran ahead of her mother and called out, with great excitement, "Come over here and look at the inside! Oh! Isn't this a wonderful place mom?"

Sarah loved Angela's enthusiasm. It always made her smile. She made her way around the pool's edge, carefully stepping on the flat stones. Just as she approached the building, she lost her footing and fell sideways into the water, momentarily submerging, only to re-emerge laughing amid a myriad of bubbles. "Come on in! The water is fine!" She sputtered, still laughing, she added, "I must say this water is a perfect temperature for swimming." She added, "Perhaps the stone building was a changing room for shy bathers."

Then Sarah, with one fluid movement, expertly raised herself up and out of the water, and sat on one of the flat stones at the edge of the pool. This allowed her feet to remain in the water.

Suddenly Sarah winced and cried out in pain, "Owwww!" She quickly raised her feet out of the water and exclaimed, "That really hurt!"

Angela ran over to where her mother sat clutching her left foot, which was now bleeding profusely from what appeared to be a tiny but very deep cut.

Sarah smiled up at her daughter, "I'm sure its nothing honey. I probably scratched it on the stone when I fell in. The water has just made it feel more tender."

Once again a strange uneasiness fell upon Angela. Did something sinister live in that beautiful pool, and was it something that wished them harm? She helped her mother to her feet, and taking her hand, led her to the entrance of the stone building.

Sarah looked in and remarked, "Why this is a good size Angela. It is much larger than it looks from the outside." She continued enthusiastically with her assessment. "My goodness! You have a window on each wall and a stone floor. I'd say you have found a perfect playhouse." She smiled impishly and added, "However, I do think a roof, window glass and a door with a lock would be definite improvements!" They both laughed.

Sarah smiled lovingly at her daughter and asked, "Would you like me to have Ivan look at the place and give us an estimate?"

Angela briefly looked away. The 'Ivan' replacement for the former, more formal, 'Mr. Strom', had not escaped her attention, and she wasn't sure if she liked the change. However, she quickly turned a smiling face to her mother and told her that the coming summer would be soon enough. It was enough for now that Sarah loved the place too, and wanted to help her fix it up. Angela was very happy.

Sarah's foot was still bleeding and her wet clothing was causing her to shiver. They decided to return to the cottage. Angela insisted that Sarah have a hot bath while she made them both a mug of cocoa.

A half hour later, a much warmer Sarah padded downstairs in her terry robe and slippers. She flopped into the comfortable old rocking chair that sat near the kitchen table, feeling wonderfully relaxed.

Angela brought a stool, which enabled Sarah to raise her injured foot, and then presented her with a mug of hot cocoa.

"Mmmmm...This really hits the spot...thanks." Sarah murmured appreciatively. After examining her wound more closely, she decided that it must be a nail puncture and had Angela pour a great deal of antiseptic over it.

Now that Angela had the opportunity to examine the injury, she had her own idea as to what had caused the wound and was becoming very angry. She murmured with barely audible vehemence. "If they dare to harm my mother they will be very, very sorry!" Her thoughts were filled with rage and vengeance.

Sarah glanced over at her daughter and could see that Angela was in one of her infamous 'Black Moods'. Since she first began to express herself, Angela, when angry, could project the fiercest energy. Sarah's husband Rory had the same dark energy to which he credited his Celtic Ancestry.

Sarah asked gently, "What has made you so angry? Do you want to talk about it?"

At just that moment Angela's face relaxed. She grinned happily as Cedric and Boris came running toward her, both losing control of their footing on the slippery linoleum and tumbling end over end, before sliding into the kitchen mat. They were such adorable little creatures. She loved them so very much. Her rage quickly vanished.

Sarah called out with some urgency in her voice, "Quick Angela! Close the door or Cedric will run out like a flash! I have never known a snoopier kitten! Heaven knows what mischief he'd get into out there!"

Angela rushed to close the door and was just in time to prevent Cedric from making his escape. Luckily, Boris was far more interested in the food she had just put out for them.

Angela had made a decision and suggested, "You look far too comfortable to disturb mom. I'll make a spaghetti supper tonight." It was the one meal she could prepare from start to finish. Sarah gratefully accepted her daughter's offer. Their dinner conversation was filled with interesting conversation and conjecture, most of which concerned the pool and the stone house.

Much later, after their nightly mug of cocoa, they prepared for bed and retired for the evening. Angela fell asleep with her kittens purring contentedly beside her.

She was awakened at dawn by a plaintive mewing. At first she couldn't tell where the sound was coming from. Then she looked over to her curtains, and there was chubby little Boris, halfway up. His claws were hopelessly caught, so that he could neither move up or down. He was such a pathetic sight!

Angela called out to him softly as she rushed to his aid, "Oh! Poor dear little Boris, I wonder how long you've been hanging there?" She gave him a long cuddle with lots of stroking. Finally he stopped shaking and began his raspy little purr. After gently placing him on her bed, Angela began her search for Cedric.

Although he was nowhere in sight, she could hear his inquisitive little meow! "Aha! There you are!" Angela laughed as she looked up to see his little black and white face, peering innocently down at her from the shelf that projected out from the top of her curtains.

She scolded him lovingly, at the same time wondering how he managed to reach his precarious perch. Then she laughed out loud! Of course, it would have been the same route that poor little Boris had tried to follow without success. Cedric would probably always lead Boris into impossible situations. She chided him gently, "Never mind, you're safe for the time being Cedric." Then lifted him down from his perch. Both kittens were soon purring contentedly.

Thanks to the kittens, Angela was awake and dressed much earlier than usual and planned to make an attempt at fixing breakfast, if her mother's foot was still bothering her.

Sarah, however, was already up. Angela could hear the sound of her melodic singing coming from the study. Sarah often sang in her wonderful cheerful voice. Her songs were a part of Angela's earliest memory. The sound always lifted her spirits.

Angela checked the warming oven to see what surprises awaited her. There were three golden waffles.

Angela and the Enchanted Bell

This was her favorite breakfast. After finishing her meal and tidying up, she called in to see how her mother was feeling.

Sarah assured her that she felt great and was inspired to write at least 3 chapters. They hugged and Angela asked if it was all right if she went out to play? Sarah nodded her head but cautioned Angela to stay away from the pool until Ivan checked it out for safety.

Angela agreed and then called out, as she ran out the cottage door, "I'll be home in time to help with the lunch. You'd better rest that foot today."

CHAPTER 7

The Report

It had rained during the night, giving the woodland surrounding the meadow an even sweeter fragrance than before. Rays of brilliant sunshine filtered through the forest canopy, causing the raindrops to glisten on the leaves and branches like prisms. The tiny droplets of water now sparkled like a million precious jewels.

Angela's imaginings placed her in the cave of "Ali Baba', and she was gazing up with awe when a huge droplet of water splotched her face and broke the spell. She chided herself for being so easily distracted from her morning's mission, and made her way swiftly to the edge of the stream. There was no sign of the now familiar golden light; she wasn't late after all.

Angela turned to face the meadow. She was relieved to see that it was impossible to see her stone house from the bank of the stream. Smiling happily she declared aloud, "Good! The Trillan Elders won't be able to view it through their crystal!"

She turned to once again face the stream just as the Royal Coach appeared. Without waiting to be told, she quickly rang the bell three times and entered the tiny craft where Darvith waited and smiled expectantly. Angela smiled back but remained silent.

Much to Darvith's annoyance, it was impossible to read anything in the Earthlings thoughts...well at least anything of value. The child seemed to be obsessed with thoughts of a stone house. Darvith was filled with curiosity.

Angela was grateful to see that only the Elders and Annwynn were there to greet them when they emerged in the shimmering lake. After all, her news might not be well received by the 'citizens' of Trillan.

Annwynn walked toward her and took her hand. Her gentle and loving manner made Angela feel very comfortable. Darvith leant toward Annwynn and whispered, "She would tell me nothing." Angela smiled up at them just as the Elders approached.

Elder Griffin was the first to speak. He scowled, and then issued a torrent of questions. "Well? What news do you have for us? Did you manage to find the entrance to their land? Did you find any evidence of their existence in the meadow? Did you even 'see' any Elgats?" His tone was derisive.

At this point Elder Planus stepped forward. "Please forgive Elder Griffin's rude behavior. He hasn't yet recovered from the fact that we made a decision without consulting him." The other Elders were about to laugh when Griffin lifted his chin and glared. There was immediate silence.

Planus was not to be discouraged and continued, "We saw you in the meadow and watched as you appeared to follow something through the grasses of the meadow. You can imagine we all hoped that it was an Elgat. Was it?"

Angela shook her head and smiled, "No. I'm afraid it was only a mouse." She could see that they were disappointed and quickly added that it wasn't an ordinary mouse. "This mouse had a collar and harness.

The type of harness field-working animals wear, when they pull ploughs and things like that." She added brightly, "I thought this was very odd and followed the little creature to another part of the meadow."

Griffin sighed loudly in exasperation then declared acidly, "We guessed that much when we lost sight of you." Then he glared at her and shouted! "Now tell us what, if anything, happened next! If it's not too much trouble!"

Angela began, "Well, on the other side of the meadow there is a natural spring that has formed a large very deep pool. Someone has built a stone structure at one side and then placed large flat stones all around its edge. It is really quite beautiful."

Griffin had heard enough. He shouted angrily, "What has this to do with Elgats! You are a waste of my time just as I said you would be! I'm leaving! I have more important work to take care of today!"

Annwynn interrupted in the child's defense. "If you will just give her a chance, I'm sure she has something of interest to tell you."

Angela sensed that for some reason, Griffin wanted her to leave without telling her story, and decided to quickly establish the fact that she had indeed met an Elgat, before Griffin had a chance to dismiss her.

She smiled up at Planus, who had just put his hand comfortingly on her shoulder, and continued. "When I followed the mouse into the stone building I met an Elgat male. He was very handsome and in no way deformed."

Angela studied their faces and all, with the exception of Griffin, were filled with anticipation and excitement. Griffin showed a complete lack of interest. No. She was wrong. He was behaving as if he had already been informed. He knew of her news and for some reason did not want the others to hear of it...but why?

Griffin felt her gaze, understood what she was thinking and quickly smiled one of his astonishing smiles. In a voice that oozed with false interest, he declared, "Well Angela, so you managed to make contact with an Elgat. My, my, I must say that I am surprised...pleasantly surprised of course. Please do carry on with your fascinating report."

Angela continued calmly but bluntly, "He believes that Princess Annwynn was kidnapped hundreds of years ago and that all Trillans are liars."

All of the Elders began to shout at once. Denying any wrong doing on the part of Trillan or of its Elders. Griffin shouted. "He is the liar! He is an outrageous liar! Annwynn was found abandoned in the Earthling meadow and she was completely alone!"

Angela felt strangely unafraid as she continued. She inquired in a calm voice, "Were you all present when she was found? If you weren't, how can you possibly report on what really happened?"

A hush fell over the group. There was a long silence and then all eyes turned to Griffin.

Griffin returned their gaze and replied coldly, "I found her, and in exactly the manner I related to you." He smiled at Angela, and in a voice filled with a false sweetness, asked, "Whom do you believe, dear Angela? After all, why should we lie to you? What would be our motive? Annwynn has lived as a Princess in Trillan and will soon Oath with a Prince. Now be honest, does that sound like ill treatment to you?" Griffin declared in a voice filled with righteousness, "Of course we haven't treated her badly. Why you have only to ask her yourself. This Elgat was obviously lying for some reason known only to his sick mind."

The Trillan Elders were all nodding their heads in agreement. Just like so many sheep, thought Angela.

Annwynn took Angela's hand in hers and announced, "I want to meet this Elgat. He is of my own community and I will be able to reassure him of my safety and well being." She added with conviction. "Don't you see? If others feel as he does, they will continue to raid Trillan. Perhaps I can bring an end to our difficulties with Elgat simply by meeting with this young man." Then she declared emphatically, "I must meet with him! Angela will accompany me."

The Elders were filled with panic. Planus stepped forward and said, in a voice filled with concern, "Dear Annwynn, it wouldn't be wise for you to meet with this man. Perhaps the disease that has disfigured the bodies of the other Elgats has instead done something to this one's brain. He might wish to harm you or even kidnap you!"

Annwynn smiled kindly at her friend and replied, "Oh Planus! Why would the Elgats want to kidnap someone that they had abandoned all those years ago? It doesn't make sense does it? Think about it!"

Griffin and the other elders remained silent.

Annwynn turned toward Angela and asked, "Would you stay close by during the meeting?" Quickly adding, "At your normal size of course."

Angela smiled and agreed. "Of course I will be more than happy to be of some help to you."

Planus still had questions of Angela. "Was there nothing more said? He just said we were all liars and kidnappers and then vanished?"

Angela smiled at Planus. She liked him and continued, her eyes now filled with mischief. "Well there were a few other things said...For instance, he believes that Annwynn is being held as a slave and forced to work in the meadow as a common field worker, for he has seen her toiling there on many occasions in the company of a frizzy haired female slave."

Darvith had heard enough and was now red with rage. "How dare he refer to the Princesses of Trillan as 'field working' slaves! I will personally slice off one of his ears for that insult!"

Another of the Elders stepped forward and scolded reproachfully, "Really Darvith! This violent streak you seem to possess and your outrageous temper, are a complete mystery to us! They are certainly not Trillan traits! Do try to calm yourself and let Angela continue with her report uninterrupted by your inappropriate outbursts!"

Darvith sulked as Angela continued, "The Elgat claims that the leadership of Trillan permanently blocked Elgat's Access to the Golden Light of the Great Crystal. He also claims that this was a deliberate action and that it took place over a thousand years ago." Angela took a deep breath and added, "He sincerely believes this and was very, very angry."

Tears began to flood Annwynn's beautiful eyes. She sobbed, "Can it be that they have been without light from the time I was found in the meadow? How have they managed without a light source? We must help them." Then she added hopefully, "Perhaps I was placed in the meadow because Elgat was in such great turmoil. Perhaps it was to keep me from some sort of danger."

The Elders, unforgivably, laughed.

Griffin spoke harshly, "Don't be ridiculous Annwynn! For you to imagine that placing a baby alone in an Earthling meadow, filled with hungry predators, an act of kindness, is ludicrous!"

Annwynn lifted her chin in a show of defiance and turned to Angela. She took the child's hand in hers and inquired with great concern, "Did he tell you how they have managed without a light source?"

Angela shook her head and replied, "I asked but he wouldn't tell me. He said it was none of my business, nor was it the business of Trillan, for whom he accused me of spying."

The elders were silent for a moment and then Planus suggested, in a voice filled with concern, "We should wait until Prince Vorden returns to the capital. He can accompany Annwynn. It isn't fitting that she should go to such a meeting unattended."

Darvith once again interrupted. "She won't be alone, for I will go with her!" She continued with great conviction, "We will be perfectly safe with Angela. She will guard both of us and there is the added bonus that he knows her."

Darvith quickly added, "If Prince Vorden were to go with Annwynn, there might be a fight. I'm not at all certain that the Prince would win. Are you? Don't forget, Elgats are trained to be warriors, practically from birth...Trillans are not!"

Griffin gathered the Elders around him and after a long and heated discussion a decision was reached. Darvith would accompany Annwynn. They would meet with Angela and be taken to interview the Elgat at two in the afternoon, Earth time. The elders left, one by one, Griffin the last.

Darvith and Annwynn were very excited about the upcoming event and were filled with questions about the mysterious Elgat.

Angela answered as many of them as she could and then added, "I liked him. I'm sure the fact that he looks so much like my father, Rory, has much to do with my impression, although his personality is nothing like dads. This Elgat is about as rude as you are Darvith, and bad tempered. But when he smiles his eyes dance and he has the most wonderful laugh. Yes, I like him. I think you both will too, at least I hope so."

Annwynn gave Angela a huge hug when she learned of the sadness that had already entered her young life, and said that she thought the silver hair was very becoming. Annwynn asked, "Do you wish it were black again?"

Angela shook her head and answered, "I used to, but I don't care anymore. The doctors think it might become black again when I'm older, but it really doesn't matter. I've grown used to it now."

Angela and the Enchanted Bell

Darvith changed the subject. There were important plans to work out. Who cares about hair anyway...nothing but a blasted nuisance! She'd shave it all off if she could. She flushed when she recalled the Elgat's insult...frizzy blond hair indeed!

However, her angry countenance quickly changed to one of calm as she inquired, "Is there an easy way to get to the stone building for our meeting with the Elgat?"

Angela beamed and replied, "Yes! I know just how I'll do it and I think you will be pleased when you see what I have in mind."

Both Princesses were very curious, but in spite of many entreaties, Angela held firm and told them that it would have to be a surprise.

At last it was time to leave and this time Annwynn accompanied Darvith and Angela to the bank of the stream. She was amazed at the awesome sight of a full-grown Angela.

Darvith laughed and then teased her friend. "Close your mouth Annwynn, you look ridiculous! Oh! If only Prince Vorden could see his Princess now!"

Annwynn turned to her friend and declared, "My word but you were brave to talk to this creature! She's enormous!"

Darvith laughed as she replied, "Ah! But you forget...when I first saw her she was sitting, and not nearly such a formidable sight."

They were all laughing when they said goodbye, promising to return at the agreed time.

Angela was suddenly very hungry. It must be time for lunch. She murmured under her breath, "Let's hope there are no unexpected visitors today."

CHAPTER 8

The Meeting In The Stone House

Sarah greeted her with a big hug when she entered the cottage and Angela was grateful to find the kitchen empty. Fresh buns and a steaming bowl of homemade soup lay waiting for her on the table, two favorite meals in one day. Life was good!

After a leisurely lunch Angela could sense that Sarah was ready to return to her work. She offered to do the dishes and mentioned that she planned to visit the meadow again after she played a while with the kittens.

Sarah agreed and asked Angela to say hello to the Trillans and Elgats for her. It wasn't long before the familiar tap...tap...of the typewriter keys could be heard.

Angela took the kittens up to her bedroom where they continued to play happily. She grinned at them and once again was grateful that she had been allowed to choose two, for they truly were good company for each other.

Now she must get down to work! She began to search through her closet and then through the big chest that rested at the end of her bed. Where was it? It had to be here somewhere.

Angela and the Enchanted Bell

At last she found what she had been searching for, the Royal Coach her father had built for her last year. The perfect conveyance made from an almost weightless wood, so it would be easy to carry with the Princesses inside.

Sarah had lined the interior with gold brocade. Beautiful pale blue velvet covered the cushioned seats and backs, and there was soft matching carpeting on the floor. Her father, Rory had carved an intricate leaf and vine motif on the outside of the coach and later painted it gold. She smiled happily and murmured to herself, "Yes! This will be perfect!"

Now she had one last task. Where were her adorable kittens? They were playing at her feet just a moment ago. She smiled when she checked their box. There they were, Cedric curled up in a neat little ball and Boris sprawled across his bunched up blanket like an exhausted Sumo Wrestler. Everything about Boris made Angela smile. She decided to leave them upstairs; it wasn't necessary to disturb them.

Two o'clock was drawing near. She must hurry to the stream, much better to be early than late. Carefully holding the coach in her arms, she walked quickly down the path. Soon she saw the familiar Golden light just under the surface of the water. The Princesses had arrived and Angela thought they both looked beautiful, like creatures from a Fairytale.

Darvith laughed. "Annwynn...I don't believe Angela will be happy until she changes us into fairies. Whatever 'they' are! Whenever she looks at me I read the thought 'Fairy', prancing around in her tiny brain."

Annwynn smiled kindly at Angela and then chided Darvith. "Don't be so rude! I think that it's charming to be compared with creatures that she obviously thinks are lovely. I shall accept the comparison as a compliment."

Darvith entered the beautiful coach without comment and urged, "Oh do hurry Annwynn! We don't want to be late! I can't wait to give this arrogant Elgat male a tongue lashing he'll never forget!"

Annwynn complimented Angela on the beauty of the Coach and then quickly stepped inside.

Angela latched the doors, warned the princesses to grasp the inside handle, and then carefully began her trek across the meadow.

Darvith and Annwynn could hardly contain their excitement and kept remarking on how incredible the meadow looked from the air, and on the magnificence of the flowering plants. Then the pool appeared before them.

Darvith gasped in surprise, "I had no idea that such a body of water existed so near to where we have been working all these years!" Then turning to Annwynn she added excitedly, "We must visit it the next time we gather our medicines."

Annwynn's eyes were bright with excitement as she replied, "Oh yes Darvith, we must!"

A vague uneasiness began to dampen Angela's enthusiasm toward this meeting, a strange feeling that something might go wrong. She carefully looked around to see if there were any large predators, like weasels, in the vicinity.

Darvith laughed and taunted, "Ring the blasted bell if you're nervous! I can assure you that I'm not afraid!" Then, realizing that she had once again been rude, she added softly, "For goodness sake Angela, your 'size' will scare any predator away."

Angela laughed and suddenly felt calmer. She smiled at the Princesses. Of course, Darvith was right. She asked, "Where would you like me to put the Coach. Darvith suggested that if it were placed just inside the door, it would be possible for Angela to guard them 'and' the entrance at the same time.

Angela placed the beautiful Coach on the floor. The Princesses remained safely inside. They waited...and waited.

After several minutes had passed, Darvith became impatient. She stepped out of the coach and exclaimed, "I knew this Elgat would be a coward! He was too frightened to return for this meeting! There is not an Elgat in sight! We have been tricked! Let's return to Trillan! Now!"

Annwynn stepped out of the Coach and gently chastised Darvith. "Do try to be more patient! We don't want to offend him; we want to make contact with him. Now let's give him a chance to see that we mean no harm, and that we have come to see if we can be of any help."

As soon as Annwynn finished speaking, the Elgat appeared from somewhere near the floor and the wall. Angela guessed that he'd been waiting there to see that it wasn't a trap.

He immediately strode over to where Annwynn stood and fell to one knee. With head down he announced, "I am Commander Stavro, Leader of your Elgat Guards, all regions." Then he rose and smiled as he stood before her. "May I say what a pleasure it is to be in your presence at last. All of Elgat is eagerly preparing for your return."

Annwynn smiled graciously. She was uncertain as to how she should respond. As a friendly gesture, she took his hand in hers and introduced him to Princess Darvith.

Stavro did not bow. Instead he gazed down into Darvith's beautiful green eyes and accused her and her fellow Trillans of keeping Annwynn a prisoner, and worse, of kidnapping a Royal Princess, the only claimant to the Elgat Throne. Then upon gazing down at her foot, he demanded to know why she wasn't limping!

Darvith, for the first time in her life was at a loss for words. She stared at him incredulously. Her voice quickly returned however, and she inquired acidly, "And why is it that you think I should be limping, you fool?"

Angela was filled with rage as she shouted, "Because yesterday he mistook my mother for a Trillan and stabbed her in the foot!" She glared at Stavro angrily, "You horrible man! My mother is a gentle, kind creature and you caused her to be in great pain!"

Instead of retreating in fear, Stavro stood his ground. In an attempt to justify his behavior, he explained that he knew the Trillans used charms and magical spells. He had often seen the animals in the meadow stand as still as stone when the tiny bells were rung. He assumed that they also had a spell that could change them into giants. After all, just minutes after he had talked to Angela and arranged a meeting with the treacherous Trillans, what did she do but bring a giant Trillan back with her. Obviously to set a trap in order to sabotage the peaceful meeting that was to take place the next day.

Angela considered all that he had said and decided that from his point of view his actions were justified. Even Planus had remarked on the likeness and in all fairness, she had to agree. However, the fact that he had caused her mother pain still angered her. She glared at Stavro again and declared hotly, "I suppose you were responsible for her plunge into the pool as well!"

Stavro nodded sheepishly, then explained, "But I set that particular trap long before you moved to the cottage." He added remorsefully, "I'm truly sorry if I've harmed an innocent." Then bowing to Angela, he said with great sincerity, "Please say you will forgive me?"

Angela graciously accepted his apology, and although she was still angry, she realized that there was far too much at stake to halt negotiations now.

Annwynn, however, was still angry with him because of his rudeness to Darvith. She declared, with a slight edge to her voice, "Commander Stavro, as you can see for yourself, I am not now, and I can assure you never have been, a prisoner in Trillan. I have always been treated as a

Royal Princess...indeed the Royal family adopted me when I first arrived in Trillan."

Her anger now spent, she smiled at Stavro and continued with great sincerity, "It has just been a misunderstanding that has divided our people. You must tell them that, for the truth is, if the Trillans hadn't found me in the Earthling meadow on that day so long ago, I most certainly would have been eaten by one of its creatures."

Annwynn smiled again and added, "We have agreed to meet with you today in that hope that we can help you regain your light source and heal your bodies."

Now it was Stavro's turn to be taken off guard. He stared at the Princesses in disbelief and demanded, "What makes you think that our bodies need healing?" Then without waiting for an answer he added, in a voice filled with disgust, "Liars! The Trillans are liars! Their lies have robbed you and your people of a thousand years! You were stolen for those discs you wear around your neck, the discs that are held in that pendant. 'That' is the truth!"

Annwynn covered the pendent with her hand as if for some kind of comfort. Huge tears welled up in her eyes as she stammered, "I don't believe you! You're...you're lying!"

Darvith was furious! She strode over to where Stavro stood and slapped his face, very hard!

Stavro immediately slapped her back!

Darvith gasped in disbelief! No one had ever dared to strike her in return. She did not cry out in spite of the fact that her cheek stung from the blow. She would not give him the satisfaction! The brute!

It was time to intervene. Nothing would be accomplished if this behavior were to escalate. Angela suggested that they all take a deep breath and then each party should tell their story without interruption. They all nodded in a silent agreement.

Angela noted that a bright red handprint now glowed on the left cheek of both Darvith and Stavro. She smiled inwardly and thought, 'two of a kind'. Darvith was distracted by darker thoughts at the moment, and didn't pick up Angela's, but Annwynn's knowing smile told her that she had, and agreed.

After a brief discussion, it was decided that Stavro would be the first to tell his tale. His handsome face projected strength and purpose as he began. "A thousand years ago Elgat was a happy and prosperous place in which to live. All of the outlying kingdoms were peaceful and productive. The 'Golden Light' still bathed our land."

Stavro smiled at Annwynn and continued, "It was a beautiful spring day when our Princess, whom you call Annwynn, was to be given her "Royal' name. She was the only child of our Royal couple and very precious to the whole realm for one day she would be Queen.

This was long before the stone structure was built and our spring made into a deep pool. The meadow belonged to us and we used it for many of our important ceremonies. At that time, the animals respected us and stayed with their own ways." He added sadly, "Unfortunately we lost our peace with the creatures of the meadow when we lost the 'Golden' light."

He continued stonily, "We were having a feast in the meadow to celebrate the 'Naming Day' of our Princess. Everyone was filled with joy and great happiness.

Quite unexpectedly, The Trillan Elders arrived uninvited and bearing gifts for our Princess. We had been trading with them for a thousand years or so, and many of our people had become the life-mates of Trillans, therefore we saw no reason to be alarmed." He added, "In fact one of the Trillan Elders had become very friendly with our Elders, and was a frequent guest in Elgat, and because of this, their presence, although unexpected was not regarded as suspicious in any way."

Angela and the Enchanted Bell

Stavro's countenance changed to reflect the rage he felt so strongly in spite of the passage of so many years. "They brought food and drink to the feast. It was a delicious addition and everyone tasted or drank some of it, for in Elgat Society it is considered very rude to refuse to eat and drink with friends." His voice was now filled with hatred as he continued with his tale. "The Trillans knew they could use this custom to their benefit. Much later we awoke to find that we had all been drugged and our Princess stolen from us. She had been wearing the Royal pendent with the five Golden Discs as part of the day's ceremony.

It was a double and devastating blow to Elgat! For when we returned to our land it stood in total darkness. The Golden light was no longer ours. All of our Crystals had been deliberately and systematically destroyed. Our Enemies had struck what was to have been the final blow...the end of Elgat! The Trillans had tricked us. Their treachery had robbed us, not only of our light source, but more importantly, of our Princess, the last of our Royal line."

Once again Stavro smiled at Annwynn. "Luckily our Elders didn't tell the Trillan thieves and liars everything about our culture. We still have some important secrets known only to a trusted few. Once you and the five discs are returned to us, we can begin our final plans for the complete restoration of Elgat."

Angela had been studying Annwynn's face to try to judge her reaction to all of this new and shocking information. She could only see great sadness.

Annwynn sighed deeply and said, "Stavro, you have twice mentioned that my pendent contains five discs, but from my earliest memory there have only been three."

Stavro's handsome face looked troubled. He shook his head and declared softly, "Well, that is most unfortunate. There were five discs. If two are missing, the Trillan Elders must have removed them when you were still a baby." He mused, "I wonder what they have been using them for...I must find out. The citizens of Elgat may be in more danger than I thought."

Annwynn began to reflect on the behavior of the Trillan Elders when she and Darvith left on this mission. They had wanted her to leave the pendent with them and became very angry when she refused. Now she understood the reason why they had behaved so badly, all but her dear friend Planus. He couldn't have had any part in this treachery.

She sighed deeply. The seed of suspicion had been planted in her heart and it was already beginning to take root. When she gazed up into Stavro's earnest, strong face she could not think of a single reason to disbelieve anything that he had said. What had he to gain by making up such an elaborate story? Annwynn felt in her heart that he was telling the truth. She both liked and trusted this brave young Elgat.

Darvith too liked Stavro, but would rather have died than admit it to anyone. Her cheek still stung hotly from where he had struck her. However, she was comforted by the fact that her tiny handprint still glowed scarlet on his cheek.

Out of the blue, Angela innocently asked, "If Elgat wishes to live in peace as you say Stavro, why does it still have armies for you to command? Trillan doesn't have armies."

Stavro raised an eyebrow and inquired, "Now how would you know whether Trillan has armies or not? I'm sure you haven't seen much of Trillan. Why, one of the outer kingdoms might well contain a great army!" Then he added kindly, "Of course you are entitled to your own beliefs Angela, but I can assure you that no Elgat will ever trust a Trillan again!"

Stavro studied Angela for a long moment and then offered a further explanation. "Unfortunately, Trillan is not our only enemy. Since the beginning of our restoration, when we were still weakened by Trillan's treachery, we have been attacked by warriors who live in a country called Tavia. It lies on our eastern Border. I would love to learn more about their country. Unfortunately, it seems they would rather die than be captured."

He added fiercely, "The threat of invasion is always present and we must remain prepared. We will never be caught off guard again!" Stavro gave Darvith a sharp glance and declared, "There will be a swift death for those who dare to attack us!"

Suddenly Angela felt an icy chill, it invaded her body and she shivered involuntarily. Stavro's fierce expression was frightening her.

Stavro sensed her discomfort at once and smiled. It was a wonderful smile that engaged his eyes in a most mischievous manner.

Angela grinned back at him, once more at ease. She liked Stavro. Yes, she liked him very much.

Stavro's eyes continued to dance with mischief as he suggested, "Perhaps as Commander of the Guards I could enlist your help in infiltrating Tavia. You share their coloring. They also have silver hair and bright blue eyes. Why you could just blend in with the population, and find out all that we need to learn." He added with a wink, "Mind you, none of our Elgat Guards have returned, but I'm sure that a bright little Earthling like you would have no trouble at all. How about it Angela?"

Annwynn rested her hand on Stavro's arm and gently scolded him. "Now stop it! Angela doesn't realize that you are just teasing her. Can't you see that you're making her nervous."

Angela admitted, "I guess I was a little. Please tell us more about Elgat?"

Stavro was just about to reply when Annwynn spoke, "I believe all that you have told me Stavro. So many things that have taken place in Trillan over the years that puzzled me now make sense. What is it you wish me to do?"

Stavro smiled at the Princess and replied, "I want you to return to Elgat with me and leave these treacherous Trillans behind, forever. I promise you will have a wonderful life in your own land, among your own people. Trillans can never be a part of your new life with us. They simply can't be trusted." He took her hand in his and continued in a voice that was firm with conviction. "You must come with me now. Your subjects have prepared a wonderful celebration in honor of your return."

Darvith quickly reached for Annwynn's other hand and cried out passionately, "Oh Annwynn, please wait a moment! Think! You have just met this Elgat! He could be lying! It could be a trick!" Darvith was pleading now. "You have lived with us for so long. You know us! You don't know him! Planus and I love you! Prince Vorden loves you! We need you! Please, please don't go with him Annwynn!" Darvith was so filled with emotion that she began to tremble.

Annwynn gently put her arms around her dearest friend, who was now sobbing bitterly. Finally she spoke. "Please try to understand Darvith, and put yourself in my place. I must go and see for myself, just as you would want to do if you were in my place. I trust Stavro and I don't believe he will let any harm come to me."

However, Darvith wasn't satisfied and pleaded, "Let me come with you. I can protect you! Please let me come with you! You must!"

Annwynn held Darvith at arms length and declared firmly, "No. I thank you dear sister, from the bottom of my heart. You are so brave and I know that you want to protect me as you always have, but this time I must go alone." She added solemnly, "However there is something to be done and only you can do it. Will you help?"

Darvith could see the resolve in Annwynn's eyes and reluctantly accepted her dear friend's decision. Her eyes were filled with tears as she asked, "What is it you wish me to do? I will help you in any way that I can."

Annwynn began slowly, forming a plan as she spoke. "I want you to see if you can find out about the two missing discs, and if they hopefully, still exist." She continued, "Also, you have access to the Great Library and all of the Birth Records. I want you to find all the information you can about my origin." She quickly added, "Perhaps at the same time you could check to see how the Trillan light source evolved."

Darvith was silent for a long moment. She looked at her dear friend sadly and replied, "You want me to become a traitor and to spy on my own people. I can't do that."

Annwynn nodded sadly in affirmation, "Yes. But surely you want to know the truth for your own piece of mind? I know that you and many other Trillans would never have condoned the offences Stavro has related to us." Annwynn's arms once again encircled Darvith in a reassuring embrace. "You are the only one who can take on this task. The only Trillan who has a chance of learning the truth! Please Darvith, as a sister, do this for me! Do it for both of us!" They held each other closely for a long moment.

Darvith pulled away and began to pace back and forth. Suddenly she stopped and declared! "Yes! I will do it! I will do it for both of us!"

Annwynn was very serious as she warned, "Do be careful of Griffin. I know you like to torment him in subtle ways, but one of these days I'm afraid you will go too far. I have heard that he has a hidden prison where he takes his enemies, and they are never seen again."

Angela shuddered and declared, "He's really scary. I had nightmares after my first meeting with him."

Then Annwynn smiled at Darvith and said lovingly, "Just be your usual bad-tempered self and I'm sure everyone will continue to leave you alone."

Darvith smiled in spite of the fact that her heart was filled with sadness. How bleak life was going to be in Trillan without the presence of her dear friend...her only friend.

Annwynn took Darvith's hand and led her to where Stavro stood. She commanded, "As your Royal Princess Stavro, I want you to formally apologize to Princess Darvith for striking her."

Stavro looked down into Darvith's beautiful eyes and gently touched her cheek with his hand. Then, much to the surprise of all who were present, he bent down and kissed the red mark that still showed there.

Something overpowering had taken hold of him, a sensation he had never before experienced. It was known in Elgat as "Bella". In a voice, husky with emotion, he said, "I am in your debt. I can see that you are a good and true friend to our Princess. I beg your forgiveness for striking you." Then he added with a rueful smile, "It was more of a reflex action than an intent to harm; I've never struck a woman before." He touched his own cheek and said, "You possess remarkable strength for a young woman!"

Once again, the talkative, anything but shy, Darvith, was at a complete loss for words. However she did manage an appeal and murmured softly, "Please take good care of her."

The Princesses embraced once more, each wondering if it would be for the last time. Then Annwynn and Stavro disappeared.

CHAPTER 9

An Uncertain Future

Darvith stood as still as stone. Tears flooded her eyes as she cried out in deep sorrow, "I miss her already! She is my dearest friend and I may never see her again!" She continued to sob as if her heart were breaking.

At last she regained her composure and began to pace back and forth, while talking out loud. "What am I going to tell the Elders? For that matter, what am I going to tell my parents?"

Angela heard Darvith gasp, and then blurt out, "What if they have been a part of the conspiracy? What if they have known of it all along?

Old memories came flooding back to her...the fact that both she and Annwynn had always felt like outsiders in the Royal court...in a strange way isolated from the others. Whereas her sister Tova, was given great respect, in spite of her youth. The respect one would give the future ruler of Trillan.

Darvith was silent for a long moment, and then she spoke softly, as if she were thinking aloud, "What if I was taken from another Kingdom as well? What if it wasn't an act of kindness that allowed us to live in the Royal Palace. What if the Palace was just an elaborate prison where our every move could be monitored?"

Suddenly remembering that she was not alone, Darvith quickly glanced up at Angela and suggested, "I think that it's time I returned to Trillan. There is much work to be done." With that said, she entered the coach and continued to talk as they crossed the meadow on the way to the stream. Angela held the coach in such a way as to allow easy conversation between the two of them.

Darvith sighed and said, "Poor Prince Vorden. How will I explain all this to him? He loves her so much and I gave my word that I would protect her and bring her back safely."

At this point Angela interrupted. "We. 'We' promised to bring her back safely."

Darvith countered, "That may be true, but I'm the one who must live in Trillan…you only visit." They were both silent for a moment. The tension that had shown in Darvith's lovely face lessened and her lips formed a sad smile. She asked, "Tell me Angela, do you think Stavro was speaking the truth?"

Angela considered the question and replied, "I think he believes it to be the truth, but Annwynn is the only one who can give an unbiased and accurate view of Elgat and its citizens." She added with great sincerity, "I think both you and Annwynn are enormously brave, and I'm so proud to have met you."

Darvith was silent for a moment and then looked up at the giant child whose expression was so earnest and sweet. She smiled and said, "Thank you for saying that Angela. I don't know why it should make me feel better, but it does."

Darvith was once again filled with her usual confidence. She declared with great enthusiasm. "Let's go! Onward to the battlefield! I will simply tell them that there was a distinguished envoy waiting to greet her, and that they insisted she return with them to Elgat where there was to be a great celebration in her honor."

Darvith smiled and continued. "I'll tell them that Annwynn felt that her refusal would be taken as an insult to the citizens of Elgat. However, she insisted that she must return by two in the afternoon on Saturday, and that everyone present agreed."

Angela was puzzled by Darvith's last statement and interrupted. "I didn't hear you agree on a time for her return? Did you just make that up?"

Darvith laughed and quickly explained that she and Annwynn agreed on the time of day while they were hugging each other. Then she smiled mischievously and raised an eyebrow. "You think I'm full of tricks don't you? I guess I am at that! However, I did not invent the time of her return. Whether or not she will be 'allowed' to return is another question." She added mysteriously, "There is something else that you haven't noticed."

Angela was once again puzzled and studied Darvith for a long moment.

Darvith smiled and held Annwynn's pendent where Angela could see it. Amazingly, the Princess was now wearing it around her neck.

Angela stopped and stared at Darvith with dismay. She stammered, "But...but don't the Elgats need it? Aren't you afraid they will hurt Annwynn when they find out that she doesn't have the discs with her?" Angela's blue eyes were now enormous, and filled with concern.

Darvith scowled and replied, "They don't need the pendent silly!" Then she smiled and added, "It's the discs they need and Annwynn has taken them with her. She gave the pendent to me so our elders will think I have brought the discs safely back to Trillan." Darvith sighed deeply and continued. "She thinks they will be less angry with me when I return without her. If she's right, it probably means that Stavro is telling the truth."

They had reached the bank of the stream at last. Angela gratefully placed the wooden coach on some moss. "Do you know, I must be tired. This coach seemed twice as heavy without Annwynn as it did when I carried you both." She scowled at Darvith and added reproachfully, "You didn't by any chance use a magic spell to add extra weight just so you could watch me suffer. You have a very wicked sense of humor!"

Darvith laughed. "Oh Angela, are you never going to trust me again? I suppose you're still angry with me about the 'bell' incident."

Angela snapped, "That 'bell' incident, as you call it, is easily the most frightened I've ever been in my life; it still makes me shiver whenever I think of it."

Darvith laughed again. "Then my dear, you must cease thinking of it! What could be simpler?"

Her rather flippant and unsympathetic remark elicited another scowl from Angela, who was in no way amused.

Darvith jumped out of the coach and shouted, "Oh all right! Dear Angela, I promise, with all that I hold dear, to never, ever, trick you in any way again." She added solemnly, "I never break my word."

Angela smiled and murmured a simple, "Thank you."

Darvith smiled back and replied, "Thank you, Angela." Now I must leave. I see the Coach approaching the surface. Don't forget our date on Saturday!"

Soon Darvith was on her way to Trillan. She was ready! Yes! She was ready for the fight of her young life!

CHAPTER 10

The Triumphant Return Of A Queen

Annwynn felt uneasy as she followed Stavro down the long corridor that seemed to be situated inside the wall of Angela's stone building. At least that's where she thought she was...She sighed resignedly, "I could be anywhere." It didn't matter. She still felt that she had made the right decision, to be with her own people in the land of her birth. Although this corridor she was now walking through was completely enclosed, it managed somehow to be as bright as the earth plane's daylight. In fact the walls seemed to glow with a wonderful iridescent light. Unlike the Golden light of Trillan, which tended to be calming this wonderful light seemed, well, playful. Yes! That was it! This light made her feel energetic and playful. It was a joyful light.

Stavro raised his hand as they approached what appeared to be a wall. It opened and allowed them access to a descending stairway, then slid swiftly and silently back into place once they had passed through.

Annwynn felt a momentary sense of panic and wished dear brave Darvith were with her.

Stavro immediately turned to face her and smiled at her reassuringly. "Please don't be frightened Princess, for I assure you, you have nothing to fear from your own people. They love you very much."

Annwynn found both the sound of his voice, and his presence to be comforting. Once again she allowed joyful feelings to invade her heart. She loved the energy this new light seemed to produce and she did feel that she was somehow returning home.

Once again they approached what appeared to be a wall, and again Stavro raised his hand, and again the wall slid away. Instantly, a rush of wondrously scented air greeted them. The air was as sweet and clean as the scent of the blossoms and leaves of the Earthling's Season of Spring.

Annwynn stood on a knoll overlooking the great capital city of Elgat. Sparkling lights like a million stars stretched out before her all bathed in the wonderful iridescent light. It was a breathtaking sight.

Stavro led her to a beautifully decorated and slightly elevated platform. There were Elgats everywhere and all were cheering for their princess. She was home at last.

Many of the Elgats had tears of joy in their eyes. Beautifully costumed groups made lovely sounds with their voices. Annwynn had never heard singing before and was both charmed and thrilled by it.

A hush fell over the gathering as nine women and one man approached her. There was something familiar about them...of course these must be the Elders. Each greeted her with words of welcome.

Annwynn was surprised to learn that she could not read their thoughts. However she smiled at them in acknowledgement, at the same time wondering how they managed to prevent mind intrusion.

One of the Elders stepped forward and said, "Forgive us. You are at a disadvantage for we are all able to read your thoughts, while ours our shielded from you. It is a simple trick. I will teach you." She smiled kindly and continued, "Our future Queen must not have unguarded thoughts."

Within minutes Annwynn had mastered the technique. She thanked the Elder and then said, "I wish I could teach this method to a friend of mine."

The Elder offered, "You needn't worry about Darvith. You are surprised that we know of her are you not? I should explain. We, the Elders, witnessed your meeting with Stavro in the old stone building. He carried a device that enabled us to both see and hear most of what took place."

She took Annwynn's hands in hers, and said comfortingly, "We have taken the precaution of sending a guard with Darvith. We understand her temperament and are fully aware of how insulting she would find this act. Therefore, he will be invisible to all for the time he is with her."

Annwynn was both amazed and delighted. She asked, "Is invisibility a gift that Elgats possess? I must have lost my power to vanish. How useful it would have been in Trillan."

She smiled warmly and added, "You have no idea of how happy I am that you've sent someone to protect Darvith. I fear she will need a guardian although she certainly wouldn't agree."

The elder continued, "He is the only brother of Commander Stavro, and a brilliant scientist, with many discoveries to his credit." Then the Elder continued, "Alas, he is the only one with the ability to remain invisible for short periods of time. It's one of his latest discoveries. Perhaps it will one day be available to all."

At this point, their conversation was interrupted by Stavro, "Please excuse me Princess, but everyone is anxious for the celebration and feast to begin. They are all longing to catch a glimpse of you."

Annwynn followed Stavro as he led her toward the banquet area and the cheering throng. And what a feast it was! There was much singing, laughing and general merriment, and soon Annwynn was lost in the joy of the celebration.

Goblets were filled with a wonderful liquid that tasted of honey, and the tables were laden with platters of delicious food.

During the Evening Annwynn walked around the vast banquet area, visiting all the tables and talking to as many of the Elgats who were present as she possibly could, laughing with them and just listening to what they had to say. She found them to be a wonderfully kind and friendly people. Annwynn had never felt so loved or so at home.

After the feasting was over and all of the dishes cleared away, the next part of the celebration began. Dance groups from each region in her Kingdom began to perform their intricate dances for her. These were performed while accompanied by wonderful sounds produced by instruments that were blown into, while in other instances by strings that were plucked.

This glorious evening would live in Annwynn's heart forever; she was overcome with happiness. Trillans did not sing or dance or have musical instruments. In her heart she knew that she would never return to that ancient Kingdom. This was her home.

Alas, too soon it was time for the celebration to end. After one last chorus of a soulfully melodic Anthem, her subjects returned to their homes.

Unknown to Annwynn, a pair of eyes had been watching her every move, all night long. Stavro had been studying her reactions carefully and was now convinced that the pleasure and joy that she exhibited throughout the event, were genuine emotions. It was obvious that in spite of her long separation from Elgat, she knew that

Elgat was her real home and these were her people. He could see it in her eyes.

Stavro wondered if she was in love with Prince Vorden, and if she could leave him and Trillan behind forever. He scowled and murmured softly, "I wish the Elders hadn't been so quick to give her the power to shield her thoughts. It would certainly be very useful to read them now."

Stavro smiled ruefully when he touched his bruised cheek. Until this day he had openly despised Trillans. Now as his thoughts turned to Darvith he found he could not hate her. He admired bravery, loyalty and passion, and this young woman had displayed all three of these virtues. Try as he may, he could not erase the memory of her from his mind. She was...he paused in thought...she was magnificent.

Stavro's thoughts drifted back to a chance meeting he once had with a Mystic near the Border of Tavia. It wasn't so much the meeting he remembered as much as it was all that she had told him. She claimed that she could predict his future by holding some tiny blue stones in one of her hands and his left hand in the other.

Stavro remembered how she had shrugged in indifference when he had laughed at her predictions, so many years ago it now seemed. Later, as more and more of her predictions unfolded, just as she said they would, he decided to revisit her. Unfortunately, he never found her again. She had disappeared. It was one of her last predictions that now filled his mind. It had been there for a long time, haunting the shadows.

'A golden creature will cast a spell and steal your heart. It will be lost to you forever, for she will never release it, or give you her heart in its place. She will be near to you but forever far. Her brilliance will weave through your lifetime like a golden thread. Only your death will bring her to your side.'

Later that evening, Stavro related the predictions to his fellow guards and remembered how they had all laughed uproariously, at even the suggestion that he, Stavro, could ever suffer from unrequited love. Young women had always thrown themselves at him, practically at his feet. There were times when he found their attentions very embarrassing.

But now, recalling the encounter, a strange uneasiness filled his senses. He frowned and mused softly, "What was the mystic's name? Was it Aleesha, or was that the name of the kingdom where she was born?" Stavro could only remember the name for some reason. In fact everything about her was more like an image from a long ago dream. Ordinarily his memory of even the most distant events was sharp and clear, but for some reason his encounter with this mystic remained cloudy. All he could really remember about her appearance was that she had golden hair. He simply couldn't remember what she looked like but he could remember the sound of her voice to this day, it was clear and melodic...it was an enchanting voice, almost hypnotic. Stavro suddenly became aware of the fact that he had heard that voice again, and recently. It was Darvith's voice. But how could that be?

Stavro was still lost in thought when Annwynn approached him. She took his hands in hers and exclaimed, "I have never been so happy! Thank you for bringing me home Stavro." She kissed him on the cheek and added, "I'm grateful to your brother too, for I was very worried about Darvith's safety. She is both brave and clever, but there is an Elder, Griffin by name, who is very powerful and presents a very real danger to her.

Annwynn continued confidingly, "He knows she is unafraid of him and will stand up to him when he is wrong, which is most of the time. She deliberately provokes him and one day I fear she will go too far. Until now she has managed to outsmart him, and while it is nothing more than a game to her, Griffin is deadly serious. I have seen the rage in his eyes and one day I fear he will make her pay."

Stavro's countenance darkened. "Ah yes! Elder Griffin is very dangerous and known to all in Elgat. It was he who often visited with us when our lands were friendly, and it was he who brought destruction to Elgat and kidnapped you, dear Princess, all those years ago."

Annwynn stared at Stavro in disbelief as he continued, "On my Oath, I swear I am telling you the truth."

Annwynn's eyes widened as she asked in a hushed voice, "How many Trillans know of this treachery?"

Stavro was silent for a long moment and replied stonily, "I honestly don't know."

Annwynn shivered involuntarily as she inquired forlornly, "Why do you suppose he didn't murder me as a baby and just keep the pendent?"

Stavro replied, "He probably felt that he couldn't take the chance. There were too many witnesses. However, I'm sure he considered the act. He may have believed that you might one day be more useful as a pawn."

Stavro took her hands in his and continued. "Tell me, did you suffer from any mysterious illnesses as a child? Were there any life threatening events such as accidents?"

Annwynn gasped in horror as she remembered. "Yes. In fact there were three accidents. Indeed, I would not be alive today if Darvith had not rescued me on each occasion." Annwynn gazed up into Stavro's eyes as she added "She very nearly lost her life the last time. How Griffin must hate her for her interference."

Stavro smiled sadly and confessed, "We owe Princess Darvith our deepest gratitude for keeping you safe. How I wish I'd left her with a better impression of Elgat Chivalry." He added comfortingly, "Try not to worry about her too much Annwynn. I realize that is easier said than done, but she has my brother Bowdren with her now. Frankly, between the two of them I don't think Griffin has a chance."

Stavro smiled down at Annwynn and said gently, "You must be exhausted. I think it's time I took you to your new home. The Royal Palace has been empty too long.

It has been carefully maintained since the death of your parents, many years ago. We all knew that you would return to us one day."

Annwynn sighed softly, "Please tell me about my parents? I wish I had a memory of them but I haven't." She added hopefully, "Do I have any brothers or sisters?"

Stavro shook his head sadly, "Unfortunately no, you do not have any living relations." He continued with pride in his voice, "However, I can tell you a great deal about your parents. They were a magnificent couple! As you can imagine, they were heartbroken when you were lost to us and never gave up hope of your eventual return, but you must realize they had all of Elgat to organize. It is a huge country with many different regions, all of which were now plunged into darkness. As our leaders, our King and Queen had to overcome their personal grief in order to help bring all of our people together once again, in a united Elgat." Stavro added with genuine admiration in his voice, "It is my belief that the restoration would not have taken place without them. They were a truly remarkable couple!"

Stavro smiled warmly at Annwynn and continued. "Once the discs are returned to us we will once again have access to the Golden light. We now have all the necessary crystals. Griffin has obviously used one of the discs you were carrying to activate the Trillan light source. I wonder what he's done with the other one. We must have all of them back!"

He continued, "Our current light is superior in every way but one, unfortunately only the golden light gives immunity to the rays of the Earth Realm's Sun. Our skin now burns with just the briefest exposure to it, thus preventing our people from visiting the meadow that had been ours since the beginning of Elgat recorded history." He added proudly, "My brother Bowdren is convinced that once the Golden light is returned to us, we will quickly be able to build up the protection we need and once again claim our meadow."

The couple had been walking slowly but steadily as they engaged in this conversation. Stavro stopped and pointed to a beautiful structure that lay just ahead of them. It resembled a huge, many faceted diamond. He announced with the sweep of his hand, "The Royal Palace of Elgat, and your new home."

The structure sparkled in Elgat's wondrous light. However, Annwynn could see no windows, doors or balconies. When she remarked on this, Stavro explained that once inside, the reverse was true everything could be seen from the windows and balconies of the Palace. This was possible because of a special shielding and it was the shielding that gave the structure its jewel like appearance.

Stavro smiled down at Annwynn and assured her that the Palace had hundreds of floor to ceiling windows each opening out to private balconies. It is a remarkable structure built to insure complete privacy for the Royal Family. Annwynn was very impressed and declared, "What a splendid idea! Just the opposite to that draughty old Palace in Trillan where there was no privacy at all."

Stavro confided, "You might be surprised to learn that Griffin designed the Palace in Trillan. He used to boast of his designing ability when he visited Elgat. I wouldn't be surprised if he had secret entrances and exits incorporated into the structure."

Annwynn shivered and said, "Now I'm beginning to worry about Darvith again. How I wish she were here with me and safe."

Stavro smiled and said with twinkling eyes, "Somehow I don't think that being 'safe' has all that much appeal to Darvith. She would soon be bored and impossible."

They laughed together as they entered the Palace and Annwynn was once again relaxed and happy. Stavro had a wonderful affect on her. He was like the older brother she had always wanted. She was filled with curiosity and walked toward one of the main floor windows, and just as he had promised, she was able to view Elgat, twinkling in the distance.

There were portraits of her parents in the main greeting hall. Stavro remarked on how much she resembled her mother. He asked, "Do you mind if I address you as Annwynn?"

Annwynn smiled and answered, "Not at all. You see Darvith chose the name for me and it is very close to my heart." She added, "Do you suppose I will be allowed to keep it now that I am in Elgat?"

Stavro smiled and said reassuringly, "I will inform the Elders that it is your wish." He added, "I shall also tell them of Darvith's efforts to keep you safe while you were living in Trillan and of the fact that she named you. I'm sure they will agree that you should continue to use the name Annwynn. It is a very pretty name and suitable for a future Queen."

Annwynn was introduced to her vast staff and everyone made her feel comfortable and at home. She turned to face Stavro and said, "It's odd, but in spite of the fact that they are lost to me, I feel for the first time in my life that I am a part of a family. It feels wonderful! Thank you again Stavro!"

At last it was time for Stavro to leave. He took Annwynn's hand in his and told her that he would return with the elders on the following afternoon, for there was much to be discussed. After advising her to get a good nights rest, he bowed, turned and left.

Annwynn felt completely at home in her new surroundings. After saying a few words to each of her staff, she decided to follow Stavro's advice and retire to her room. She was very, very happy as she walked over to the balcony and gazed out over Elgat. The wondrously scented air combined with the magnificent view brought tears of joy to her eyes. She sighed deeply, drinking in the moment. She was home. There was only one thing more she could have wished for, Darvith's presence here beside her. She sighed again. "I will find a way to bring her here. I will find a way."

CHAPTER 11

The Magic Of Invisibility

Unfortunately for Darvith, she was now back in Trillan and just as she had expected, was greeted with angry recriminations.

The Elders were unrelenting in questioning everything that had taken place during her absence. Every detail was brought forward and then discussed. Why had she returned without Annwynn when she had promised to guard her and bring her back safely? Why hadn't Angela, the Earthling, been of more assistance? Why had they trusted an Earthling in the first place? The questioning went on and on until Darvith thought her head would split.

As a distraction she casually displayed Annwynn's pendant by running her fingers around its edge absentmindedly. Darvith hoped that there would be no reaction from the Elders, but she was to be disappointed. There was an immediate change in tone. Now there were trite murmurs. "Oh well, perhaps it's for the best." Followed by, "She was never really one of us. Now the Elgat raids will stop."

At this point Griffin added slyly, "I was never totally convinced that Annwynn wasn't in some way helping the Elgats steal from us."

Darvith could feel her cheeks turning red with rage and was about to say something in Annwynn's defense when Griffin seized the opportunity to try to snatch the Royal pendent from around her neck.

He had been quick, but Darvith was greatly relieved to find that the pendant had somehow managed to catch on something at the back of her dress.

Quick as thought Darvith explained to the Elders that she had given her Royal vow to Annwynn that she would personally keep the pendent safe. She smiled innocently at Griffin and declared, "So you see, 'I' must keep it. As you are well aware I'm sure, a Royal oath is unbreakable." She deliberately said this loudly and clearly in front of all who stood there in order to thwart any future plans that Griffin might have to obtain the pendent by force.

One glance into his cold green eyes showed her the fury that lived there. However his lips formed a kindly smile as he said evenly, "Well of course Darvith, it will be as safe as you are until she returns to us."

Darvith knew with chilling certainty that this was a threat to her very existence. No one else seemed to notice and she wondered at their complete lack of perception. Griffin seemed to have a special power over everyone but her. Why couldn't they see how evil he was? All at once she felt very alone and strangely tired.

Darvith knew that all of her thoughts could be read and was therefore being very careful.

As a child she had learned when adults were near, to focus her thoughts on one object, any object, the more uninteresting the better. They would soon become bored and would leave her presence. The ease, with which she had fooled them over the years, never failed to amuse her. She used this ruse often and was using it now. She smiled as the Elders began to leave one by one, they were satisfied that there was nothing more to be learned.

Griffin however, was not satisfied. He was angry. He had hoped to uncover plans or strategies that he was as yet unaware of, but could discover nothing. Darvith was blocking her thoughts with a mental image of the Earthling brat, Angela, because she knew it would anger him. Although he was infuriated and filled with rage, he smiled and said, "Well goodbye Darvith. Perhaps I'll see you at the Great Hall tomorrow. Take good care of the pendant."

Darvith smiled at him knowingly and then put her hand to her mouth to cover a yawn. She said tonelessly, "I'm going to see my parents and sister and then climb into my bed. I doubt if I'll see you tomorrow. Goodbye"

This was the Darvith that infuriated Griffin the most! She was reverting to the 'don't bother me, I have other, more important things to do,' Darvith. It made him want to strike her. Everyone else in the Kingdom feared him. He knew this and used it to his advantage. He smiled wickedly. The power it granted him was thrilling.

Annwynn was terrified of him; he had seen it in her eyes countless times. That timid little Elgat would be dead by now if it weren't for Darvith's interventions. Darvith! Even as a child, she showed no fear at all. His most recent threat, and he knew she knew it was just that, seemed to have no effect on her. Yes! He decided at that moment, one way or another, Darvith would have to be dealt with, and soon. Griffin turned on his heel and angrily strode away, deep in dark thoughts.

Darvith was left with the depressing feeling that at least part of what Stavro had said, was true. No one seemed to care in the least about Annwynn's safety. The possession of the pendant was all that mattered to them.

Bowdren was very impressed with the way Darvith had handled the Elders and most especially Griffin. Until now he had no idea of Griffin's appearance or of his ability to control others. Now it was much easier to understand how this man could intimidate weaker individuals. Only Darvith and the Elder named Planus, seemed immune to his strong will. Bowdren found Griffin's handsome face and winning smile to be more than a little frightening. It was a benign mask that covered an unspeakably evil Aura and was a deadly combination to the unsuspecting.

Bowdren smiled as he studied Darvith's Aura. Now there was an Aura to be reckoned with, and so much like his brother Stavro's, that they could have been twins. They were bold, passionate and utterly fearless.

Bowdren began to read Darvith thoughts as she tried to sort out in her mind who was friend and who was foe. She decided that only a few of the Elders knew the truth of what happened in the Earthling meadow. It was Griffin who found Annwynn, none of the current Elders were there…perhaps he is the only one to fear. She was certain that Planus wouldn't know. He would never do anything to hurt Annwynn.

Darvith was very fond of Planus, in a sisterly way. For a long time during their childhood, Annwynn, Darvith and Planus were inseparable. She sighed deeply, her thoughts now filled with happy memories of her seemingly endless childhood, filled with golden days. She sighed deeply. Now they were both lost to her.

All at once she began to scold herself aloud. "Grow up Darvith! Nothing stays the same and wouldn't I be bored silly if it did! Of course I would!" She laughed out loud as she continued on her way to the palace and her family. "Tomorrow I will check the Birth Records and see what I can discover about Griffin's arrival. How I despise him! If only Trillan could be free of his presence!"

Darvith knew that one could never tell a Trillan's age by his or her appearance until they had reached 2000 years Earth Time. At that time hair would begin to turn white and eyesight and hearing would be lost to some degree. Therefore, it was difficult to guess Griffin's age with any hope of accuracy. He looked so young but he always had, since Darvith's earliest memory of him. Yet, he should look at least as old as her parents. If she could pin point his time of birth she would then be able to check with the Trillans who were living at that time and perhaps gain some insight into the events that took place preceding Annwynn's arrival.

Darvith had never been interested enough in Griffin to wonder about his age before, but now she was intrigued. She had never heard of anyone living beyond 3,000 years Earth Time and that was considered a Great age. Could he be that old?

Bowdren was walking along with Darvith and reading her thoughts as they quickly made their way to the palace.

He watched with interest as her family greeted her and thought her parents' attitude toward her was very strange. Her sister Tova grinned at her and gave her a welcoming hug, but her parents seemed distant and cold, and by the lack of questions, completely disinterested in learning anything of what had taken place that day. Most surprising of all, they did not once ask about Annwynn.

This seemed incredible to him. Was it possible that they had already been informed...and if so, by whom?

Darvith was obviously used to this lack of affection from her parents for when she mentioned that she planned to retire, they just nodded and said goodnight. Whereas Princess Tova, hugged her sister again and chattered on and on, asking a million questions. Darvith lovingly answered each and every one.

Finally, after a long chat with Tova, she tucked the child in bed, kissed her on the forehead and left the room. Tova quickly fell asleep.

At last Darvith allowed herself to relax. She murmured softly, "I must rest. I will need my wits about me tomorrow if I'm to check the birth records without arousing Griffin's curiosity." With that said, she lay down and fell into a troubled sleep.

Bowdren gazed down at this young woman and was unsure of just how he felt about her. She was so unlike any of the young women he knew.

His thoughts drifted to a remembrance of the other young woman he saw so briefly in the stone house. She was magnificent! His heart had almost stopped beating when he first caught sight of her. He had always scoffed at the notion of 'love at first sight'. He laughed softly and shook his head. "As if a beautiful Princess would be interested in a humble scientist. Forget it Bowdren! She is way beyond your reach." He added, barely audibly, "However, I will do everything I can to help her friend and keep her safe. In fact I shall start by giving Griffin an illness that will put him in his bed for a few days and give her some freedom of movement in the Great Hall of Records." Bowdren smiled to himself as he reflected on the pleasure he would take in making Griffin sick. As an added benefit, the brief, but incapacitating illness, would give him the opportunity to search the private residence of the evil one. Bowdren was soon on his way.

CHAPTER 12

A Playhouse At Last

Angela had already decided that she would spend the next three days away from the meadow. Mr. Strom and Eric were to be coming out tomorrow with the new cupboards and would no doubt stay the whole day.

Sarah and Angela had spent the greater part of this day preparing the food they expected their guests would eat. Finally the refrigerator and pantry were both filled with enough food to feed two hungry visitors. "That should do it!" Sarah exclaimed with a smile. "Now I think it's time we had our nightly cocoa and then prepare for bed. I'm tired and I'm sure you must be as well."

Angela agreed. It wasn't long before Angela and her kittens retreated to her bedroom. Sarah entered the room to kiss her daughter goodnight only to find her fast asleep.

Angela was awakened the following morning by the loud thump! Thump! Thump! of someone's boots running noisily up the stairs. "No doubt with a boy's body attached!" She declared angrily, under her breath. She was very annoyed.

Suddenly Eric's cheeky, freckled face peeked into her room. He grinned at her.

"Well really!" Angela declared peevishly as Eric began to roar with laughter. Her face flushed red with rage as she shouted angrily, "Don't you have any manners at all? You should never enter anyone's bedroom unannounced!"

She added hotly, "Especially a lady's bedroom! Haven't you been taught anything?" She picked up one of her stuffed toys and threw it at him. "Now get out and stay out, you...you little savage!"

Eric roared with laughter as he ran down the stairs.

"Boys!" Angela shouted loudly. She continued talking as she climbed out of bed. "Well I might as well get up and get this day over with!"

Her kittens raced over to her and she gave them a long cuddle. They rewarded her by purring loudly and grooming her fingers. It was then that she happened to glance up and catch her reflection in the dresser mirror. She laughed in spite of herself. She did look funny! No wonder Eric laughed!

Her long silver hair stood up in tangled masses and she had funny black marks all over her face. She was instantly filled with panic and concern. What had caused those black marks? Had she caught some sort of disease from the Trillans?

Upon closer inspection, Angela knew without a doubt exactly what had caused the marks. They were tiny paw prints. One of her kittens, or perhaps both, had been playing in the inkpad she carelessly left open yesterday afternoon. She smiled and murmured, "It's a good thing the ink isn't permanent."

Within minutes, she had brushed her hair, washed her face, dressed, and clasping a kitten in each hand, was on her way down the stairs.

Angela quickly ate her breakfast while chatting happily with Eric. Her anger had vanished and she was enjoying herself. The pair decided that they would ride their bikes to one of the playgrounds in town where they would spend the rest of the morning.

Mr. Strom, with Sarah's help, had already begun to work on the cupboards. Sarah called out as the children were about to leave, "Don't be late for lunch!"

Angela and Eric replied in unison, "We won't be late!" Then left the house talking and laughing.

The morning passed quickly and in no time the pair returned, hungry and full of chatter. Sarah and Ivan were outside in the garden talking when they arrived. Within minutes they were all enjoying a delicious meal.

Angela thought the cupboards looked perfect. Mr. Strom said Sarah had been a big help and that he was amazed at her strength. The compliment pleased Sarah; she hated the way so many people treated her as if she were some sort of Dresden doll, just because she was small.

Angela smiled inwardly. Mr. Strom had just scored some major points. She secretly watched him and was amazed to see that he finished a whole loaf of bread all by himself, just as Sarah had predicted. He also had three helpings of stew and three slices of apple pie. What an amazing appetite!"

It was time for the Strom's to leave. Sarah walked with Ivan and Eric out to their truck and Angela overheard her mother suggest that Ivan take a look at the old stone building in the meadow. She wanted him to give her an estimate as to how much it would cost to make it into a playhouse. She had added in a hushed tone, "Would be possible to finish it by Friday? It's Angela's Birthday?"

Ivan smiled warmly at Sarah. "Sure! I remember the place. I'll just take some quick measurements and have it finished in a couple of days." Soon the Stroms were on their way to fetch wood and window glass.

Angela felt an anxious moment but then quickly reassessed the situation. After all, if the renovations were to be ready before her birthday on Friday, they wouldn't interfere with her meeting with Darvith and Annwynn on Saturday. Suddenly, Angela was filled with excitement and expectation. At last she would have a playhouse…a space that would be hers alone.

CHAPTER 13

Confessions

Stavro arrived at the Palace the next day accompanied by all of the Elders and a young woman Annwynn hadn't yet seen. She would have been remembered for she was a lovely young Elgat with a beautiful heart-shaped face and thickly lashed large blue eyes that tilted up at the outer corners. Her hair was held back from her face, as Stavro's was, by a long braid down her back.

The stranger smiled and stepped forward. "Greetings Princess. My name is Rowena, and I am a professor at the Elgat institute of Science." Her large beautiful eyes were filled with concern as she asked, "I was hoping you might be able to tell me more about Trillan, and if you think my fellow scientist, Bowdren, will be in any danger there?"

Annwynn returned the young woman's smile and replied, "He should be quite safe as long as he remains invisible. As you all know of Griffin, and of just how dangerous he is, I'm sure Bowdren will be very careful." She quickly added, "It will certainly be for the best if Darvith never learns of his presence. She's a very independent young woman and would not appreciate anyone acting as her guardian. I'm afraid she would consider it an insulting interference."

Rowena frowned and gave an exasperated little sigh. "Please forgive me for asking this, but why have we risked the life of one of Elgat's greatest scientists for one who obviously doesn't want, or possibly need, protection?"

Annwynn could hear the hostility in Rowena's voice but decided to ignore it for the time being. After all, from her point of view Bowdren's involvement would seem unnecessary and possibly even foolish. Annwynn too wondered why it had been necessary to send such an important scientist. She explained, "I can't tell you why they chose to send Bowdren as a guard to Darvith. I can tell you that Darvith...'Princess' Darvith is carrying out a very dangerous search for me and indeed for all of Elgat. She has access to records that will hopefully explain the details of my arrival in Trillan and the whereabouts of the two Discs that are now missing from my pendant."

Annwynn continued, "I owe Princess Darvith my life for she has rescued me from certain death on three occasions. I consider her to be my sister, and when all of this trouble and treachery are behind us, I want her to visit with me in Elgat."

Annwynn smiled kindly at Rowena who was still visibly upset. "I want Darvith as a Trillan, to see what a wonderful country Elgat is, and how very attractive its citizens."

She smiled sadly, "Unfortunately, most Trillans are now convinced that Elgats are cruel and sadistic raiders of peaceful countries like Trillan. They also believe that the Elgats have recently undergone some illness that has distorted their bodies. Indeed the most recent sightings during the raids have all confirmed that many Elgats now have a toad-like appearance."

There was absolute silence as Annwynn gazed out at her visitors who were now staring back at her with incredulous eyes?

Stavro was the first to speak. "Princess, as Commander of the Elgat Guards, I can assure you that we have not been raiding Trillan, and as you have seen for yourself, we are certainly not toad-like in appearance." He added questioningly, "What makes the Trillans think that we look like toads?"

Rowena scowled. "Now I'm certain the stories about Trillans must be true. They are all delusional and lost in the dreams the Golden Light produces." She added derisively, "There lies your answer! They can no longer reason! Toads indeed!"

Stavro put his arm around Rowena in an affectionate, brotherly way. Then he smiled at Annwynn and explained, "Many Elgats, in fact I would say most, feel as we do about the Trillans. Please forgive us if we sound a little harsh."

Annwynn was puzzled. "Well if the Elgats aren't raiding Trillan and stealing valuable artifacts, then who are the toad-like people so many of us have seen?"

Stavro was very serious as he asked, "Have you actually seen these raiders with your own eyes?" Quickly adding, "Can you give us a description?"

Annwynn nodded her head. "Yes, I can." She continued, "Darvith and I were in the Earthling meadow gathering flowers and roots for our medicines when we noticed a strange looking creature standing on the bank of the stream. It had its back to us but was moving about in an upright manner. The bells had not affected it in any way, therefore we knew it couldn't be one of the creatures of the meadow."

They all listened with great interest as she continued. "We dropped to our knees and moved toward it as stealthily as we could. We were as close as I am to you now, when quite suddenly a strange buzzing noise filled the air, and forced us to put our hands over our ears to block the sound. The noise was more penetrating than loud." She added, "The creature's response to the noise was to dive into the stream and disappear from sight. I suppose it was frightened."

She smiled as she continued. "Darvith, bravely dove in after it and searched the bottom of the stream in the area, but could find no sign of anything unusual. It had simply vanished without a trace."

Annwynn was silent for a moment and then added, "As far as its appearance goes, it did have a body shape similar to our people, both Elgat and Trillan, but its skin was definitely toad-like and when it dove into the water we noticed that its feet were very large and webbed." She quickly added, "Many have seen the creatures. There have been sightings in Trillan near the lake. They do exist."

Stavro was the first to break the silence. "Well if they exist, and I certainly don't doubt your word Princess, who can they be?" He paused thoughtfully and then added, "It is certainly possible that another kingdom exists. However it is odd that they would be able to gain entry into Trillan without some help from the inside." He queried, "Has anyone been under suspicion?"

Annwynn nodded sadly. "Many suspected that I might be helping them in some way. Griffin was the first one to bring that rumor into focus, and by doing so, made me sound guilty. He has a way of making a defense turn into an accusation."

Stavro raised an eyebrow and remarked, "I think, dear Princess, that you have had another very narrow escape. Griffin no doubt had a plan in place that involved your execution for treason."

Annwynn was inclined to agree and once again began to worry about Darvith. She turned to Stavro and asked, "How long will Bowdren be in Trillan with Darvith? Does he intend to stay until the Discs are recovered?"

Stavro took her hand in his and remarked, "I don't think you need to worry about Darvith. Did you say that she dove into the stream in order to find a trace of that mysterious creature? What a brave young woman!" There was unguarded admiration in his voice.

Rowena retorted angrily, "More likely too ignorant to understand the danger!"

Annwynn had heard enough and jumped to her friend's defense. "Rowena! I will not have you speak of Darvith this way!" She continued with pride. "It's true that she likes to live on the edge of danger, but it is equally true that she has the most brilliant intellect in Trillan. There has never been a problem presented to her that she has been unable to solve. Unfortunately Trillan law forbids women to use their gifts in any of the professions, but I can assure you that everyone admires her intelligence, Griffin included."

Annwynn was very grateful that the Elders had shown her how to block mind intrusion last evening. This new skill was serving her well today.

The Elgat Elders were still unaware of where she had hidden the Elgat Discs and she intended to keep the hiding place a secret for a while longer. She had just met an Elgat that she didn't quite like.

It had been a long meeting and the Elders asked to leave in order to complete their duties for the day. Rowena was quick to follow after first saying a somewhat 'frosty' goodbye to Annwynn.

Stavro smiled warmly at his Princess, and explained, "Rowena is a wonderful young woman but she does have very strong opinions and rarely keeps them to herself. Please don't judge her too harshly; her life thus far has not been an easy one."

Annwynn returned his smile and remarked, "It would seem that we both have dear friends who lack that rather precious commodity called 'tact'...I don't believe Darvith ever thinks before she speaks." Then Annwynn tilted her

Angela and the Enchanted Bell

head to one side and teased, "Is Rowena soon to be your life-mate? You seem to be very fond of her."

Stavro smiled and replied, "Oh yes, I am, very fond of her, but her heart belongs to another, as mine now does." He added, "The truth is, I can't get Darvith out of my thoughts. She keeps invading my mind and leaves me with no peace. I am here to seek your advice. Tell me, is she promised to another?"

Annwynn smiled sadly and softly sighed. "Oh dear." She took Stavro's hands in hers and confided in a gentle tone, "I'm afraid the best advice I can give you is to involve yourself with someone new, and as soon as possible. Darvith is not for you, or for any other young man. I honestly believe that she will never oath. She regards 'Oathings' with terror, just as others might fear a horrible death...slow and painful. There are many broken hearted young men in Trillan who can testify to her resolve."

Annwynn explained further, "I love Darvith with all my heart but I could never share a roof with her. She would be impossible to live with in harmony! She is completely unpredictable, hates any kind of routine and has the most outrageous temper." She laughed lovingly as she continued, "She also takes far too many chances. Why I could tell you tales that would make your hair stand on end!"

Stavro interrupted, "But don't you see, that's exactly why I find her so bewitching! What a splendid and exciting life-mate she would be! What brave children we would have!" He continued with growing excitement in his voice. "I completely understand her wish to be free for it has been my own, and I will never force her to do anything against her will. We will have a wonderful life together that will be filled with adventure!"

Annwynn was silent for a long moment. She smiled warmly at Stavro and said with great sincerity, "Personally, I think you would be a splendid life-mate for

Darvith. I believe your love and admiration for her to be strong and true. However, because I know her so well, I fear that it will be a hopeless pursuit. Darvith loves but in a comradely impersonal way. She is very loyal to anyone she considers to be her friend. However, I don't believe she understands the kind of love one feels when one wants to Oath with someone forever, or if she does, she doesn't want to experience it in any way."

Annwynn took his hand in hers and added kindly, "Please believe what I say Stavro. I don't want to see you with a broken heart." She could see resolve in Stavro's eyes and knew she had not convinced him to abandon his pursuit. She felt great sadness for him.

Stavro, still filled with hopes and dreams, smiled at Annwynn and changed the subject. "There is something I'd like to tell you about my brother Bowdren." He continued, "There were two prerequisites for the guardianship of Darvith in Trillan. Firstly, the obvious strength combined with intelligence, and secondly, appearance. What you are unaware of is that Bowdren is as fair as Darvith."

Annwynn's eyes widened in surprise as Stavro continued with his explanation. "Every once in a great while, fair hair and green eyes show up in an Elgat birth. Apparently Bowdren was quite a shock to our parents because they had both been led to believe that their family lines were pure Elgat. However, it has long been considered a good omen when 'Golden Ones', as they are called, are presented. They are considered to be an important part of Elgat Society."

Stavro was strangely silent for a moment then added sadly, "As our future Queen, I must inform you that there was so much hostility toward Trillan at the beginning of our restoration, all 'Golden Ones' who were born were immediately terminated. When your parents learned of these tragic deaths, they put an immediate stop to the procedure. This is a part of our history that we remember with great shame."

Annwynn's beautiful eyes reflected the sadness she felt as she murmured a barely audible, "How terrible." She couldn't imagine how anyone could kill an innocent baby. Then she said, "It's odd that I have never seen a Trillan with Elgat coloring. There were many Oathings, surely some must have been born." Then she added, "Of course it's possible that some exist in the outer kingdoms."

Annwynn smiled and changed the subject. "Please tell me more about your brother Bowdren? How wonderful it must be to be invisible for a time! Was his coloring considered important in case his invisibility failed in Trillan's golden light?"

Stavro laughed and said, "Yes to both of your questions." It would be fun to be invisible, however, it's a recent discovery of Bowdren's and he's still perfecting it. And yes, we knew we would have to send a Golden one in case the invisibility failed, Bowdren was the most logical choice.

Although we had no way of knowing if there would be a way for him to enter Trillan, we assumed they would not let you visit with me unattended, and that person would need to return. Bowdren intended to follow him back into Trillan and see if he could recover the missing discs." He added, "We knew nothing of Darvith. We expected a burly Trillan Guard."

Annwynn laughed and declared, "I'm afraid such a Trillan does not exist. A burly Trillan!" She laughed again. "You must forgive me for laughing, it's just that Trillan males are not overly robust, most are very tall and slender." She considered thoughtfully, "Although I'm sure they could be, if they were trained to use their muscles in some type of vigorous exercise." She added, "However they are very attractive in their own way".

Stavro smiled at the Princess and bowed. "I must be on my way. If you have any questions please send for me. I am at your service night or day."

Annwynn returned his smile and said, "I look forward to seeing you soon with good news from Trillan."

CHAPTER 14

Dangerous Information

Meanwhile, in Trillan, Darvith was surprised and delighted to find that the Great Hall and Library were almost empty of Elders and students...and better still Griffin was nowhere in sight. How wonderful! She could have skipped! She smiled inwardly as she slowly made her way to the Birth Records. The few who were present in the hall, did not acknowledge her presence in any way.

Darvith seated herself in one of the high-backed chairs and switched on the attached crystal. Soon the earliest records were displayed on the screen that lay directly in front of her. The unseen Bowdren could also see them clearly.

Trillan records were first recorded at 10,000 ET, Earth Time. Darvith had never understood why Trillan records were kept according to Earth years. It was a complete mystery to her and to this day she had not received a satisfactory explanation. For some obscure reason it was considered to be easier. It was Griffin who insisted on using the System and no one seemed willing to invite his wrath by confronting him about its usefulness.

At last names and dates were now appearing on the screen. Darvith didn't recognize any of them. She concluded. "Of course I won't know any of these people." She murmured. "They all died long ago."

She continued to watch the screen, uncertain of just what she hoped to find, when suddenly, at 5,000 years ET, a tiny blur appeared and then just as quickly, disappeared from the screen. It was such a brief event that it would have been missed, unless the Trillan inspecting the records was actually looking for some discrepancy. Darvith was intrigued. She immediately tried to force the screen to reverse so she could check the blur more closely but it continued moving forward. Undaunted, she moved it forward as quickly as possible to the current year and then began again at 10,000 ET. When it reached about 6,000 ET, she put the records on slow scan. "Now!" She said to herself softly, "We shall see if there is something sinister about the blur."

All at once, there it was, Griffin's name and birth date appeared, unbelievably at 5,000 years ET. Darvith felt her heart race with excitement. The writing was very faint, barely visible. In fact a casual observer browsing through the records would most certainly miss seeing it. Darvith put the screen on hold and ordered magnification. She wanted to see why the writing was so faint. On closer inspection the reason was obvious. The record of his birth had been tampered with. This was a criminal offence. Of course there was no way of proving Griffin had done it...but would anyone else have a reason?

Darvith stared at the screen for a long silent moment. How could Griffin be that old? It was impossible! No one lives to be that age...and he looks so young...as young as Planus and others her age.

Darvith decided to continue to check the records and ran them forward. It wasn't until 3,000 ET that some of the other Elders appeared, followed by her parents the King and Queen. There were thousands and thousands more names and births, some that she knew of and some that she didn't, when suddenly an impossible event appeared, Griffin's name clearly recorded this time, at 3,000 ET.

Darvith's lips formed a wicked smile. "Well...Well...Well, it seems that I have you at last Griffin. The question is how will I make use of this information?" She switched off the Crystal and sat thinking. She sighed deeply, and murmured, "You obviously possess very special knowledge Griffin. I have been in greater danger than I had believed, I must be much more careful in the future. I wonder how you have managed to extend your lifetime to five thousand years?" Darvith shivered and whispered softly, "Perhaps you intend to live forever."

Finally she rose from her chair and ascended the circular staircase that led to the upper rooms and the Trillan History files. The room Darvith entered was spacious and thankfully, empty of Trillans. Bowdren decided to remain outside the door and act as a sort of Guard. After all, that was what he was supposed to be doing. He would read her thoughts later and learn of any important information.

Bowdren was very pleased with himself. Thanks to his intervention, Griffin was too ill to leave his bed. He seemed to be suffering from a mysterious illness that none of the Trillan healers were acquainted with. Bowdren laughed softly. The thought of Griffin's discomfort pleased him greatly.

Last night he had searched Griffin's rooms thoroughly but could find nothing of interest. He had already decided that once Darvith had all the information she needed from the crystals, he would allow Griffin to become well again. Bowdren concluded that Griffin must have a private laboratory hidden away somewhere, and he wanted a newly recovered Griffin to lead him to it.

Bowdren too was astounded to learn of Griffin's great age. As far as he knew, the oldest recorded Elgat was a mere 3,000 years and she looked every year of it. It seemed impossible and more than a little frightening to think that an evil force like Griffin could live possibly, forever.

Last night Bowdren had made several other discoveries concerning the many faceted Griffin. For one thing, he had night-sight. In spite of the fact that Trillan was almost continually bathed in golden light and therefore the interior of most buildings was bright as well, Griffin kept the inside of his private quarters in absolute darkness. Bowdren watched in amazement as Griffin not only entered the sealed darkened rooms, moving about with ease, but also searched for and retrieved items from various shelves where it was completely dark.

Bowdren found the sight of this evil man walking about in the darkness, chilling. A cloud of malevolence seemed to encircle Griffin. This ancient Trillan was a formidable enemy.

Another surprise came in the form of a haunting melody. Griffin had hummed a song that Bowdren had heard before, but couldn't remember where. Trillans did not have music in any form, where would Griffin have heard the melody.

Later he found his way to Griffin's bedroom and put the drug he carried into a goblet containing an amber liquid that sat next to his bed. Although he had no way of knowing of Griffin's great age, he was angry with himself for not taking a sample before tampering with it. As a scientist he shouldn't have been so careless. The mysterious amber liquid might very well be some sort of 'Elixir of Youth'.

Bowdren's thoughts turned to Elgat. Now as he stood guarding this doorway, in a strange building, in the land of his enemy, he wondered if he would be able to return safely to Elgat. Would he see his family again? He would miss his family, but there were no young women who had claimed or even touched his heart. Until today, he thought he was immune to love.

It was true that he admired some women in Elgat. His fellow professor Rowena was lovely and possessed great intelligence, but she was more like a sister to him. Bowdren frowned when he recalled their last conversation. She was unreasonably angry with him for volunteering for this mission to Trillan. Her usual calm and cool manner had turned to one of utter rage when he refused to give up the mission. Her behavior had been so out of character that it had made him laugh. She became furious and left the room, slamming the door behind her.

Bowdren smiled as his thoughts turned to Annwynn. She had captured his every sense. He could remember everything about her, from the way she looked, to the sound of her voice, to every word of her conversation. In the brief time he was able to study her, she had captured his heart. She was perfection!

On the other side of the door, Darvith was now in the process of reviewing Trillan history. She had never been given access to this room before, but today, thanks to the invisible Bowdren, she found the door unlocked. She couldn't believe her good luck.

According to the Crystal, Trillan history began at 10,000 ET, which coincided with the birth records. It was a fairly predictable beginning, tiny groups trying to survive with no great technological advances other than the surprising and unexplained ability to use crystals.

Larger centers gradually evolved and Elders were brought in as a ruling body and they in turn appointed a King and Queen to begin the Royal Dynasty. This was at 8,000 years ET. Life continued to progress predictably.

She sat up straight and murmured, "What's this at 4,000 ET?" The Trillan light source was beginning to fade causing general panic among Trillan citizens. By this time contact had been made with another Kingdom with whom they had begun to trade. Trillan Elders had visited this new Kingdom and found it to be very interesting. There was no explanation as to what the Elders had found so interesting about the new Kingdom.

Darvith frowned and muttered, "Now I know why these records have been off limits, they're incomplete!" She added scornfully, "I suspect the same hand that tampered with the Birth Records, has been playing in the History files as well."

She continued to read and was surprised to learn that there had been a revolt in Trillan at about 2,000 ET. All of the Elders but one were executed for treason. Elder Griffin, the youngest, was found innocent of the charges and was allowed to personally select the replacement elders.

Darvith sighed. "Well that sure explains a lot!"

No wonder all but Planus are terrified of him. I wonder why the text isn't more explicit, after all treason is a very serious charge." Then she laughed softly and added, "They probably dared to disagree with him." Darvith sank back into her chair sighing deeply as she did so; this was all too depressing.

Just then she noticed a special chapter devoted entirely to Trillan's renewed light source, brought about in large part by adherence to Griffin's extensive study on light emission. It was a glowingly flattering chapter extolling the great genius of Griffin, and the fact that he worked tirelessly for the benefit of all Trillans. "He probably wrote the blasted chapter himself." Darvith declared scornfully.

She paused when she caught a glimpse of Annwynn's name. She was soon filled with bitter disappointment as she read the brief notation aloud. "A female child, believed to be Elgat, was found in the Earthling's meadow. The Child was apparently abandoned by her own people, perhaps as some kind of primitive sacrifice." There was nothing more.

Darvith was very discouraged. She felt certain now that everything that Stavro had said was true. The only important information to have come from her research was Griffin's true Birth Date and the fact that he had tampered with both sets of records. Darvith knew that this was very dangerous information and she must guard it very, very carefully. She stood up and stretched. Suddenly she felt very tired. It was time to return to the palace. She needed to think.

Bowdren decided that he should make his presence known to Darvith. He didn't want her to do anything that would jeopardize his search for the discs, such as confront Griffin with her new knowledge. However, there was the question of her terrible temper. He muttered just below Darvith's hearing, "I'll just appear before her and take my chances. Who knows, she might be shocked into silence." He continued to formulate a plan as he followed her back to the Royal Palace. When she was safely in her room he swallowed the tablet that had been concealed in a ring he wore, and became visible.

Darvith gasped in surprise and then immediately regained her composure. "Who are you?" She demanded! "What are you doing in my room? If you don't answer this minute, I will call the guards!"

Bowdren caught her hand just as she reached to pull a velvet cord hanging next to her bed. He called out softly, "Please Princess, let me explain. Then if you still wish to call the guards, I will be your prisoner." Adding with a smile, "After all, where can I go?"

There was something about Bowdren's manner that made her hesitate. She decided to let him speak. If, as she suspected, this was a trap, she might learn more about it from the 'bait' that now stood before her; he was an interesting little piece of cheese. She declared hotly, "Well! Get on with it!"

Bowdren smiled his most winning smile. "Please allow me to introduce myself. I am Bowdren, the only brother of Commander Stavro of the Elgat Guards. I have been sent to help you recover the Elgat Discs."

Darvith raised her chin as she declared victoriously, "I knew you would tell me a lie! You may be surprised to learn that I have recently met with Commander Stavro, and you in no way resemble him." She added angrily, "This is obviously some kind of trick, instigated no doubt by Elder Griffin. Although it's hard to understand why he would try to pass you off as Stavro's brother when he knows of my meeting with the Commander today." She added grimly, "There is some devious plan within this plan, I can be certain of it! I shall call the guards!" Then once again she reconsidered.

Darvith's attention had been drawn to an unusual crescent birthmark on Bowdren's forearm. She possessed the same mark, in the same place and had never expected to see it on a stranger's arm. It made her feel uneasy...no not uneasy, but sad. Why should the sight of this mark on a stranger's arm make her feel sad?

Darvith was intrigued and decided to allow him to give a further explanation of his presence in her room. She gestured for him to continue, adding, "I have always understood that Elgats are dark-haired, fair-skinned and blue eyed. Tell me, how do you explain your appearance? You look like a Trillan, you are even dressed like one, and how did you get into Trillan from Elgat?"

Bowdren knew his best chance would be to give as brief an explanation as he could...brief and to the point. He began, "I am called a 'Golden One', there are many like me, who have been born into families who once had a blood tie through a Trillan-Elgat Oathing. In the case of my family, it must have been an Oathing that took place before our "Restoration', for there is no record of it. I was quite a surprise to them."

Darvith knew of these Oathings from Stavro's account of Annwynn's abduction. She nodded her head and agreed. "I'm sure you were." She told him to continue.

Bowdren, feeling more confident now, smiled at her as he continued. "Well, 'Golden Ones' make up about fifteen percent of the population and except for our exclusion from the military, we are treated equally and with respect. In fact, we are considered to be a 'Good Omen' and very good luck to the family who presents one."

Darvith commented dryly, "How very nice for you." Then she smiled an astonishing smile as she gazed up into Bowdren's earnest eyes. "I believe you. Griffin would never have had the imagination to dream up this story." She added candidly, "I have great admiration for your brother Stavro, although I'd appreciate it if you would just keep that bit of information to yourself."

Suddenly and quite unexpectedly, Darvith laughed. She gave Bowdren another of her astonishing smiles and exclaimed, "You! You caught the pendant at the back of my dress when Griffin tried to remove it!" Thank you!" She chuckled, "And you were the extra weight that poor little Angela had to carry across the meadow. Why, you've been with me since our meeting with Stavro in the stone house, haven't you?"

Darvith was suddenly serious. "Were you with me today when I was checking the records in the Great Hall?"

Bowdren nodded affirmatively. "As you are aware, the information you now possess is very dangerous." He offered, "Although I must say I'm impressed with your ingenious method of blocking mind intrusion, I would like to teach you an easier and perhaps more effective method. It wouldn't do to have this information known to all."

Darvith gratefully agreed and quickly mastered the technique. She felt more relaxed, not only because she could now block mind intrusion but also because she was no longer alone in the struggle against the evil Griffin.

Darvith asked, "Do you think the missing discs have something to do with Griffin's youthful appearance?"

Bowdren looked thoughtful for a moment and then replied, "I won't know of their powers until I've had the opportunity to study them in a scientific manner. I only know that they are believed to possess magical properties and were forged by ancient Mystics."

He added sadly, "Unfortunately, the Great Library that contained many volumes devoted to the Discs alone was destroyed at the time we lost our light source." Bowdren continued gravely, "As this was a direct result of Griffin's treachery, I suppose it is reasonable to assume that he now has any important volumes tucked away safely, somewhere in Trillan, although I didn't notice any books in his home last night. In fact there was nothing of interest there."

Again Darvith laughed and declared, "I take it then, that his absence today from the Great Hall was no accident. What did you do to him? Did you give him some unspeakably painful drug, or is that too much to hope for?" She quickly added with a playful smile, "Ah! How the thought of Griffin's suffering brings tears of joy to my eyes."

Bowdren laughed wickedly. "Yes Darvith, I can say with all honesty that Griffin suffered greatly." He added, "And alas, poor fellow, no one could ease his discomfort. I gave his sleeping draught a little extra kick. He will be fully recovered by tomorrow, when I hope to follow him and see if he has some hidden laboratory."

Bowdren was serious as he continued, "Tell me Darvith, were you aware that he has night-sight and can see Auras?"

Darvith shook her head. "Somehow that fact that he possesses night-sight doesn't surprise me but what is an Aura, I've never heard the term before?"

Bowdren was surprised to learn that Trillans, all but Griffin that is, were unaware of something that was so helpful in charting illness. He quickly explained. "An Aura is a luminous array of colors that surrounds every living creature. However not everyone can see them, fortunately I can. It is a fascinating study that I've been involved with for the last few years."

Suddenly Darvith asked, "What is the plan? How can I help you?"

Bowdren was quick with his reply. He snatched a pen and paper from Darvith's desk and made up a list of compounds and asked, "Can you obtain these items for me, and four medium sized mixing containers...oh yes and some measuring instruments meant for liquids?"

Darvith quickly scanned the list and said "yes."

Bowdren was very serious now as he asked, "Will it be safe if I work here in your room? Is there any danger of a visit from your parents perhaps? There must be no interruptions or the mixture will fail. This is very important!"

"Don't worry, there won't be any visitors." She assured. "What are you going to do? Will it be dangerous to anyone else in the Palace? My sister Tova is next door and I don't want her to be hurt."

Bowdren's attitude towards Darvith had changed. He was now playing the teacher role and she the student. He answered her last question impatiently, "I'm going to be doing something very important that will harm no one! Now off with you! Don't just stand there! Hurry! We have no time to waste in idle chatter!"

Darvith did not appreciate this dismissal. How dare he treat her as if she were a stupid child! However, she managed a sweet, submissive smile before she left the room. Annwynn would have recognized that smile and been worried. Bowdren did not.

Darvith quickly returned with all the compounds, the suitable mixing containers and the instruments for measuring liquids. It didn't occur to him to ask where she found these items so quickly and Darvith had no intention of telling him. The arrogant twit!

Bowdren proceeded to prepare two potions, one for invisibility and one to block his aura. He declared, "Well that's done!" Then he turned to Darvith and said, "All of this extra work could have been avoided had I not felt it was imperative to materialize in order to prevent you from doing something foolhardy and irrational." He might just as well have said 'stupid'.

Bowdren became alarmed at the fury now visible in Darvith's aura. He decided to try to placate her in some way. In the same patronizing tone he had been using, he said, "Now Darvith, I want you to stay near the Palace and behave just as you normally would. Griffin must not suspect your behavior is in any way different. You do understand don't you?"

Again Darvith smiled, she felt like answering with 'whatever you say, oh mighty and great one'...but instead she agreed with his plan while carefully documenting the ingredients, measurements and mixing procedures in her quick brain. At last it was time for Bowdren to leave. He said goodbye, drank the liquid and vanished from her sight.

CHAPTER 15

The Trap Is Sprung

Darvith quickly rushed to her private study where she had left the identical compounds Bowdren had used. She mixed them expertly, drank the liquid and instantly disappeared. Then after leaving a note for her parents, she left the palace.

She felt wonderfully free and could think of countless ways that she would be able to use this new gift. Now however, she must search Griffin's residence. She hoped that she wouldn't accidentally bump into the pompous Bowdren. He would be furious! The thought of his face, red with rage, made her laugh out loud! "I should have put a bell around his blasted neck!" She laughed again.

Darvith had taken a shortcut to Griffin's cottage and when she reached the top of the hill overlooking his property, she was just in time to see him leave by the back door. She wondered where he could be going. A wall made from stone encircled the tiny backyard. To her amazement she watched as he walked right through the wall and disappeared. Without hesitation she ran to follow him.

Griffin proceeded down a long wide tunnel and she continued after him. Every so often he glanced back in her direction, as if he expected to see someone.

At first it was unnerving but soon Darvith dismissed it as the action of someone, who is always trying to hide his evil deeds from others. Still, it was almost as if he expected to see something or someone, but who?

All at once the wall they were approaching slid downwards and without a moment's hesitation, Darvith followed Griffin into a well-lit corridor. There was no obvious source for the light. The wall slid quickly back into place. Darvith pressed her hand against it and noted that this was one wall that no one was going to walk through. She felt a momentary surge of panic but there was no time for hesitation for another wall immediately slid downwards as Griffin approached. Again Darvith and she assumed Bowdren, passed through.

Darvith immediately stepped sideways and pressed herself against the wall of what appeared to be a large and very well equipped laboratory. She reasoned that if she stayed where she was, she wouldn't accidentally trip Bowdren.

The Door slid closed in an instant like a trap! An exultant Griffin spun around to face the wall frighteningly close to where Darvith stood. He laughed malevolently and shouted, "I have you Bowdren! You were no challenge at all! You are an incompetent fool!"

Griffin chuckled and continued derisively, "You have no idea of how very difficult it was for me to remain silent, and not fill the corridor with hysterical laughter each time I turned and saw you tip-toeing behind me. As if I couldn't see you! I saw you that first day when you stood beside Darvith and prevented me from removing the pendant from around her beautiful neck."

Griffin raised his chin and scowled at Bowdren. "When did you decide to poison me? That wasn't supposed to be a part of your plan...just a bit of improvisation on your part, I suppose. Not a wise decision to have made, for you will pay for that bit of treachery with your life!" He added coldly, "I had intended to allow you to return to Elgat, but of course it is out of the question now...quite out of the question."

With the last of his tirade over, he produced a bottle of liquid from his pocket and threw it at the blank space beside Darvith. Bowdren appeared for all to see. Griffin shouted, "Seize him! Put him in chains!"

Darvith pressed herself against the wall and waited for the same exposure, but nothing happened. For some inexplicable reason Griffin was unable to see her. She was ecstatic!

Griffin continued to torment Bowdren with still more taunts. Then all at once he smiled an astonishing smile. "I see you are wondering how I managed to trap you so easily. I knew of your coming you fool! I knew everything about it, of your quest for the missing discs and the books from the Elgat Library. Oh I have them all right, but you'd never have found them."

Griffin frowned and said, in a voice filled with disdain, "Did you really think that you could protect Darvith? A fool like you would have difficulty protecting much of anything, I would think...at least judging from your efforts in Trillan.

Griffin laughed and continued, "Darvith would never have been as easily caught. I alone know of her real worth. And soon she will belong to me. I have waited a long time for her to grow to maturity, a very long time." His tone was sinister and Darvith shuddered at the sound of it. Then he laughed sadistically as if he alone were aware of some private joke.

Griffin continued in a new and strangely hushed tone, almost as if he was talking to himself, "As a matter of fact, I have recently asked the King of Trillan for the Princess as my life-mate and he has given his consent." He added slyly, "Of course King Tallis could not deny my request. No one, not even the King, can say 'no' to any request from me. We've decided to keep the news of the 'Oathing' a secret from the Princess. It will be so much easier for everyone."

Darvith was stunned by this terrible news and wanted to strike him!

Suddenly a loud penetrating Buzzzzzzzzzz filled the air. Darvith and the others in the room immediately put their hands over their ears. She recognized the noise and remembered where she had last heard it. When she glanced over to where Bowdren stood chained to the wall; she could see that he was in great discomfort from the dreadful noise. There was nothing she could do to help him.

Finally the buzzing ceased and the wall directly behind Darvith began to slide downwards. She quickly moved aside as ten toad-like creatures entered the room. Instantly they began to strip off their outer coverings along with their huge webbed feet. Darvith was amazed to see that Elgats now stood directly in front of her, and one of them was a lovely young woman.

Bowdren shouted from across the room, "I demand to know where you have found Elgats who are willing to work with you, our sworn enemy?"

Griffin smiled triumphantly as he replied. "My dear boy, these are but ten of more than a thousand, and they are not Elgats, but Trillans. I have named them Elgans." He continued with obvious pride now rising in his voice. "For several thousand years I have had every child in Trillan shown at birth to have Elgat coloring, brought to me. I became aware early on that Elgat-Trillan children are brighter, and more gifted in special and varied insights than the pure Elgat or Trillan." He quickly added, "I am of course the exception, as there must be to every rule."

Bowdren interrupted, "Darvith seems to be very bright and I can't believe there aren't other Trillans who possess special gifts. My brother Stavro is an Elgat and I can assure you he is very intelligent." He added defiantly. "You are wrong in your assessment of the pure-blooded populations of each Kingdom."

Griffin was silent for a long moment then declared hotly, "I am never wrong!" Then he smiled slyly and said, "How could I assess your brother's intelligence, after all, we've never met. However I can tell you that Darvith is brilliant. I would say that her intelligence is even greater than your own." Then he smiled one of his astonishing smiles as he continued. "She is not a Trillan, Elgat or Elgan. Only I know of her true identity, of her true worth." He added with a sly smile, "I placed her in the care of the Royal Family just before Annwynn arrived, and swore them to secrecy. It's a secret that they will keep till death because the life of their only child, Princess Tova, depends on it."

Darvith was grateful that she was invisible to all. These revelations were beginning to take their toll and she felt tears rolling down her cheeks. She silently scolded herself and slowly began to formulate a plan for her escape with Bowdren. She vowed then and there that once they were safe, she would investigate the mystery of her existence.

Griffin continued with a confident smile. "As you are soon to die, I will tell you about my plan. In fact it will give me great pleasure to tell about an elite Society, a Society that would never have included you.

I've been training my Elgans for a thousand years and will soon be ready to build my new kingdom where Elgat and Trillan now stand." He smiled and added coldly, "Of course I will have to rid both countries of most of their population. Not much of a loss really, most of them are stupid, incompetent wastrels." He added. "We'll keep the strongest physical specimens for our heavier work, but the rest will have to be terminated, unless I can think of a better use for them before the magic day arrives." His voice began to rise with excitement as he continued, "My new Kingdom will be headed by brilliant scientists and 'I' will be in control!"

'Of everything but your mind', thought Darvith, she was not impressed and wished that she could tell him so, but there would be time for that later.

Griffin laughed. "When I presented an idea similar to this to the former Elders of Trillan, they dared to disagree with me! Can you believe it?"

He smiled wickedly as he continued. "I then set an elaborate trap for them that was later interpreted as treason, on their part of course, and of their own doing. No one believed their pleas of innocence and they were all executed. It was so easy!" Griffin added, "I had a similar trap in place for Annwynn. She too would have been executed for treason had she remained in Trillan but alas, she has escaped, at least for the moment."

Bowdren was horrified by this latest revelation; he quickly decided to change the topic in case Griffin could read anything from his thoughts. He asked, "How do you hope to execute this takeover? There are many more Elgats and Trillans than there could ever be of your Hybrids."

Griffin replied tonelessly, "Of course it would help if I could double our numbers by adding the 'Golden' ones, but right from the beginning I found them to be too volatile in temperament and illogical to be of any use to the new society."

Bowdren lifted his chin in defiance. "Perhaps we are just too intelligent for you to train."

Griffin laughed derisively and said, "Your pride is out of place here, don't you think, where you were caught as easily as a mouse in a trap. How inferior you must feel! Foolish...foolish Bowdren, you have been a great disappointment to me. There was a time when I had other plans for you. Now I'm grateful that I didn't waste the energy."

Griffin was about to turn away when Bowdren called out to him. "I thought you were going to tell me all about the 'Takeover'...your great plan." He added slyly, "As you stated, I am soon to die, so please enlighten me. I am after all, a captive audience in the truest sense."

Griffin once again smiled. "Of course...of course I will be happy to tell you all about it, in fact it will give me great pleasure." I shall tell it from the beginning.

"Thousands of years ago, I had two entrances to Elgat, this was long before your famous 'Restoration'. Rather than trying to learn of a way to penetrate Elgat's shielding, which may have aroused suspicions, I discovered a way to tunnel into Elgat in an area that was completely unprotected. We have always used rodents, even the occasional rat, to do our digging for us."

He snorted derisively! "That horrid little Earthling brat saw one of my mice and reported the sighting to the Trillan Elders, but none of them thought it was important enough to investigate. They are so unbelievably stupid." He added, "Of course their temperament might be slightly different if they weren't under the influence of the Golden Light."

Griffin smiled slyly. "My special additive to the light is one of the ways I have kept control of Trillan all these years 'and' robbed them of night sight...only Annwynn has somehow managed to retain the ability."

Suddenly Griffin's face changed from its benign expression to one of absolute rage! He had read Bowdren's thoughts and learned of Darvith's recent and important discovery. His voice was now cold and filled with menace. "So Darvith has checked the Birth Records and discovered my Birth date. She will pay for that knowledge with her life. The fact that she is a 'Daughter of Aleesha' will not save her now...not this time!"

Griffin angrily strode across the room and gave the order for Darvith's immediate arrest. He commanded, "Bring her to my study in the Great Hall as soon as you find her! I don't want to hear any of your excuses! Find her at once!"

Bowdren was overcome with despair and filled with anger at his own stupidity. He was indeed pathetic. He had just placed Darvith in the gravest of danger and there was nothing he could do to help her. What an arrogant fool he had been, and now she must pay for his stupidity.

During this brief moment, Griffin had turned his back to Bowdren; in fact no one was paying any attention to the prisoner, all were busy with other tasks.

Taking the moment, Darvith squeezed his hand and whispered in his ear, "Better dead than Life-mate to Griffin!" Bowdren's spirits soared! He was filled with awe; Darvith was truly remarkable; he would never make the mistake of underestimating her again. She whispered in his ear, "Try my trick to block mind intrusion." Then he felt soft lips touch his cheek and the release of his hand as Griffin once again turned toward him.

Bowdren decided to occupy his mind with questions for the ancient tyrant. He began, "How could you see me when I was following you? I know for a fact that no one in Elgat has ever detected my presence when I am invisible."

Griffin noticed a definite change in Bowdren Aura. The fool was happy! Why should he be happy? Griffin laughed, "I have no idea why it happened, but wasn't it lucky for me that it did."

Then out of the blue he asked, "Why are you so happy Bowdren? Auras never lie and yours fairly bubbles with happiness and good spirits. Are you hoping to make me angry?"

Suddenly Griffin grabbed Bowdren by the throat and spat out contemptuously, "You're going to die you fool! I can assure you there is no way out for you now!"

Bowdren quickly began to think of times when he'd been truly frightened and his Aura quickly changed to one that satisfied Griffin. The Ancient Trillan was happy once more and his fingers released their grip on the young man's throat.

Undaunted, Bowdren decided to continue with his questions. If there was a chance that he might be able to escape he wanted to have every bit of information he could get. He asked. "How do you hope to control the Elgats without the help of the Golden light?" He added, "The Elgat light source gives great energy and initiative and has a built in safety device to protect it. You will never conquer Elgat."

Griffin laughed and declared haughtily, "You are a fool! There is nothing and no one I can't conquer if I so choose! I have done it time and again! I always win!" He continued in the same arrogant manner. "For a thousand or more years my Elgans have infiltrated Elgat Society at every level. There are many thousands in strategic positions all over the kingdom." He smiled wickedly and added, "Many of whom you know personally."

At just that moment, one of the Elgans who had arrived through the waterway stepped forward and out of the shadows. Bowdren couldn't believe his eyes. It was Rowena.

The beautiful Elgan smiled her icy little smile and said evenly, "You would insist on volunteering for this ridiculous mission. I did try to dissuade you. Griffin's elders were willing to send an ordinary Golden One, but oh no, you had to make the big gesture; well now you will pay the price for your stupidity and arrogance. You are such an egotist Bowdren!" She continued coldly, "It's such a waste of a gifted scientist, and we still had a use for you in Elgat."

Rowena's eyes narrowed as she added, "I'm looking forward to meeting this 'Darvith' creature; everyone seems so in awe of her. I will enjoy dissecting her brain to see if anything unusual lives there." Then she laughed wickedly. "Oh get that horrified look off your face Bowdren; she will be dead after all."

Rowena then turned away from him, and after receiving some orders and papers from Griffin, she and the other nine Elgans from her group entered a corridor in the wall next to Bowdren and disappeared.

At just that moment a message appeared on Griffin's crystal. Darvith it seemed was not in the Palace. She had left a note for the King and Queen, informing them of her intention to visit Prince Vorden in order to give him the news of Annwynn's departure from Trillan. She promised to return within a week.

Griffin paced in silence for a long moment and then sent a return message "Find Darvith and arrest her for treason! I don't care where she is or with whom! Get her back here!"

Bowdren called out, "Wait! Why must Darvith die? How can she be of any real threat to you; she is only a woman."

Griffin studied Bowdren for a long moment and then smiled. It was an odd smile, almost sad. "Only a woman you say. Who are you to judge the worth of another creature?" Griffin was about to say something else when suddenly he turned from Bowdren walked over to the Crystal and sent another message. "I've changed my mind. I no longer want Princess Darvith to be arrested. Instead I want to have her watched. I must know where she is and what she is doing every minute of the day! Do you understand?" He added menacingly, "Your lives and the lives of your families depend on an accurate accounting of everything she does from this time forward!"

Griffin stood before the exit tunnel to Trillan. He turned toward his prisoner, as he was about to leave. "Goodnight, dear boy. I trust you will have a very uncomfortable night. I do hope the mice don't find you, chained up as you are; they probably wouldn't leave very much for me to experiment with tomorrow." He smiled wickedly and continued, "Still, I mustn't be selfish, and I can manage my experiments with surprisingly small amounts of tissue. The poor creatures must have their daily nourishment." With this last comment Griffin began to chuckle. It was a low menacing sound that was far more like a growl. He added, "You see, I leave the tunnels open to the Earthling meadow at night, thus allowing the rodents to forage for food and enjoy any tasty, uninvited trespassers." After another burst of raucous laughter, the door slid open and then quickly closed behind him.

Bowdren took a deep breath and tried to calm himself. The thought of a hungry rat from the Earthling's meadow racing toward him filled him with fear.

Darvith spoke softly to him. "I have the keys to your chains. I'll release your hands first so you can help me. Be quick! We've no time to lose." She gave an exasperated little sigh. "Blast Griffin! There must be at least 20 separate locks on your chains. I hope it's just a simple matter of matching the numbers on the keys to each lock."

They worked quickly and in a short time Bowdren was free. He stretched and then laughed. "I'd give you a hug if I could see you. Please accept my apology." He added with a note of anxiety in his voice, "How do you know Griffin isn't still here and invisible to us?"

Darvith answered quickly, "I think the device on the wall by his crystal is a sort of display of his tunnel system. I'm sure that light you see moving along the shorter tunnel is Griffin on his way back to Trillan. I noticed when Rowena and the other Elgans went into the tunnel to your right that ten lights moved away from this area. The conclusion seems obvious." She added briskly, "Your apology is accepted. Just don't do it again."

Darvith was silent for a moment and then laughed as she teased, "Tell me all about dear, sweet little Rowena? It seems you must learn to choose your playmates with greater care. Is she a jilted once to be life-mate of yours? I thought I detected a certain tension between the two of you."

Bowdren shook his head as he answered, "I have known her and worked with her on projects at the Institute for many years. I thought we were good friends." He added sadly, "Now it seems that I didn't know her at all."

He asked, "How do you feel about being Aleesha's daughter? Have you ever heard the name before? I haven't. Griffin seems to attach great importance to your birthing. Did you know that he desired you as his Life-Mate?"

The invisible Darvith shuddered as she declared vehemently "I will never belong to Griffin or to anyone else! I can assure you that he will never see me again now that I have had this warning of his plans! I will never return to Trillan; I'd make my life in the Realm of the Earthlings first."

Darvith's voice lost its hard edge when she began to talk of Aleesha. "Anyway I think you misheard Bowdren. Griffin didn't say I was Aleesha's daughter, he said I was a Daughter of Aleesha. I interpret that to mean that either I was taken from some secret order, perhaps Mystics, or from a Kingdom that no longer exists." She added sadly, "I wonder how many other innocent babies he has stolen? How I despise him!"

The invisible Darvith clasped Bowdren's hand and declared, "However, I must say that it pleases me to learn that I am not a Trillan!" She added joyfully, "It's also wonderful to imagine that I might have a family waiting for me somewhere. Yes! Without intending to, Griffin has given me very good news!"

CHAPTER 16

Release From Captivity

Darvith traced the crescent birthmark on Bowdren's forearm with her finger and asked, "Tell me, have you always had this mark on your arm? And have you ever seen another just like it on any other Elgat?"

Bowdren shook his head and inquired, "Why? Is it important?"

Darvith was silent for a moment and then answered, "I don't know yet, but it might be."

Bowdren laughed and teased, "But what I really can't understand Darvith, is why you aren't thrilled at the prospect of becoming Griffin's Life-Mate? After all he is handsome, powerful, brilliant and the list goes on and on."

Darvith interrupted, "And let's not forget sadistic, devious, and very, very old." They laughed together and the laughter seemed to ease some of the tension they felt.

The still invisible Darvith gazed at Bowdren openly and critically. She decided that while he was handsome, he did not have the presence and authority of his brother Stavro. Griffin had been correct in his assessment of Bowdren. She too felt that he had made some very stupid mistakes, mistakes that could have taken her life. But most of all she remembered with anger that he had treated her as a lesser creature.

She made a decision! She would now take charge. She commanded, "Bowdren, I want you to make yourself invisible again immediately! I'm sure all the necessary compounds are here in this laboratory. Then I want you to remove any papers that you think might be useful. Perhaps the formula that keeps Griffin so young is hidden here. What a find that would be!" She continued enthusiastically, "It's even possible that the Elgat discs are here, within our grasp."

She pulled at Bowdren's arm and commanded, "Don't just stand there! Get busy! We've wasted enough time!" Quickly adding, "I'm going to check the tunnels."

Bowdren called out after her. "I don't think I'd do that if I were you!" His words of concern fell on deaf ears. He searched and found all the ingredients and quickly began the mixing process. After all, Darvith could take care of herself! She had proven that.

Moments later Darvith returned to find Bowdren nowhere to be seen. She called out to him but there was no response.

Unable to restrain himself any longer, Bowdren laughed.

Darvith was filled with rage at his childishness. She stamped her invisible foot and yelled, "Will you please stop being such a fool! There is too much to be done to be wasting time in this manner! I've reached the end of my patience with you! I mean it!"

Suitably chastised, Bowdren put on his most serious voice and they began to discuss the fact that they could find nothing of interest or even of value.

Bowdren remembered that Griffin had said the discs and books were somewhere safe and no Trillan or Elgat would ever be able to find them. He suggested, "Griffin obviously has another laboratory that is absolutely private. I wonder where it is?"

Darvith offered, "Perhaps Griffin wears the discs around his neck as Annwynn did."

Bowdren muttered, "More likely they're in that pouch that hangs from his belt. He sleeps wearing it. I tried to get into I but he rolled over onto it and was impossible to move him back again."

"Bowdren!" Darvith shouted angrily! "You make me want to strike you! Why didn't you just cut his belt off and pull it through? How could you have been so unimaginative?"

Bowdren was beginning to feel dreadfully inadequate. He was about to apologize yet again when they both heard a loud shuffling noise. They glanced at the tunnel maps but could see nothing. Could Griffin be returning by another route? No. The noise was far too loud to be an Elgat or Trillan.

Bowdren shouted to Darvith, "Quickly! Climb up out of reach; climb as high as you can!" The urgency in his voice quickened her speed. Unseen to each other, they managed to jump toward different rings that hung mysteriously from the ceiling.

Darvith wondered what possible use Griffin could have for ceiling rings, but not for long. Something else now had all of her attention.

A huge rat had entered the room and was slowly moving about the area just below her. She was grateful to be well out of reach and hoped with all her heart that Bowdren was as fortunate.

Darvith shivered as she recalled that only moments before, she had exited the same tunnel the rat beneath her had used to enter the laboratory.

Although the massive rodent seemed to sense that something edible was near, their invisibility made him uncertain and nervous. After sniffing the air and once nearly touching Darvith with his whiskers, it slowly shuffled off to one of the other tunnels, much to the relief of the invisible captives.

"We've got to get out of here!" declared Darvith in a shaky voice." She whispered, "I thought Griffin said that mice were in the tunnels at night. I wonder how many of them there are? Can you think of a way to frighten them off?"

Bowdren laughed then asked in mock disbelief, "What's this? Oh but surely this can't be the great Darvith asking for Advice?"

Darvith was filled with exasperation and sighed audibly and with great impatience. "Really Bowdren! This is not the time for silly Ego games! Can you, or can't you, think of a way to frighten them off!"

A contrite Bowdren answered with a simple, "Can and will."

Darvith heard the sound of his feet when they touched the floor and watched as bottles of liquid were poured into a large basin. A dreadful odor soon wafted to the upper portion of the room. She jumped down to the floor. "Ugh!" She grimaced, now holding her nose, "What is that terrible smell?"

Bowdren replied with a burst of laughter, "That, my dear, is weasel, pure weasel!"

They both laughed loudly as they covered their bodies with the dreadful scent; then raced down the tunnel toward Elgat.

Only minutes later they entered a large well-lit room. Darvith asked, "Where are we? Do you know?"

"Yes." Bowdren replied. "Yes, I know where we are. It's my home away from home. We are in the Institute of Science." He added incredulously, "It's amazing to learn that I have worked this near to Griffin and Trillan all of these years." Bowdren ordered, "Follow me! It's time to get rid of the weasel scent. We haven't a moment to waste!"

"Idiot!" Darvith snapped peevishly, "How can I follow you! I can't see you!" She added derisively, "You have the logic of an infant!" She immediately felt his arm grab at her body, and on finding her arm he yanked her swiftly down the hallway.

Darvith whispered loudly, in a voice filled with indignation, "You brute! All you had to say was a simple right or left! Let me go! You're hurting my arm! Let go of me! Do you hear me?"

Bowdren had reached the end of his patience and told Darvith to 'shut up' or she might attract unwanted attention. He then pulled her into a room filled with archways made from some type of yellow metal tubing and ordered her to stand under one of them. He declared, "Soon you will smell as good as ever, probably better, and you will feel wonderful."

"Why this does feel wonderful Bowdren!" She exclaimed, "I feel so relaxed and rested. I'm not even angry with you anymore. What a marvelous invention!"

Bowdren laughed and said, "At last some praise from Darvith. Of course you weren't to know that it is one of 'my' inventions." He explained, "We work with so many dreadful odors here at the institute that I felt it was necessary to find a quick and easy way to cleans both our bodies and our clothing." He added, "For some reason the procedure tends to leave the individual using the process, feeling relaxed, rested, and as you pointed out, in a much better frame of mind. In other words it's a great way to end a work day."

Darvith decided to ask Bowdren about something that had puzzled her since becoming invisible. She asked, "How is it that our clothing becomes invisible when we drink the potion? It doesn't seem logical."

Bowdren was quick with his reply. "Apparently it's because of an invisible vapor that is emitted through the individual's pores when the potion is integrated into the cells of the body."

Then he laughed as he went on to explain, "When I first began my experiments with the potion, I felt as you did, that my clothing would encase my invisible body, so I took the precaution of testing while not wearing any." He continued, "My experiments with invisibility have always been carried out in my private laboratory in my mother's home." He laughed again. "To make a long story short, I made a rather spectacular and unforgettable appearance at a luncheon my mother was giving at our home when my invisibility failed."

They both laughed uproariously. Bowdren loved the sound of Darvith's laugh and for some strange reason it made him feel protective of her. He said apologetically, "I'm sorry I was so rough with you in the hall and for making such a mess of things. There is no excuse for my behavior."

Darvith replied, "Your apology is accepted. Please accept mine. I know how impossible I must seem at times...well all the time, really."

They laughed together once more, and then Darvith's voice became serious as she suggested, "If you take my hand I will gladly walk out of this building with you. We can't be very safe here. Griffin may know of your escape. We must leave now." Soon they were on their way to the Royal Palace and Annwynn.

Meanwhile, just as Darvith had predicted, Griffin had discovered Bowdren's escape and was filled with rage. He growled, "How could he have escaped? It was an impossible feat! I had him here! Why didn't I finish him off when I had the chance?"

All at once a malicious smile appeared on Griffin's handsome face and he grew strangely calm as he continued his soliloquy, "Of course it really doesn't matter. I will soon have him back. After all, where can he go? And who can the poor, dear boy trust?" His sinister chuckle bubbled forth like some ancient spring of evil intent. Griffin ceased to pace and declared jubilantly,

"I will alert my Elgans at once and let them find and return Bowdren to me. He won't escape from me again for it will be our 'final' encounter." Satisfied, he smiled wickedly and abruptly left for Trillan.

At this same moment, Darvith and Bowdren entered Annwynn's room in the Palace. As they approached the Princess who was standing on the Balcony, Annwynn turned and called out softly, "Darvith, dear sister, are you here with me?" She was startled but filled with happiness when Darvith hugged her and asked, "How did you know I was here?"

Annwynn answered, "I have no idea." Then asked in a hushed voice, "How is it that you are invisible? Is it the work of Griffin?"

Darvith explained, "Well, no. It wasn't Griffin, but Stavro's brother Bowdren who gave me this great and useful gift...although he wasn't exactly aware of it at the time."

Annwynn was mystified and asked Darvith to explain more fully. When Darvith had related all that had taken place since their last meeting, she added one further detail. "It seems that one of Bowdren's colleagues at the institute, a young woman by the name of Rowena, is one of the Elgans working for Griffin."

Annwynn gasped, "She knew all about the quest, no wonder Bowdren was so easily caught."

Darvith shook her head and suggested solemnly, "I'm not sure that she played a significant part in his capture. As you now know, Griffin has his Elgans placed in every important post in your Kingdom. I'm sure he would have been able to trap Bowdren whenever he wished."

She added thoughtfully, "The question is, why was Bowdren sent at all? The mission was designed to fail right from the start. What had Griffin to gain? There had to be a reason! As you and I both know, Griffin never does anything without a reason." She sighed and said, "It must be some kind of cover-up or smokescreen to hide another of his devious activities, perhaps even from his own Elgans."

Annwynn asked, "Where is Bowdren now? I suppose with Stavro and their mother. They'll certainly be glad to see him."

In truth, Bowdren was in another dimension, completely lost in Annwynn's loveliness. She was even more beautiful than when he first saw her in the Stone House. He had been unable to speak from the moment they entered the room.

It was not just her outer beauty, the visible perfection of her face and form, but her inner beauty and gentle spirit that shone forth in her magnificent Aura. He was her captive. Bowdren knew that he had fallen in love. It was what the Elgats called 'Bella', love at first sight, and was considered the most fortunate of events if the love was returned in the same way. It meant everlasting love for the couple...a life of bliss. But what if Annwynn didn't return his love when she saw him for the first time?

Darvith grew impatient with his silence and declared tartly, "Bowdren is here Annwynn. I can't imagine why he has remained silent. He must be hoarse from all of the orders he has given me since we met! Do this! Do that! There has been an endless stream of commands!" She added with a pathetic little sigh, "I don't know how I have managed to cope with his overbearing and completely unreasonable attitude!"

Bowdren roared with laughter and replied, "Princess Annwynn, as you know Darvith so well, you can well imagine which of us should now be suffering from a sore throat!"

Soon they were all laughing and the room was filled with warmth and love.

Darvith was suddenly serious as she remembered aloud, "Today is the day we are to meet with Angela. I had almost forgotten. Do you think we will need Stavro

Angela and the Enchanted Bell

to help us get out of Elgat, or can we slip through the shielding on our own?"

Bowdren was quick with his reply, "We will need Stavro. I will go to see him now." They heard the door close as he left the room.

Annwynn was overcome with curiosity as she questioned the invisible Darvith. "Now! You must tell me all about Bowdren! Everything that you know!" Then she added softly, "I must say he has a wonderful voice."

Darvith began slowly, "How can I describe him...? Well, he is nothing like his brother Stavro, either in personality or appearance; he looks like a very muscular Trillan, and he is quite handsome, I suppose. However he has an arrogant way about him that I find very annoying."

Darvith laughed softly and continued; a hint of derision was now present in her voice. "Had I remained in Trillan like 'a good little girl', as he advised, he would now, without question, be 'a dead little boy'!"

Annwynn interrupted with gales of laughter. "Oh! But surely he didn't say 'like a good little girl', not to 'Darvith the Terrible'? Has he no sense of danger?"

Annwynn sighed deeply and was suddenly serious as she said, "I wish I could actually see you again. Will you ever be visible while you're in Elgat?"

Darvith replied softly, "It isn't likely. There is danger in Elgat for Bowdren and me. We'll have a better idea of just how much danger, when Bowdren returns with or without Stavro."

CHAPTER 17

Astonishing Revelations

Bowdren was at this moment entering his family's home and was about to make his presence known, when he heard the sound of a strangely familiar melody coming from the next room. An icy chill invaded his body when he remembered where he had last heard it. Griffin had been humming that very tune just two nights ago in his darkened library.

The invisible Bowdren was filled first with disbelief and then profound despair as he gazed, heartbroken, at his brother Stavro who was now whistling that same haunting melody. It was a melody that Stavro often whistled but Bowdren had never attached any importance to it...that is, until now. He knew it wasn't an Elgat tune therefore it must be Elgan. Could his brother, whom he loved more than anyone, be an Elgan?

Bowdren recalled all that Griffin had said when he was sure his victim would soon die. How he'd mentioned that there were highly placed Elgans in important positions throughout the kingdom, many of whom, he assured, Bowdren knew, personally. Bowdren sighed sadly. Certainly the Commander of the Elgat Guards was about as 'highly placed' as an Elgat male could hope to achieve. With the exception of the Royal Family, no one had more power, not even the Elders. But it couldn't be true! Stavro hated Griffin!

Bowdren's thoughts now turned to Annwynn. Why was she brought to Elgat? Griffin had already planned for her execution in Trillan and had his trap set, at least so he said. There was no need for him to lie to a man that was soon to die. Why then bring her to Elgat? There had to be a reason!

A new and startling thought came to his mind. Could it have been a decision that Stavro had made without consulting Griffin? If so, Stavro would be risking his position in Elgat.

Perhaps Griffin doesn't actually have power in Elgat, he can only manipulate those who do. Of course that's it! And Stavro made a decision of his own. He had saved Annwynn's life! But why would he do that, was he hoping to use her as a pawn against Griffin? More and more questions flooded Bowdren's thoughts, more questions than answers. Of course and that's why I appeared in this supposedly pure Elgat family. One of my parents must be an Elgan!

At just that moment his mother Theda rushed into the room and declared, "Stavro! There is news of Bowdren. For some reason Griffin had been holding him as a prisoner in the laboratory that lies between Trillan and Elgat. One who was there said Griffin had Bowdren chained to a wall and left him for the mice and rats." She continued in a voice filled with both anguish and hope. "He was chained! Why would Griffin do such a thing when he promised to return him to us."

Stavro scowled, "Perhaps he just didn't intend to return him alive."

Theda murmured softly, "I wonder how he managed to escape? Griffin promises to severely punish those who helped him."

Stavro pronounced stonily, "Well we all know who will be at the top of his suspect list. I hope she has a good alibi."

Stavro pulled his mother toward him and held her close. "No tears now. Bowdren is out of Griffin's clutches. We must be grateful for that." Then he added, "Rowena has to be the one who helped him; none of his other friends has access to the Trillan laboratory."

Stavro was deep in thought for a long moment. Then he said in a voice filled with concern, Bowdren should be here by now! What can be keeping him?" He began to pace back and forth and confided, "You know mother, there is the possibility Griffin, confident that Bowdren would soon be dead, told him about us and the Elgan Society, and now he no longer trusts us."

Theda began to sob as if her heart were breaking. "No. He can't think that, I love him like a son. Surely he couldn't believe that we would wish him harm. He couldn't believe that! He must know that he lives in our hearts!"

Stavro frowned as he put his arms around his mother in comfort and said softly, "If only we could alert him in some way. I know we could help him. Griffin has no reason to suspect our behavior." He added, "Why he didn't even doubt my motives when I explained why I felt that Annwynn should return to Elgat, and accepted my explanation that it would save a messy trial in Trillan and accomplish the same end." Stavro laughed derisively. "In the end, he took it as all part of 'his' plan. That Ego of his will bring him down one day."

Stavro was silent for a moment and then said, "We should try to warn Rowena; you could be her alibi mother, if she hasn't one."

Theda agreed and then declared angrily! "One thing is certain; we know that we can never trust Griffin! He promised that no harm would come to Bowdren, yet we now know that he would have killed him in cold blood, without a moments hesitation."

Bowdren had heard enough. Although it was true that they had kept the existence of the Elgan Society from him, it was obvious that they loved him. He put his arms around their shoulders and pulled them toward him in an enormous hug.

Stavro continued to hold Theda and explained, "We are most certainly being watched. To an outsider it will appear that I'm consoling mother and if she and I continue to face each other while we engage in this three-sided conversation, all watchers should be fooled." Stavro asked, "Now tell us Bowdren, how did you manage to escape? I understand you were chained to the wall."

Bowdren was quick with his response, "Darvith rescued me. I owe her my life. She is amazing!" Then he went on to relate all that had happened in Griffin's laboratory and added. "There are things about Darvith that you may not know. For one, she isn't a Trillan. She's a 'Daughter of Aleesha', whatever that means, and she was stolen as a babe, just as Annwynn. Also, Griffin has asked for, and received, permission from the King of Trillan to obtain Darvith as his Life-Mate."

Bowdren was very serious as he continued. "I was studying Griffin's Aura when he spoke of Darvith, in glowing terms I might add, he thinks she is brilliant. His Aura showed a deep but troubling affection for her. I would hesitate to say love, but it's very close. I don't believe he has ever before experienced the type of feelings he has for Darvith. If she were a different type of young woman she could certainly use it to her advantage."

Stavro was filled with rage and unreasonable jealousy, but he managed to keep his temper. He asked, "How did Darvith react to all of this shocking information?"

Bowdren noticed Stavro's flaring Aura and smiled as he answered, "She doesn't react to anything in what you would call a 'normal' way. Just when I think that I'm beginning to understand her manner of thinking, she behaves in just the opposite way to what I had expected. She's a puzzle, but a lot of fun to be around." He added, "I love her laugh! It's infectious and always brings the same response from me. As far as the 'Oathing' with Griffin, she just said that he'd have to catch her first. She has no intention of returning to Trillan and was very happy to learn that it isn't the Kingdom of her birth.

Stavro was silent for a moment as he once again tried to remember more of Aleesha but it was no use, he could only remember the name. It was too long ago."

Bowdren tapped Stavro on the shoulder and said, "I'm off to my laboratory. I'll take all the invisibility pills I've stored there and share them with Darvith, Red to disappear and blue to reappear, enough to last for years if the need should arise." Then he sighed deeply, "Surely not for years."

Just before leaving he clasped one of his mother's hands in his and asked softly, "Tell me mother, am I not your son?"

Stavro gazed at Theda questioningly, "I heard you say it too mother. You said, 'I love him 'like' a son'."

Theda frowned and replied hotly, "This is what Griffin's influence is doing to all of us! He infects us all with mistrust! Of course you are my son Bowdren!"

She sighed and continued. "I'm truly sorry that you must leave us. However, you may be able to return sooner than you now believe. I want you to know that there are many Elgans, thousands in fact, who only pretend to follow Griffin, just as we do."

She explained further, "I head a special group, and our numbers grow every day thanks to Elgat's wonderful light source. Our time is drawing near and we will be ready. What Griffin does not understand, or perhaps can't understand because he lives in Trillan, is that the Elgat light source produces and encourages independent thought. One cannot live here for more than five hundred years without changing for the better."

Bowdren flushed and retorted, "Well how do you account for Rowena's actions? You both seem to think she is with you, but I saw her arrive with ten others in Griffin's laboratory, complete with toad-skin coverings. The kind the raiders of Trillan wear. She must have been a part of the plot to implicate Annwynn as a traitor to Trillan."

Bowdren was filled with indignation, as he added with a hint of sarcasm, "Earlier today, as I stood chained to a wall in Griffin's laboratory, soon to be left as a choice little meal for the mice and rats that search the tunnels at night, your 'precious' Rowena was 'very' comforting. Do you know what she said to me before she took the tunnel back to Elgat? She looked at me coldly and said that she'd advised me not to take the assignment and that now I must pay for my foolhardy decision. There was no attempt to help me, not so much as a glass of water!"

Stavro exploded with ironic laughter. "Poor little Bowdren! Dear brother, what did you expect the poor woman to do? Griffin was standing beside her! Think man! She had tried to warn you before you left; that act alone has put her in grave danger thanks to your recent escape." Stavro continued and his voice was now filled with admiration. "She even went so far as to make a formal protest to Princess Annwynn in front of the Elders, three of whom she knows are Elgans. She is a very brave young woman who happens to love a young man who, sadly, appears to be totally unaware of her existence as anything but a scientist."

He scowled at Bowdren and added somewhat harshly, "The fact that she has been working on a secret project alters nothing. We will learn of it eventually. We always learn of any new projects. She has to wait until it is safe for her; she knows she is of no use to our cause if she's dead."

Bowdren was silent then murmured softly, "I had no idea that she cared for me. I thought we were just very good friends. It seems that I am not a very good judge of women."

He added solemnly, "I certainly underestimated Darvith. I actually ordered her to stay in Trillan, while I, 'The Hero', would take care of Griffin and find the missing Discs."

Theda was very curious and asked, "Tell me more about this young woman? Will I have the opportunity to meet her? It seems that as well as being courageous and intelligent she is something of a sorceress, capturing the admiration of both of my sons. Yes. I would certainly like to meet her!"

Before Stavro could answer, Bowdren replied, "Darvith is beautiful, blond and green eyed. She is brighter than the rest of us and knows it. You will like her mother, but she would be a completely unsuitable life-mate for either of your sons...if that was in your mind."

Stavro smiled broadly and added, "I reserve the right to disagree! She is the only young woman I have ever desired as a Life-Mate. The more I learn of her the more desirable she becomes."

Bowdren laughed softly and said, "That may well be, but I suggest you save yourself while you still can! Darvith will never be a Life-Mate to you or to anyone else." He added sadly, "Admire her as you would a wild creature, but do not seek to possess her for it will never happen...of this I am certain."

The invisible Bowdren put his hand on Stavro's shoulder and asked, "Will you help us to enter the earth plane and allow us to use your private shelter?"

Stavro replied immediately, "Of course, and I think you should leave as soon as possible. As you know there is great danger for you here and in Trillan. The Elgans are on full alert and it's possible that some of them will be able to see your Aura in spite of your invisibility. I suggest we leave now.

After saying goodbye to Theda they swiftly made their way to the Royal Palace. No one questioned Stavro's entrance into the Main Hall where he awaited permission to see the Princess. She soon sent word that she would receive him in her sitting room and added that they weren't to be disturbed.

Moments later Annwynn greeted Stavro with a warm smile. Once the door was closed Bowdren took one of his pills, became visible, and called to Darvith to do the same. There was no answer.

Annwynn extended her hand to Bowdren. "It is so good to meet you at last. I've heard so much about you." Then, while still holding Bowdren's hand she turned to Stavro and said, "You are both just in time, Darvith has a plan."

Bowdren replied dryly, "Why am I not surprised."

Darvith's lovely laughter filled the air and she teased, "Now Bowdren, you must try to keep your enthusiasm for my enterprises under some kind of control, lest it be misinterpreted as praise." Everyone laughed.

Darvith took the pill Bowdren was holding in his upright hand and appeared for all to see. She gazed up into Stavro's eyes and smiled as she murmured, "Hello again."

Stavro felt that his heart was going to stop beating. He bent to the floor as if to retrieve something in order to hide the emotions that he was certain would have shown on his face. Never had he felt so exposed and vulnerable.

Darvith appeared not to notice and began talking of escape plans. "I believe we are thinking along the same lines Stavro. Bowdren and I must leave Elgat immediately. Luckily, we are to meet with the Earthling Angela, this very day."

She continued with great enthusiasm, "I'm sure we can make some sort of shelter, perhaps in the stone house, and stay in the Realm of the Earthlings for a few days, or even a week." She added, "Actually, we could probably stay there indefinitely. It might even be fun!"

Darvith was filled with the excitement of the moment. "Perhaps we should try to return to Trillan. You can let us know when it would be possible. Bowdren and I can then enter through a secret entrance in the Stream. Annwynn and I have used it on many occasions. Even if Griffin has guards at the main entrance we can still enter undetected." She added triumphantly, "Then it's off to the safety of the Velds. I have a hideout there that no one will ever find! Why we might even try to find the great Sea that is supposed to exist to the distant east! Adventure at last!"

All through Darvith's elaborate plan making Annwynn and Bowdren were holding hands and gazing into each other's eyes, seemingly unaware of the others in the room. Bowdren's dreams had come true. Annwynn had experienced 'Bella' when she first looked into his eyes.

"Annwynnnnnnnnn!" Darvith dragged out with obvious annoyance in her voice. "Bowdren!" She added acidly, "Give the lady back her hand! Have you two been listening at all? This is important!"

Annwynn answered as if awakened from a dream, "Will Bowdren be able to enter through the stream? We are used to doing it; he is not. Have you forgotten how frightened Angela was when she first saw it?"

Darvith laughed and scoffed, "Oh don't be silly Annwynn! Angela is just a frightened Earthling child. Bowdren is a big, strong, young man."

She asked mockingly, "You aren't afraid of a little water are you Bowdren?" And without waiting for him to answer, she declared, "Of course you're not." Darvith was impatient and motioned that they should leave.

Annwynn turned to her, hugged her and as she released her said, "I wish you didn't have to leave so soon. I know it is necessary but I wish it were different. Please be careful dearest sister."

Annwynn then turned to Bowdren. Had Stavro and Darvith been able to see Auras, they would have been amazed by the brilliance before them.

Bowdren kissed Annwynn's hand and said with great feeling, "You must be very careful too, trust no one, for there are those who wish you harm. I wish I could stay here to protect you."

Annwynn smiled back at him sadly and said, "Yes. I wish you could stay with me." She then slipped off the ring she wore on her middle finger and whispered softly, "Here, please accept this ring as a token of my intent." They kissed. Darvith and Stavro stood silent in amazement.

Within minutes Stavro and his invisible companions were on their way and no one noticed them as they slipped through the shielding and entered the brightly lit corridor that Annwynn had traveled through just a few days before.

Once safely through the shielding, Stavro suggested that the pair should once again become visible. In truth he longed to actually 'see' Darvith again, in order to take some memories of her, back to Elgat with him.

They approached the last of several walls, and it slid downward as the others had, but instead of continuing onward toward the pool, Stavro stopped and allowed the door to slide back to once again form a wall.

He smiled as he explained, "That is the only exit my guards know of and as you could see, it leads to the deep pool. However, I have a private entrance to the stone house where I have a rustic retreat that I use when I want to be completely alone." He added, "You see Darvith, we all need a place where we can be alone when we choose to be…like your hideaway in the Velds of Trillan. I'm sure Griffin has several such places. As he is unable to detect your Aura, it might be fun for you to try to find them should you ever return to Trillan."

Darvith agreed enthusiastically, "What a good idea! I would make his life a misery!"

Bowdren laughed and interjected, "Why not! Why should 'he' be spared?" They all laughed together and there was a good feeling of comradeship and purpose. These were three friends who liked each other very much.

Stavro turned to face the stone house wall and placed his foot against a small wedge of wood near the floor. An opening slightly larger than the size of a normal doorway appeared as a door slid downward. But to Stavro's surprise, something was now blocking his entrance to the Stone Building!

Stavro commanded, in a voice that was very familiar with giving orders, "Both of you, help me push whatever this is away from the entrance!" They all pushed at the count of three and at that very moment it moved away, leaving them to tumble and slide across a very slippery floor and land in a heap at the opposite wall.

Deafening laughter filled the tiny room. Then Angela quickly knelt beside them and apologized. "I'm sorry for laughing at you but you looked so funny. Please forgive me?"

They were all laughing now as they straightened out their clothing.

As always, Darvith was the first to speak. She was amazed at the changes that had taken place and asked incredulously, "What have you done to this building Angela? I would hardly recognize it as the same place."

Angela was now sitting cross-legged on the floor, grinning at her guests. She explained excitedly, "Isn't the room great! A friend of my mother is a carpenter and he's made the stone building into a playhouse for me. They did it for my birthday. As you can see it now has a roof, glass windows, linoleum on the floor and best of all a door that I can lock! No one else can use it! Isn't it wonderful?"

After taking a deep breath, Angela frowned and asked, "How did you get here Darvith? I was expecting to see Annwynn with Stavro." Then she pointed to Bowdren and asked, "Who is he?"

Darvith laughed and declared, "At last you've stopped talking!" She gave Angela an affectionate pat on the leg. "I do enjoy your company; I love your enthusiasm!" Then she introduced Bowdren and asked if it would be possible for the two of them to stay with her for a few days.

However, before Angela could answer, Darvith's attention was caught by something that was standing against the end wall. She asked, while motioning to the structure, "What is that?" She was pointing toward Angela's new Dollhouse. Mr. Strom had built it for her birthday. It was the perfect size for the newly homeless Darvith and Bowdren, and was completely furnished with wooden furniture, rugs, curtains and everything else a well-to-do doll family might require.

Angela explained, half apologetically, "I'm afraid it was the Dollhouse that blocked your way into the room until I moved it. Although I had Mr. Strom remove the baseboard he'd placed around the room; I had no way of knowing just where you were going to enter."

Then she turned to Darvith and added reproachfully, "I waited at the stream all morning and was very worried when you didn't appear. I was terrified that Griffin might have harmed you."

Darvith smiled at the oh so earnest little Earthling with great affection and said, "I'm truly sorry, but I had no way of reaching you to tell you of our narrow escape from Griffin." She then went on to relate all that had taken place during the last few days as Angela sat listening, quietly spellbound.

When Darvith had finished she looked up at Angela and asked, "Would you do something very important for us now?"

Angela jumped up enthusiastically. "Anything! Anything at all! I want to help!"

Darvith smiled in appreciation, "That's great; I knew we could count on you!" Then she asked, "Would you go up to the cottage and bring back some suitable food for us?

It is possible that we might have to stay here for many days." She continued, "Also, could you place the food in containers that we can open and close?" Then Darvith smiled her most dazzling smile and said, "Thanks Angela, you are very kind...hurry back!"

Angela was completely unaware of the fact that she had just been dismissed. She left smiling happily, closing and locking the door behind her.

Darvith immediately ran over to the Dollhouse. She bounced on one of the quilt-covered beds and declared with a smile, "This will do nicely! As a matter of fact it is perfect! What luck! It was if it were made for us!" Then she pointed to another room at the other end of the house and issued an order to Bowdren, "You take that one!"

Darvith's spirits were high as she continued, "We can stay here as long as we want! Don't you agree Stavro? Then when you tell us that Griffin is no longer searching Trillan; we could enter and explore its outer regions. As I mentioned there is a Legend that tells of a great Sea beyond the Velds. Angela could take us to the bank of the stream."

Stavro felt in his heart that Darvith was slipping away from him, from where he could help her, and it bothered him unreasonably. He replied gruffly, "She can't take you! The Elders would see her!"

Darvith frowned. "Of course, you're right they would see us unless...unless we entered the stream at night!" Once more Darvith was filled with excitement.

Stavro shook his head and declared, "Surely that is out of the question! You can't expect an Earthling child to come down here at night and escort you to the stream! No! It is out of the question! I will take you both to the stream! There is no other way! As soon as it is safe; I will return!"

Darvith was amazed and surprised by her reaction to Stavro's commands. She reasoned that she wasn't filled with resentment or anger at his taking control now and then, because his decisions were always logical and not ruled by male vanity. Yes, that was it! She decided that she liked this young man very much. He would be a good friend.

There was a look of profound sadness in Stavro's eyes. For some reason that Darvith herself was unaware of, she ran over to where he stood, put her arms around his neck and kissed him tenderly on the lips. It was the kiss one would give an injured child. She gently pushed back a tendril of black curly hair that had fallen against his forehead and murmured softly, "Please don't look so sad Stavro. I will take good care of your brother. I promise to return him to you safe and sound." Then she laughed her lovely laugh and added, "Well 'safe' anyway. I can't perform magic!"

Bowdren's response to this insult was a pillow thrown at Darvith's head.

Stavro caught her off balance, swept her up in his arms and kissed her passionately. A kiss so deeply felt by both that for a brief moment they were lost to all but themselves. Upon releasing her, Stavro declared, in a voice husky with emotion, "I'm not in the least worried about Bowdren." With that he turned and left the room.

Darvith was at a complete loss for words and just stood still for a moment. Then she turned and glared at Bowdren who was now grinning at her.

He declared, "It's your own fault Darvith. You did kiss him first and my brother has a very passionate nature."

Darvith responded by throwing the pillow back at him. She was annoyed and more than a little upset. Her kiss was one of comfort. Stavro had no right to take advantage of the situation. How dare he! She could still feel the pressure of his lips on hers and it troubled her. There was a time during that brief moment when she was not in complete control of her emotions and it had threatened her precious freedom, a freedom that Darvith had made a vow long ago to protect. She must remain single and free to come and go as she pleased. She would never become a Life-Mate! Never!

Bowdren had been reading her unguarded thoughts and knew of her great resolve. He had been astonished at the sight of Darvith's Aura blending with Stavro's when they had kissed. What a wonderful love match it could be. Bowdren knew his brother well and knew without a doubt that Stavro would love Darvith for the rest of his life. And he was just as certain that his love would never be returned. Bowdren was filled with a great sadness and wished with all his heart that Stavro had never met Darvith.

All at once the quiet was broken by the sound of Angela turning the key in the lock. She entered the room carrying a large box and pushed the door closed with her foot. Glancing quickly around the room she asked, "Where's Stavro? Did he have to return to Elgat?"

Darvith flushed a brilliant pink but said nothing leaving Bowdren to explain that Stavro had important business to attend to and would return in a few days.

Angela nodded in understanding. Then she knelt by the box and said, "Now, what I'll do is put everything I've brought, out on the floor. Then you can inspect it, and take whatever you think will be useful."

Darvith was very pleased. "Why this is wonderful Angela!" She exclaimed as she walked among the treasures. After tasting the various offerings, they made their selections and chose the containers most appropriate for each. Angela had also brought fresh water for them to use and promised to refill it every day.

Bowdren then asked if it would be possible to have access to the table that sat under one of the windows. He explained, "Then we could look out at the meadow." Angela replied with an instant, "Sure! I'll be right back!" She warned, "I'll just be a moment, but the door will have to remain open. Keep a watch out for unwanted guests."

Angela quickly returned with a short piece of board that had been left behind after the renovations to her playhouse. She placed it at an angle to the table and secured it against the far wall, thus making a long, gradual ramp.

"This is splendid!" Exclaimed Bowdren, while running up the plank. "What a view!"

Darvith was already gazing out at the meadow and declared gratefully, "This is wonderful Angela! Thank you so much for all that you've done for us. You are an exceptional Earthling!"

Angela was delighted to receive praise from Darvith. She grinned happily and replied, "You're welcome." Then she frowned and added, "Are you sure that you will be all right? I could easily take both of you up to the cottage. No one would see you, I promise." She continued in the same worried tone. "I don't think either of you realize just how dark it will be in a few hours. It will be impossible to see anything in this room."

They both smiled at her. She was treating them as if they were her children. It was sweet.

Darvith said kindly, "You must try not to worry about us Angela. You have been a wonderful help and we are very grateful. However, you told us yourself that the room is safe, and you have promised to lock the door. What is there left to fear?"

Angela reluctantly agreed. She said goodbye, closed the door, locking it carefully from the outside and was soon on her way to the cottage.

CHAPTER 18

Stavro's Dreams Fulfilled

Darvith and Bowdren sat in the comfortable armchairs that Angela had taken from the Dollhouse and placed on the table for them. They gazed out of the window each temporarily lost in thought.

Darvith was filled with awe and murmured aloud, "The Realm of the Earthlings is so beautiful but at the same time so frightening and unpredictable."

Bowdren nodded solemnly in agreement and smiled as he said, "Like you."

Darvith turned to face him and gave him an enchanting smile. "Why thank you Bowdren. I'm going to take that as a compliment."

Bowdren answered simply, "I meant it as one."

Darvith smiled graciously and then asked, "May I see the ring Annwynn gave you?"

Bowdren lifted his left hand and showed her the ring he was now wearing on his little finger. He kissed it tenderly.

Darvith was silent for a long moment, and then looked deeply into his eyes. She asked, "Do you seek Annwynn as your Life-Mate? You do understand that this was her intent when she gave you her ring. As a Royal Princess, she must make the choice." Darvith's eyes flashed as she continued. "If you hurt her in any way, I will make your life intolerable! That is a promise! She is more dear to me than anyone I have ever known."

Bowdren smiled at Darvith and replied in a voice filled with love and admiration, "Annwynn has held my heart from the first time I saw her in this very room. I know to my depths that she will always be my only love. I feel I have known her longer than I have lived. We are as one."

Bowdren's obvious sincerity brought tears of happiness to Darvith's eyes. She smiled and exclaimed joyfully, "I'm so happy for you both!"

Dusk was beginning to settle on the meadow. They continued to watch with wonder the many creatures now preparing for the cover of night, the hunters and the hunted.

Bowdren turned to gaze at Darvith, who was transfixed by the events taking place within their view. Just another of the wild creatures, he thought. A spirit so wild and free cannot be contained. He smiled sadly when he thought of his brother Stavro and of his love for Darvith.

Bowdren wondered about Aleesha...was it a place or a person, or perhaps a group of Mystics as Darvith had suggested? He scowled, Griffin knows. How he wished he could learn of all the secrets that rested in that Ancient Trillan's brain.

Bowdren broke the silence by asking, "Have you ever considered becoming a Life-Mate?" Quickly adding, "I don't mean Griffin's but perhaps with some handsome young man...?"

Darvith looked deeply into his eyes for a moment then replied. "No. I will remain free forever. I love children and I will miss having my own, but I simply cannot pay the price. I shall have to content myself with spoiling Annwynn's babies." She continued resolutely, "The idea of belonging to someone has always been a terrifying prospect. I compare it to a slow and painful death. As it is now, my life is my own; I could have it no other way."

Darvith scowled as she continued, "Anyway, most young men are not only stupid, boring to be around, and oh so predictable, they also have the annoying habit of playing 'Lord and Master', whenever they get the chance. The arrogant fools!" Darvith had not bothered to hide the contempt in her voice as she added angrily, "I will not be treated as a lesser creature!"

Bowdren immediately jumped up and then knelt at Darvith's feet. "Speaking as one who has most grievously offended, I can only humbly apologize and promise to never, NEVER do it again." Bowdren gazed up at her with mock submissiveness. "Oh please say you will forgive me, dear, DEAR Darvith?"

Darvith burst into laughter and pushed him over with her foot. "You are an idiot Bowdren but I do like you; I'm very glad that you and Annwynn have found each other. You are a much better mate for her than Prince Vorden, and that's the truth."

On a sudden impulse, Bowdren looked straight into Darvith's eyes and asked, "What do you think of Stavro?"

Darvith's beautiful eyes flashed a quick warning and she turned away from his direct gaze. She had been caught off guard by the bluntness of his question and was silent for a long moment. Bowdren could not read her thoughts.

Finally she turned to him and replied, "As we are being so honest with each other I will tell you the truth. Your brother Stavro is the only young man I have thought about for longer than a few minutes. I find him exciting, maddening, interesting and completely unpredictable. If I did plan to choose a Life-Mate, and you must understand 'I never will', it would have to be someone like Stavro." She added almost inaudibly, "Although I doubt if there is anyone like him."

Bowdren suggested, "It seems you and Stavro have a great deal in common. Freedom has always been very important to him. Many hundreds of maidens have tried to win his heart but he has never wanted to be tied to anyone..." He was about to add "until now." When Darvith quickly interjected, "Then we are in absolute agreement!" That statement, it seemed to Bowdren, effectively ended the conversation.

Deep shadows were now beginning to fall across the meadow and it was rapidly becoming a darkly forbidding place.

Once again it was Bowdren who broke the silence. "Here, before it gets dark, I want to give you half of the pill supply."

Darvith immediately put hers in the small pouch that hung from the belt she wore about her tiny waist. She smiled at Bowdren and suggested, "Let's divide the coverlets from the other bedrooms; we might be cold later." The task was quickly accomplished and soon they were both asleep.

Unfortunately Darvith had a nightmare and woke from it to find herself in total darkness. The nightmare of being Griffin's Life-Mate was bad enough, but to awaken in total darkness was terrifying. She shivered uncontrollably. "This won't do." She murmured. After taking a deep breath she decided to focus her thoughts on the happy, golden days of her childhood.

Just as she was beginning to feel calm she heard a noise, and the sound was moving toward her. Her mind raced and her heart pounded, then mercifully she heard the familiar sound of Bowdren's deep voice calling out to her. "Are you all right? I thought I heard you scream."

Darvith sighed in relief. "You probably did. I was having a terrible nightmare." She shivered again at the memory of it. "Thanks for coming to my rescue Bowdren. I'm fine now. Good night."

Bowdren chuckled and said, "Oh no you don't Darvith, that wasn't a normal scream I heard; it was one of pure terror." He continued, "You are very good at dismissing people but I think I should sleep here on this soft carpet tonight just in case you need me."

Now it was Darvith's turn to laugh. "Really Bowdren, you sound just like Angela. I don't need a caretaker! Please go!"

Darvith moved to sit up in bed, leaving her shoulders and arms bare just long enough for Bowdren to notice something that both surprised and intrigued him. She possessed the same strange crescent shaped birthmark, placed on the same area of her arm. Was it just a coincidence?

Then he recalled how curious she had been about his birthmark. She had even asked if he had seen anyone else with such a mark. He smiled to himself. She probably hadn't the slightest intention of telling him of the crescent on 'her' arm.

Darvith was annoyed as she called out softly. "Bowdren! I know you're still here. Now go away! I want to sleep!"

Bowdren laughed in spite of himself and declared, "You are such a grouch Darvith! I'll go in a minute but first I must ask you about something. Why didn't you tell me that you had a mark just like mine on your arm?

Darvith snapped peevishly, "You and your blasted night-sight!" Then she added impatiently, "I don't know why I didn't tell you. I suppose the idea that we might be related was far too horrifying a prospect for me to accept! I'm too tired to talk about it now! Let's get some sleep! We can discuss it in the morning if you still feel that it's necessary." She added with great emphasis. "GOOD NIGHT BOWDREN! NOW GO AWAY!"

They both awoke at first light. And just as Angela had predicted, the stone house was very, very cold. Darvith burrowed down into her blankets for more warmth.

Bowdren walked into her room and sat on the edge of her bed. He was wrapped in a quilt, but in spite of this he was shivering from the cold. Darvith gazed up at him with sleepy eyes and murmured sympathetically, "Poor Bowdren. We'll ask Angela for more blankets when she comes to see us today."

At just that moment they heard the key turn in the lock and Angela entered with another large box. She grinned at them and said, "You poor things; you must be very cold!"

Angela produced a thermos that she had filled with hot sweetened tea and poured the liquid into some tiny cups from the Dollhouse, presenting a cup to each of her guests and suggesting that they could have more whenever they wished. She explained that the thermos would keep the liquid hot for a long time.

Her tiny guests drank many more cups of the steaming liquid and slowly began to feel warmer.

Darvith was unable to contain her curiosity any longer and asked, "What surprises have you brought with you today?"

Angela grinned and replied, "I've brought some warm clothing for you to wear and more blankets. I'm sure you need them." She then produced two wooden wardrobes filled with clothing, neatly hung on tiny hangers, and a doll's trunk that was filled with blankets and sweaters.

"These are doll clothes, but I'm certain they will fit you." Angela explained as she placed the wardrobes closer to her guests. She held up two dolls that were almost exact replicas of the amazed Darvith and Bowdren. "See? They are just your size."

Darvith's eyes were wide with curiosity as she queried, "Did you say that these 'dolls' as you call them, are toys that Earthling children play with?" She declared. "Why they look just like Trillans!" Then she asked, "Do you have any that look like Elgats?"

Angela tilted her head to one side and answered, "Yes, lots of them. Why?"

Darvith didn't answer, instead she asked, "Would it be possible for us to borrow some of them in the near future? They will come to no harm."

Angela was very curious but answered with a quick, "Sure! No problem." She understood the futility of questioning the little blond tyrant.

Darvith smiled at the little Earthling knowingly and opened one of the wooden wardrobes, carefully examining the clothing inside. She pulled out a white lace and satin dress with a long full skirt, long sleeves and delicate crystal and pearl beadwork on the bodice. "This is lovely!" She exclaimed as she placed the attached crystal hair ornament on her head. Then holding the dress to her body she spun around in a circle showing off the fullness of the lace and satin skirt. However, when Angela explained that it was a Wedding dress to be worn at a ceremony similar to an Oathing, Darvith quickly put it back into the closet.

Angela smiled at the pair and said, "I'll leave the wardrobes and trunk here and you can try on things and take whatever you might find useful." Then she asked? "Is there anything I can do for you before I go back to the cottage for my breakfast?"

Darvith was quick to respond. "Yes there is! I have an idea! If Bowdren and I give you our clothing, could you see if it will fit the two dolls you brought with you today?"

The exchange was quickly made and with little difficulty. Darvith was very happy! The dolls could certainly be used to fool Griffin and the Elders of Trillan, and she had already begun to formulate a plan.

Again Angela smiled at the pair and said, "Well, if there's nothing else I can do for you, I'll be on my way. As I said before, I haven't had my breakfast yet and I'm very hungry. I'll be in to see you later in the afternoon."

Then she added knowingly, "I'm sure there are important plans to be made." With that said, Angela left the room and locked the door.

Just as the door closed Stavro burst into the room. "I have very bad news! Annwynn has been kidnapped. She must have been taken from the palace during the night. None of the servants heard or saw anything. I believe they're telling the truth." Stavro added, "I can only think that there must be some unknown passageway into the Palace, unknown to all but the kidnapper. It is my belief that Griffin has her." Stavro continued stonily, "I thought I should let you know immediately. The most trusted of my guards are out searching the Kingdom. I shall join them when I return."

Bowdren was heart-broken and declared, "I shall return to Elgat immediately! I must find her! I will find her! Let's be on our way! We have no time to waste!"

Stavro put his hand on his brother's shoulder and stated calmly, "You dear brother, are not going anywhere! They are calling for your death in Elgat. It seems there are many important papers missing from the Institute, and several of your former colleagues are telling anyone who will listen, that you have stolen them."

Stavro scowled as he continued, "They have also loudly insinuated that you have kidnapped Annwynn, and fled to Trillan with the Princess and the papers, in the hope that the Trillan Institute of Science will give you an important position."

Bowdren stared at his brother in disbelief. "Surely no one believes this lie?"

Stavro nodded his head sadly and replied, "Yes. They do believe it." Then he added kindly, "Look at it for a moment as they do. You are an Elgat Scientist who looks like a Trillan. You were one of the few who had access to the missing papers. Now you, the documents and Princess Annwynn are missing, and highly placed and well-respected scientists, all Elgan I might add, at the

Angela and the Enchanted Bell

Institute claim that you are a thief." He added emphatically, "Of course they believe the lie!"

Bowdren was furious! He stamped his foot and shouted, "I will return to Elgat and prove my innocence. I will find my beloved Annwynn!"

Darvith grabbed his arm as he turned to leave and announced, "I will find Annwynn, and I will go alone. You will only be in my way Bowdren." Then taking his hands in hers, she smiled sympathetically and added, "I'm sorry to be so blunt, but you know in your heart that I am right. There will always be those who can see your Aura, even when you are invisible. You would endanger both of us." She continued evenly, "As a matter of fact you can be very useful here, and might even save my life."

Bowdren was not convinced and growled, "I must go with you. How can I be of any possible use if I stay here?"

Darvith was quick with her reply, "Don't you see Bowdren? Why your presence by the stream with my look-alike doll and Angela, will give a completely believable image to those in Trillan who will be viewing you through the great crystal. It will be much more realistic than it would have been with Angela trying to manipulate both dolls." She added with great seriousness, "It is essential that they believe I am here with you. Your performance will enable me to survive in Elgat where I know I will be able to find our beloved Annwynn."

Stavro interjected forcefully, "She's right Bowdren! You must realize that this is the way it must be done. Griffin and the Elders can't see Auras through the Crystal and won't realize that the Doll hasn't one, or even a voice for that matter. The plan is brilliant!"

Stavro turned toward Darvith and said in a grave voice, "You realize that you will be in great danger until Griffin is convinced that you are here with Angela and Bowdren. At the moment, all of Griffin's allies are looking for both of you in Trillan and in Elgat." He added, "It's obvious that at least part of the reason for kidnapping Princess Annwynn has to do with setting a trap for you Darvith. He knows that you will try to rescue her."

Stavro studied Darvith's reaction to this news and saw her shudder when he spoke of Griffin's plan to trap her. His voice was calm and studied as he continued, "I have a plan. I want you to listen without interruption until I have finished explaining it to you. Do you agree?"

Darvith nodded her head in agreement. Although she was still very angry with him, Annwynn's safety was more important than petty disputes.

Stavro continued solemnly, "For purely practical purposes, I suggest that you become 'my' Life-Mate." When he saw the horrified look on her face he quickly added, "In name only of course. I promise. It would just mean that Griffin would then be unable to claim you if you should somehow fall into his hands."

He went on to explain, "As you know, the taking of another's Mate carries the penalty of death in both our lands. He would not dare to break our laws."

Stavro gazed down into Darvith's eyes and smiled warmly as he continued, "Just as you, my plan has always been to remain free. Please understand and believe me Darvith, and Bowdren is my witness, I will make no demands of you, not even of kisses. You must admit that it would be a good cover for both of us, and in many ways."

Darvith was now convinced that his passionate kiss had just been an impulse of the moment and that he did feel just as she did about freedom. She smiled up at him mischievously and said, "Now Stavro, are you sure you are not being just a bit too romantic?"

The statement was meant to be ironic but Stavro was completely caught off guard by it and reacted to his shock by laughing a little too loudly. Sudden questions flooded his mind. Had she guessed? Did she know of his great love for her? Was she aware that he would accept any kind of Oathing with her if it insured that she could never belong to anyone else?

Darvith found Stavro's reaction curious and gazed up into his eyes in a long silent appraisal. She could read nothing; his passionate thoughts were blocked to her. He smiled down at her warmly; he could see that she thought of him as a friend and that would do for now.

Finally Darvith spoke, "I wish we had more time. From my point of view Stavro, your plan has many advantages. However, I cannot believe that you would not one day desire a Life-Mate and children. Therefore I must decline your kind offer of protection. It is too much to ask of you. I will take my chances."

Stavro declared solemnly, "I can assure you Darvith, my situation remains the same, whether it is legal or not. I will remain free and alone. As Bowdren will tell you; it has always been the path I intended to follow." He added, "Of course there is always the chance that you may one day wish to become a Life-Mate?"

Darvith shook her head as she looked deeply into his eyes. "No. I never will. And if this is your absolute wish, I will be comforted by it." Then slipping a ring from her middle finger, she placed it in Stavro's hand and murmured softly, "I give you this ring to show my intent." Although the thought of Oathing still made her uneasy, she trusted Stavro. Perhaps her nightmares of Griffin would end at last.

Bowdren smiled, it seemed a good plan. He suggested. "I can perform the ceremony. Oathing ceremonies were one of my more pleasant tasks at the Institute. I can even make up the proper forms."

Darvith laughed and teased, "Will you never cease to amaze me Bowdren? Perhaps we are related after all."

Stavro felt excluded and asked the laughing pair to let him in on the joke.

Bowdren replied with a grin. "It's nothing. We're just being silly. I guess we've spent too much time together." He added cheerfully, "You know, I think the Realm of the Earthlings suits you both perfectly."

Stavro agreed and added with a rueful smile, "After all, it was here where we first made contact, in the broadest sense of the word!"

Darvith, meanwhile, had walked over to the doll closet and withdrawn the beautiful white dress that she had admired earlier in the day. She smiled one of her most dazzling smiles at the two young men and announced, "I shall wear this!"

The Ceremony took place on the sturdy little table, where Darvith and Bowdren had sat the evening before, discussing her resolve to remain forever free.

Darvith was shivering involuntarily. Then she silently scolded herself. This had nothing to do with losing her freedom; this had everything to do with keeping it. When she glanced over at Stavro she felt calm and safe once more.

The handsome pair stood on a silken carpet borrowed from the dollhouse. It represented the traditional flower petals used in Oathing Ceremonies and was woven from gold and silver thread and bordered with an intricate pattern of blossoms and leaves.

The couple held a lock of each other's hair carefully contained in individual, tiny golden cases. Stavro had brought them from Elgat in the hope that Darvith would agree with his plan. The exchange of these tiny cases was a traditional and important part of both Trillan and Elgat Oathing Ceremonies. Stavro held the tiny case containing the lock of Darvith's hair, tightly in his hand. He resolved then and there that he would wear it always, on a chain next to his heart.

The rose vines that Angela had rescued from the weeds, were now covered with blooms, and framed the view of the meadow beyond the window, as a frame for a painting. It was an exquisite backdrop for the event that was now taking place.

Bowdren smiled warmly at the pair and continued with the vows.

Darvith projected a delicate, fragility that belied her strength and fearlessness; while Stavro, beyond mere handsome, shone with his secret and profound love for her. They repeated all the Ancient vows with great solemnity and Bowdren watched as their Auras flickered together. Stavro's filled with so much love and passion, and Darvith's filled first with panic and then very gradually with a calm serenity.

Bowdren could see that Darvith trusted Stavro completely and thought of him as a dear friend. He smiled inwardly and decided that this was a very good beginning for any ceremony.

With the last of the vows completed, Darvith gazed up into Stavro's eyes and murmured softly, "I hope you will never regret this generous act."

Stavro kissed her gently on the lips and responded huskily, "I never will." And meant it with all his heart. He then turned to Bowdren and gave him an enormous hug. "Thanks brother! Wish us luck!"

Darvith smiled at Bowdren and declared, "Well now we are legally related at least!" Then she quickly left to change into more suitable clothing.

When she returned to where the two young men stood, she asked Stavro, "Does Griffin suspect that you have helped us in any way?"

Stavro laughed and replied, "I'm sure it will occur to him when he sees the record of our Oathing. He will be furious! But what can he say or do; he isn't an Elgat!" He added proudly, "Although he still controls many Elgans, immodest as this may sound, I am the most powerful of them, and the most loved."

Darvith smiled at him fondly and gave him a sweeping curtsy. She declared softly, "We who serve you, love you."

They all laughed and it felt good to break some of the tension that had crept into this farewell.

Stavro was more serious as he continued, "I've decided to make a public announcement of our Oathing to all of Elgat. I'll say that we first met when I claimed our Princess and brought her home, and that we both experienced 'Bella', love at first sight, at that meeting. I'll explain that Bowdren brought Darvith back to Elgat at my request and performed a legal Oathing Ceremony, joining us forever."

Stavro smiled confidently as he continued. "I will further explain that Darvith saved Annwynn's life on several occasions and that all Elgats should love her, as Princess Annwynn does. And I will add that it was Darvith who insisted on taking Bowdren to the Realm of the Earthlings for his own safety, until I can uncover who has spread the lies about my brother. It was an act of family love and love for me that inspired her action."

Darvith gently squeezed Bowdren's hand and murmured softly, "Try not to worry. I will find Annwynn for you and bring her back safely. I know I will."

Bowdren turned to Stavro and asked, "Do you think you should tell the Citizens of Elgat that Annwynn has chosen me as her Life-Mate, and that I have her ring?"

Stavro was silent for a moment and then replied, "No. They might decide that you took the ring from her when you kidnapped her. It would prove nothing and might make matters worse."

They all agreed and soon the newly invisible Darvith and Stavro made their way to Elgat.

CHAPTER 19

News Of Annwynn At Last

Early in the afternoon of the same day, Angela opened the Playhouse door to find a desolate Bowdren slumped in one of the chairs that sat on the table. He was staring sadly out of the window and humming a very haunting melody.

Angela was filled with concern and asked, "Whatever is wrong? Where are Darvith and Stavro?"

Bowdren related all that had taken place excluding the Ceremony, to a very sympathetic Angela who said comfortingly, "Don't worry Bowdren, I'm sure that Darvith and Stavro will be able to find Annwynn. They are both fearless and very clever, and Stavro, as Commander of the Guards, will have many contacts that will help him."

Bowdren gazed at the little Earthling affectionately, she was trying so hard to cheer him up, and it was sweet. He said softly, "I hope you're right. I just wish I could help to find Annwynn in some way. I feel so useless sitting here." He added, "They insisted that I stay behind and implement Darvith's plan. I'll need your help Angela. Will you help us?"

Angela immediately nodded her head in agreement and declared, "Of course I'll help. What would you like me to do?"

Bowdren liked this little Earthling. He smiled as he explained, "Darvith wants us to appear at the bank of the stream with her look-alike doll. She wants the Trillan Elders to get a good look at us so they will think Darvith is here and we are planning to enter Trillan."

Angela smiled, happy to be of some assistance and said confidently, "We'll fool them." Then she motioned to the Golden Coach that sat on the floor next to the Dollhouse and told him to climb in. She placed the doll now dressed in Darvith's clothing on the seat opposite his.

Bowdren was amazed at the resemblance and commented, "Between the two of us, we should be able to put on a convincing performance. The resemblance is uncanny." He laughed and added, "Of course this Darvith does sort of look like she's gone into shock. Just as if someone had dared to tell the real Princess to shut up!" They both laughed and he continued, "All I can say is it's a good thing they can only see us...no one would believe in a silent Darvith!"

Angela smiled then told Bowdren to 'hold on' as she picked the Golden Coach up with one hand and then opened and closed the door of the playhouse with the other. This maneuver tilted the conveyance and one of its occupants fell to the ground, while the other hung for his life from the door of the tiny Coach.

Angela helped him back in with her hand and scolded, "I told you to hold on! You're not going to be of any use with broken bones!"

Bowdren exploded with laughter and exclaimed, "Angela! I swear you're as unsympathetic as Darvith!"

Angela stuck her tongue out at him and then grinned. She liked Bowdren. After locking the door to the stone house, she slowly began to make her way across the meadow.

Bowdren carefully wrapped his arm around the partition between the coach doors and felt secure enough to project his head and shoulders out from the window of the coach. He was astonished by the vastness of the meadow, and by its great beauty. It was even more magnificent than it had appeared from the window of the playhouse. It was breathtaking!

All the flowers in the meadow were now in bloom with a great profusion of color. Their combined scents were heady and almost overpowering to his senses. This was a paradise!

There were colorful butterflies everywhere. He had never seen such spectacular creatures before and longed to examine them more closely. He murmured in awe, "What must it be like to fly?"

Bowdren called out with great excitement. "Can we explore more of the meadow once our task at the bank of the stream has been completed? I love your meadow Angela! I'd love to see more of it and perhaps examine some plants."

Angela smiled and nodded head in agreement. She would be happy to spend more time with him. Bowdren was great company and best of all he made her laugh.

At last they reached their destination. Angela thoughtfully sat in such a way as to give Bowdren shade from the direct rays of the sun. This was just a temporary measure for the sun would soon drop behind some tall trees.

When Bowdren gazed into the raging torrent, he was very grateful that there was no longer a need for him to dive into it. Annwynn had been correct in her assessment. As he studied the rapids and whirlpools he wasn't at all certain that he could have followed Darvith into the depths. It seemed a formidable shielding.

Angela glanced over at him; it was time to begin the show. Their first performance was a good one. Angela moved the Darvith doll in a life-like way, rarely showing it face-on and Bowdren did his best to look like he was carrying on an animated conversation with it.

The Trillan Elders were watching with great interest. One of them suggested, "They appear to be discussing their entry into the stream."

All but one of the Elders believed that Darvith had helped an Elgat spy, called Bowdren, to escape from Trillan, and that it was this same villain now speaking with her at the bank of the stream.

Griffin had explained his capture of the enemy as dramatically as he could. According to him, the spy Bowdren, with Darvith's help, had entered Trillan in the Royal Coach. Although the spy was invisible to all, Darvith knew he was there and intended to help him steal some important documents from the Great Hall. Griffin discovered him there and held him under arrest.

Of course he neglected to tell the Elders where Bowdren had been held. Instead he just added that the traitorous Darvith rescued him and fled with him to the Realm of the Earthlings where the Earthling Angela would protect them. It was neatly told.

Elder Planus didn't believe a word of it! What he could not understand was why Darvith was flaunting herself with the 'spy' Bowdren at the bank of the stream in such an outrageous manner. Planus decided that he would do some investigating of his own once this stupid meeting was over.

Planus smiled sadly as his thoughts turned to Annwynn, his beloved Annwynn. She was lost to him forever now. He had loved her since their childhood; for her part she thought of him as a good friend, which of course he was and would always be. He sighed deeply as he recalled those long golden days of childhood when

Annwynn, Darvith and he were inseparable. Could there have been a more perfect time...? He smiled dreamily.

Elder Koron, who was now shouting at him in anger, rudely awakened Planus from his daydreams. "If it's not too much to ask, would you wipe that silly smile off your face and give us some of your attention? This is a very important meeting!" Then he added snidely, "Or do you know more about the events that have taken place than you care to share with us? We know that you and Darvith are close friends." He demanded, "Do you have information that you are not sharing with us? Tell us!"

Now it was Planus who was filled with anger. He jumped to his feet and shouted, "What more is there to discuss? I suggest we bring this meeting to a close and get back to the Institute! Surely none of you are so stupid as to believe that Griffin needs 'our' help. Griffin has everything under control! We can best serve Trillan by getting on with our work at the Institute!"

The meeting was over and the Elders one by one meekly left the room. They knew the truth when they heard it.

Meanwhile, in Elgat, after having left Stavro with a gentle kiss, Darvith had already made her way toward the outer kingdoms in her search for Annwynn. She was filled with optimism and felt certain that she would find her friend. Her invisibility gave her great confidence, it made her feel invincible, but more than that she treasured the sensation of absolute freedom she now possessed.

When she had first left Stavro, she had given a brief moment's thought to him and to his sacrifice on her behalf, but it was a 'very brief' moment's thought. She was very accustomed to young men and their elaborate gestures toward winning her affection.

On the exciting evenings she had experienced since leaving him, she thought of him less and less. Now he was little more to her than any of the others, for she was on an important quest and was traveling into unknown country, possibly dangerous country. This was the ultimate pleasure!

The Kingdom of Elgat was so much more interesting than Trillan; its spectacular light exhilarated Darvith. It made her feel joyous, energetic and full of hope.

She was hearing music for the first time in her young life. The sounds were so beautiful that they brought tears to her eyes as nothing before; and the singing, she was learning to sing beautiful melodies that made her spirits fly. With the beautiful music came dancing, and she was quickly learning to master all the intricate steps. Whenever she had a chance, she would join in, at times accidentally tripping other dancers when she moved in the wrong direction.

Darvith was enchanted. She had fallen in love...not with a mere Elgat or Trillan, but with this Kingdom and its citizens. While traveling unseen among them she began to appreciate the way their society was structured and the way they honestly seemed to care about each other. She had no intention of ever returning to Trillan.

Her quest to find Annwynn had now become doubly important because Griffin might be with her and Darvith intended to destroy him. Why should 'she' spend the rest of her life running away? She could easily catch him unawares; he could not see her or her Aura.

As had been her habit during this last week, Darvith had stopped at one of the charming Inns that were stationed throughout the magnificent countryside. She enjoyed sampling the new and tasty foods and loved sleeping undetected, wherever she wished.

On this particular evening, Darvith was sitting on a low roof where she could listen to the conversations of the guests beneath her in the hope that she might hear news of Annwynn. There were dancers performing nearby. She felt relaxed and happy and sighed, "I think I shall stay invisible for the rest of my life. What a wonderful gift Bowdren has given me."

Two young men moved to a position just below her and she could hear their conversation clearly. 'Griffin' was the name that had caught her attention. Her heart raced! Could this be news at last? One said softly, "He wants us to watch out for a beautiful 'Golden one' with a crescent shaped mark on her forearm. He thinks she will appear some time in the next two weeks."

There was peevishness in the other man's voice when he asked, "Didn't he say anything else? What are we supposed to do with her? Arrest her? Kill her? What?"

The first speaker replied somewhat guardedly, "He wants us to alert him and that's all. We aren't to make her suspicious in any way." He added quickly, "Speaking of Griffin, I suppose it's time we checked in at the Canyon."

With that said the two young men began to walk at a brisk pace across the vast plain to the east, with the invisible Darvith close behind. She was certain that they would lead her to Annwynn.

Only a few days earlier, Stavro was given some heartbreaking news. Theda had informed him that his Oathing with Darvith was illegal.

Griffin had found an obscure Elgat Law that forbade Ceremonies involving siblings conducting or taking oaths in the same ceremony. Griffin then passed the information on to his Elgans in the Institute, giving them the order to inform the citizens of Elgat that the Oathing between the Elgat Stavro and the Trillan Darvith was illegal and void.

Stavro had reacted badly to the news and was momentarily filled with an almost uncontrollable rage. But Theda had managed to convince him that the time for a takeover was too near to jeopardize its success by an act of personal revenge. She had explained that Darvith was quite possibly in more danger as his Life-Mate than she would be if she were free because of Griffin's obsession to have her as his own.

Stavro had grudgingly agreed. He knew Theda was right and quickly left the room. There was no time to waste; he must find Darvith and warn her.

While changing into his hunting clothes his shirt had accidentally caught against the chain that held the tiny Golden case, containing the lock of Darvith's hair. He held it in his hand for a brief moment and then kissed it tenderly. He did not remove it, and he knew in his secret heart that he never would.

When Stavro returned to where Theda had been waiting he left important orders for General Ulvang in her care. It was then he'd suggested that Theda tell Griffin that her son was angry and depressed about the annulment of his Oathing with Princess Darvith. He decided to take his usual two weeks leave early with the hope of some diversion, perhaps some hunting near the Elgat border with Tavia.

This was his third day of travel and he was on his way to Ilsted. There were some files he wanted to check before his search for Darvith. She would want all the information he could give her.

Just as he reached the vast plain that preceded the compound, two young men approached him. Stavro knew both of them; they were young Elgan Guards. They smiled at him and saluted.

Stavro greeted them warmly and then thrust a sealed envelope into the hand of the Guard nearest him and ordered, "Here! Take this to Ilsted and give it to Griffin immediately! If he isn't in Ilsted, send it to his headquarters in Trillan!" Then he smiled at the pair winningly and added, "You will save me a great deal of time and enable me to reach the hunting grounds near Tavia by this evening. I want to begin my leave with a good start in the morning."

The Young men beamed at Stavro, happy to be of service. It was obvious that they held their leader in high regard. They wished him good luck and after another salute, they were quickly on their way to Griffin and Ilsted.

Stavro was pleased. Everyone would think he was on his way to the Border. Now he could easily search all the files in Ilsted.

CHAPTER 20

Plans To Be Made

Just as the guards disappeared from sight, Stavro felt someone squeeze his hand and soft lips touch his cheek. Darvith whispered, "Stavro, you must have important news for me. Tell me? What has happened?"

Stavro's face shone with joy. His beloved was safe. He continued to hold her hand as he related all that had taken place.

When he'd finished Darvith was silent for a moment and then said softly, "I'm glad the Oathing wasn't legal. You deserve so much more Stavro. A wonderful Life-Mate and lots of children."

Darvith could read nothing in his thoughts, but now as she gazed up into his handsome face she was amazed at how good it felt to be with him again.

It was time to leave. Stavro took the blue pill that Darvith gave him and soon they invisibly made their way to the Inn where Darvith had overheard the conversation that had led her to Stavro. They were both hungry and decided to eat, rest and make plans before they visited Ilsted.

As they made their way, Darvith commented, "Do you realize Stavro, that you are the only young man I have ever enjoyed being with for longer than a few minutes?"

Stavro laughed softly and replied, "And you, dear Darvith, are the only young woman I have ever met who doesn't bore me to tears!"

"What a pair!" They declared in unison and then walked hand in hand to the Inn while engaged in hushed animated conversation punctuated with soft bursts of laughter.

They reached the Inn at last. After eating their fill and drinking the delicious beverage that Darvith had grown to love, they stretched out on the low roof and watched the dancing.

Stavro's heart was filled with joy. The magic of this evening, of Darvith's presence beside him would live in his heart forever.

Darvith sighed with pleasure and murmured, "I have grown to love this land Stavro and its people. We can't allow Griffin to turn Elgat into another Trillan."

Stavro interrupted gruffly, "He hasn't any intention of creating another Trillan. Griffin plans to be the dominant force in an absolutely ruthless and unfeeling society, a society that will be controlled by brilliant scientists." He continued, "There will be no singing, music or dancing and our joyous light source will be taken from us and replaced by a violet light, designed to encourage scientific thought and nothing else."

Darvith's voice had a hard edge to it as she declared coldly, "Griffin is a truly evil man. I despise him! I will take his life before he takes mine, it is the only way I will ever have any peace. As he can't see me or my Aura, it should be an easy task." She added bravely, "I look forward to it! The sooner the better!"

Stavro decided that it was time to tell Darvith of Theda's plan to overthrow Griffin. After explaining why Griffin must remain alive for the time being Stavro added

"But that doesn't mean we can't help her to gather all the information we can to aid her, or find Annwynn and set her free. I'm certain that Annwynn must be in Ilsted. I've had the whole Kingdom searched by my most trusted guards and there has not been a sign of her."

Stavro continued enthusiastically, "Griffin is unable to detect my Aura when invisible, I've tested it on many occasions. Therefore, you and I should be able to access all of his most important documents." Stavro laughed softly and added, "As a matter of fact, we should be able to find enough incriminating evidence to have Griffin sentenced to death for treason in both Trillan and Elgat!"

Darvith liked the way Stavro kept saying 'we'. It pleased her to know that he didn't think she was a lesser creature. His great strength didn't depend on making another weak. She asked, "Tell me more about the Canyon and Ilsted? Is it another of Griffin's entrances into Elgat?"

"Yes." Stavro replied, "However, it is by far the most important of three, and leads from Ilsted to the Velds. Griffin set it up years ago in order to facilitate an easy transfer of babies from Trillan. Much less dangerous than bringing them into Trillan's capital and much easier to keep things quiet."

Stavro continued, "Ilsted is a small city that lies at the base of a canyon where for over a thousand years ET, Elgans have been brought from Trillan when they are still babies. They grow up in Ilsted where as soon as possible they are tested to see where they might best serve the new order. As you know, Elgans are brighter than the average Elgat or Trillan and often possess unusual gifts."

Darvith was puzzled and asked, "Well how can they infiltrate Elgat society if they grow up in Ilsted?"

"Very easily." Stavro explained, "Every year a selected group of Elgans from Elgat return to Ilsted for a day. During the preceding year they are each obliged to find a suitable and important position for any of the newly ready Elgans." He added, "As you can imagine there are always many more positions than there are Elgans to take them. Once the most suitable positions are selected, each Elgan is given false papers of birth...to this date not one had ever been questioned. It has been so easy for Griffin."

Darvith was filled with curiosity. She stated, "Obviously the city must be shielded in some way." When Stavro nodded his head in agreement, she asked, "How many new Elgans leave Ilsted each year?"

"Usually ten." Stavro replied and then added, "The thing is, any Elgan who lives in Elgat's Light for 500 years ET, changes profoundly, and for the better. Griffin is completely unaware of the power of our light and its ability to transform his Elgans into creatures who truly care for one another. Who would tell him?"

Darvith offered hopefully, "Well that means that we don't have to worry about all of the Elgans, just the most recent ones, say 5 or 6 thousand."

Stavro agreed and then confided, "If we can discover the names of Griffin's most active and important followers, I'm certain that Theda's group will be able to control them. She has thousands in her organization."

Stavro added with pride, "And now Bowdren will be able to join us! As a golden one he was ineligible, in fact until his return to Elgat with you, he had no idea that an Elgan society existed or that Theda and I belonged to it." He added, "You may not like him Darvith, but he is brilliant, and best of all he hasn't been programmed by Griffin. I'm convinced that he'll be able to help the young Elgans toward a quicker understanding of Elgat society and all that it has to offer them."

Darvith was very interested in learning all she could about Ilsted. She asked, "Please tell me more about the Elgans at Ilsted? Did you spend time there as a child?" Then without waiting for his answer, She added, "It's odd, but the whole time I lived in Trillan, I never heard of a single birth that wasn't blond and green-eyed. How did Griffin manage to keep his secret?"

"It was easy." Stavro replied gravely, "He has informants everywhere. As soon as he learned of any Elgan births he had his lackeys eliminate all evidence of them, including the parents. As you know, most Trillans are terrified of Griffin; no one would dare mention the births."

Stavro continued with his chilling account. "He moved the parents to an area he kept for the breeding of Elgans. From the day they first presented an Elgan he kept all parents as virtual prisoners, and sent the potentially useful Elgan births through the Velds shielded entrance to Ilsted."

Stavro's tone changed to one of jubilance, "Until now, nothing has stood in his way. We are about to change his luck, forever!"

Darvith was silent for a long moment, shocked by all that Stavro had told her. She murmured, "I knew Griffin was inclined to be sadistic, but I had no idea that he was completely devoid of compassion for his fellow creatures." Then she declared softly, "Yes Stavro, we will change his luck, forever!"

Stavro continued, "Fortunately Bowdren and I were allowed to grow up with Theda, our Elgan parent and were thus able to have a normal Elgat childhood. She and Rowena were not as lucky; both of them spent their childhood in Ilsted. The Elgans who grow up there have a bleak existence. Independent thought is discouraged by severe punishment, usually a type of solitary confinement in a windowless cell."

Darvith sighed softly, "Those poor little babies. I guess it's little wonder that Rowena grew up, shall we say, 'a little strange'." She explained, "When Bowdren was chained up in Griffin's Laboratory she confided to him that she was eagerly looking forward to examining my brain, after I was nicely dead of course. It seems she wanted to learn if anything interesting lived there. She was so cold and unfeeling."

Stavro explained sadly, "She's not like that really. It was an act she was putting on for Griffin's benefit. You may not know that she tried to prevent Bowdren from taking the mission to Trillan. And while Griffin's Elders were willing enough to send another Golden one, her concern for Bowdren, an outsider, caused Griffin to question her loyalty." Stavro added with admiration, "Rowena is very dear to me; I think of her as a sister.

Unfortunately, Bowdren does not return her love, and as I've only recently discovered, was completely unaware of her feelings toward him."

Stavro continued with pride, "My mother Theda was one of the most brilliant students Griffin ever had at Ilsted and very gifted. However even she was forced to follow his plan for the 'New Order' as he calls it. My father was one of her first assignments; she was ordered to Oath with him. However, I know for a fact that she grew to love him. He was a wonderful man. At least part of mother's plan for Griffin's overthrow has to do with the fact that Griffin had him killed. She only recently told me of this. I was very young when he left us."

Darvith could tell by the tone of his voice that he still felt the pain of his loss and reached to touch his hand in comfort.

Stavro was both surprised and warmed by her touch. He was about to tell her of how much he was enjoying her company when he felt her move away.

Darvith sighed and said, "I'm sorry that I misjudged Rowena, I must say her act certainly fooled me." She added sympathetically, "I'm also sorry that Bowdren has been lost to her, but I must tell you, I have never seen two people more perfect for each other than Annwynn and Bowdren."

Once again Darvith touched Stavro's hand as she said, "You are wrong to think I dislike Bowdren. I happen to like him very much."

Then quite unexpectedly she yawned and murmured sleepily, "Dear Stavro, I think it's time we found a place to sleep for the night. Suddenly I feel very tired." She pressed her lips to his hand with a tender little kiss and whispered, "Good night dear friend; we will need our wits about us tomorrow. I'll meet you here in the morning."

Stavro held on to her hand to prevent her from leaving. He did not want this evening to end and asked softly, "Stay here with me. This is a perfect spot. I'll get some blankets and pillows from one of the guest-rooms. The night sky show is spectacular in this area."

Darvith happily agreed and declared softly, "I think it's a wonderful idea! I love to sleep out of doors!"

A few minutes later Stavro returned and they made up their beds. Darvith was the first to fall asleep. Stavro lay gazing up at the sky unable to sleep because his mind was filled with plans for the next day. They were close to the Elgat-Tavia border where the combined light of the two kingdoms met and bounced against each other, producing a fantastic show of sparkling color in constantly changing shapes. It was a wondrous sight.

Darvith's arm had fallen across his chest during the night. Instead of moving it away as a distraction, he found it made him feel very protective of her and overcome with love. He wished he could actually see her sleeping, but for now her presence would have to be enough. Darvith was here beside him, just where she should be, and hopefully one day soon would always be, as his Life-Mate.

Finally Stavro yawned and closed his eyes; a plan had been put in place. He soon fell into a deep sleep with Darvith's arm still resting on his chest.

Although they had no way of knowing it, Annwynn was not to be rescued by them. Angela and Bowdren would find her from their vantage in the Earthling's Realm, and very soon.

CHAPTER 21

Annwynn's Ordeal

As she had promised, Angela continued to show the rest of the meadow to Bowdren. It was decided that today they would visit the 'boggy' section of the lower meadow. This was the area of the property Angela had saved as the last to be explored. She was very, very excited. There were certain to be frogs and even some garter snakes in such a paradise.

Angela had traded the somewhat cumbersome golden coach for an old plastic peanut butter jar that she had lined with a soft cloth. Bowdren found it was very comfortable; he could rest his arms on the upper rim.

Although Bowdren was very concerned about Annwynn's safety he was aware that there was nothing more he could do other than continue with his show on the bank of the stream.

As a scientist he was fascinated by the complexities of the Earth Realm's Flora and Fauna, and the study of the various plants and creatures made a very welcome distraction.

Bowdren requested that Angela make frequent stops during her journey across the meadow. There were so many interesting plants and insects that he wanted to examine at close range. After an hour had passed, Angela became a little impatient with his studies and every stop now elicited a deep sigh. Bowdren appeared not to notice.

They continued to slowly make their way through the meadow when suddenly their nostrils were assaulted by the unmistakable and pungent odor of Skunk Cabbages. They had reached their destination.

Bowdren wanted to make a thorough study of these very unusual plants. Agreeably, Angela placed the plastic jar, with its diminutive occupant, on the moist ground next to one of the larger specimens. She advised him to stay inside the jar, although she didn't explain why and Bowdren would have been too distracted to listen to her reason anyway.

After five very long minutes had past, she became restless and bored with the study and wanted to continue with the exploration of the swampy paradise. It was such a magical place; it was even more wonderful than she had imagined. Bowdren, however stubbornly insisted that they must stay longer. He needed more time. There was no arguing with him.

An exasperated Angela shifted her seating position to one where she could better shield Bowdren from the sun. Tiny rivulets of perspiration ran down her back. It was such a hot day! Why, oh why, didn't she wear her sun-hat? She longed to feel the cool water of the stream ripple across her bare feet.

Just as she was about to suggest, once again, that they should continue with their exploration, her eyes were drawn to a flash of color off to her right. Yes! There it was, a small, brightly striped garter snake, leisurely making its way across the boggy ground. Angela caught it easily and began to examine every inch of the tiny reptile. She marveled at its great beauty as it wound itself around her wrist and arm. Then on sudden impulse, she moved her arm and lowered it to where Bowdren could view her newly found prize.

A startled Bowdren was horrified as the snake's tongue darted toward him! With a loud yell he jumped backward in an effort to get away from this frightening creature! Angela just managed to catch the jar before it hit the ground. Bowdren was red with rage and glared at her. He shouted that they should move on, and no, he did not wish to touch the blasted thing! Angela giggled.

Bowdren scowled at her for a long moment then shouted angrily, "Angela! How would you feel if a creature you had never seen before, with a head larger than your own and an enormously long tongue were unexpectedly placed next to you? I'll bet you wouldn't think it was very funny either!"

Angela apologized, "No. I'm sure I wouldn't. I'm sorry for being so thoughtless. I won't do it again."

Then unexpectedly Bowdren laughed. He grinned up at Angela and declared good-naturedly, "I'll bet the picture of horror I presented to you was hilarious!" They laughed together like old friends. Angela liked Bowdren. He was great fun! He could laugh at himself!

Bowdren touched her arm and confided, "Actually I would like to examine it Angela. It is a very beautiful creature, but please keep the sharp end away from me, that's all I ask." Finally, after a lengthy study, the tiny snake was given its freedom and quickly disappeared into the reeds.

A short distance from where they now sat, talking and laughing, and one hour earlier, Annwynn had awakened to find herself lying on a Lily Pad that was situated near the edge of a large swampy body of water somewhere in the Realm of the Earthlings, judging by the size of the plants. In truth she had no idea as to where she was; she only knew that she was too tired to move. The warm sun combined with the sweet spring air, added to her drowsiness and she once again fell into a deep sleep.

Angela was the first one to see her. Bowdren, who was once again held safely in the jar in her left hand, was gazing in the other direction when she noticed the sleeping Princess on the Lily Pad. She pointed to the figure and cried out in disbelief, "Look Bowdren! It's Annwynn!" She added in a hushed tone, "How did she get here? Oh Bowdren, what if we hadn't visited the swamp today?"

As it happened, it seemed their arrival was perfectly timed because a weasel, the same weasel that Angela had seen earlier in the week, was now pacing back and forth along the shoreline. He jumped into the water and was swimming toward his dinner when Angela managed to make a direct hit with a clump of well-aimed mud. He was soon on his way when he saw the size of his enemy.

Angela immediately began her rescue. While carrying Bowdren carefully in one hand, she waded into the water, sinking to well above her waist, thanks to the mud that was slowly imprisoning her feet. She carefully placed Bowdren on Annwynn's Lily pad while she used both free hands to cut the stem beneath them with his dagger. Then she once again picked up Bowdren's jar in one hand and Annwynn's Lily Pad in the other and slowly made her way back to the edge of the pond.

This took considerable effort as her legs were now beginning to be drawn into the sticky goo. Angela felt a brief moment of panic as she wondered if this was how it felt to be in quicksand.

At last she reached the safety of the bank where she collapsed thankfully on the moist earth. She gasped, still out of breath from the exertion, "I don't think I'll be doing that again soon."

Annwynn had not moved or made a sound during the rescue. At first Angela and Bowdren were afraid that she might be dead, she was so still. There were deep blue marks on her throat and arms, and her dress was badly torn and covered with bloodstains.

Bowdren took her pulse and was alarmed by the weakness of it. He commanded, "We must get her to the playhouse immediately!"

Angela shook her head and suggested, "I think we'd better take her to the cottage. It will be much warmer and much safer. We have no way of knowing what has taken place in Elgat." Her lovely young face was a mask of worry as she continued, "I mean, what if Griffin has Darvith and Stavro as his prisoners and has learned about the playhouse and its secret entrance. I don't think we should take the chance, do you?"

Bowdren agreed and then drew her attention to a small, now empty knife sheath that Annwynn was wearing on her lower arm and murmured, "I wonder if this means that Annwynn was somehow able to flee from her captors, and the knife was the instrument of her release." He turned to Angela and added with urgency, "We must get her to the cottage at once!

Sarah was shopping in Goldenrod on this day and the cottage was quiet, with only the monotonous ticking of the huge Grandfather clock to break the silence.

Angela quickly climbed the stairs to her bedroom and opened the door to find two adorable kittens waiting for her entrance. Each dove at her ankles and began biting, growling and kicking with their back paws.

Bowdren was startled by both the sight and sounds of Angela's kittens and sincerely hoped he was well out reach of their teeth and claws. He laughed nervously and commented dryly, "These are what Earthlings call 'pets'? They are meant to be your friends and companions? I shudder to think how your enemies must behave!"

Angela gazed down at her two adorable kittens with different eyes. Bowdren was right. Even though they were still tiny, they could seriously hurt of even kill her guests. Different sleeping arrangements would have to be made. She turned to Bowdren and said comfortingly, "Don't worry I'll keep them out of my bedroom and take the added precaution of putting you in an area that they can't reach."

She moved to the center of her bedroom where another, even more elaborate dollhouse sat majestically on a table. She gently placed Annwynn on one of the ornate doll beds and covered her with a tiny blanket. Annwynn didn't wake or even move.

Bowdren held Annwynn's hand and murmured, "I only hope that it's just exhaustion that makes her so still."

Angela was about to comment when she heard her mother call from downstairs. She turned to Bowdren and whispered, "I must leave you for a little while. I'll take the kittens with me, don't worry." She added, "I'll bring something up for you to eat and drink when I come to bed."

The kittens did sleep downstairs that night and when Angela saw them in the morning she was relieved to see that they had been more than happy to explore the main floor and showed no interest in climbing the stairs.

After visiting with her mother over breakfast, and finishing her chores, Angela hurried upstairs with more suitable food and a thermos of sweetened tea. She hoped that both of her guests would be hungry and thirsty.

To her happy surprise, Annwynn and Bowdren were sitting in the kitchen of the dollhouse and were deep in conversation when she entered the room.

Bowdren immediately stood up and declared, "You're just in time! Annwynn has awakened at last and was about to tell me of all that has taken place. Now we can both listen."

Then he beamed and added happily, "Before she begins, I'd like you to know that Annwynn and I are to become Life-Mates. It was 'Bella', love at first sight, for both of us." Each reached for the others hand. Annwynn smiled at Bowdren lovingly.

Angela grinned broadly and said, "Congratulations! I'm so pleased for you both. When is the Oathing to take place?"

Annwynn smiled a little sadly and replied, "As soon as Griffin has been caught and executed for treason. I'm afraid none of us is safe until then."

Annwynn turned to Bowdren and confided, "I'm not sure if Angela should hear all that I will relate to you. I fear it is not a tale for tender young ears."

Bowdren smiled up at Angela and asked, "How do you feel about it Angela? You're a sensible girl and able to make quick decisions. Would you rather not listen?"

Immediately Angela pulled a chair up to the Dollhouse and declared with great anticipation, "Oh! I would love to hear of all that has taken place. Please? I don't frighten easily and you are safe now. Please tell me everything that happened?" She added, her eyes now wide with excitement, "I love to hear dangerous tales that end happily. My dad Rory always said it was because of my Celtic Ancestry."

Annwynn smiled at Angela with great affection. It was impossible not to be amused by the child's obvious relish of a good story. However she was still not entirely convinced that Angela should be listening.

The lovely face of the Princess was filled with sadness. It was as if she had just awakened from a terrible nightmare. Her voice was thin and flat, almost inaudible as she began, "On the same evening that Darvith, Stavro and Bowdren left for the Stone house and about one hour later, I received a message from Darvith. It was written in her hand. The message read, 'Meet me at the Institute, Room 9, urgent!'"

Annwynn sighed deeply then continued, "I didn't know what to do. I did consider ignoring the message, but not only was it in her handwriting; it also displayed the special mark that Darvith and I have used on our letters to each other since childhood. The mark is always placed in an obscure area therefore I felt certain that the message was genuine, no one else knew of those marks.

Annwynn continued stonily, "Although I couldn't imagine why she would have stayed in Elgat, I had to see her. I'm not a particularly brave person but my concern for Darvith overcame my fear. I donned a dark cloak and as it was late the palace workers were asleep. I made my way to the Institute unnoticed. I remember wishing that I had one of Bowdren's invisibility tablets. When I arrived I found the front entrance to be unlocked, an event I credited to Darvith."

Annwynn felt suddenly cold and began to shiver. Bowdren wrapped a shawl around her shoulders and she continued, "From the moment I entered the building I had the eerie feeling that I was being watched. At last I reached the door marked 9 and upon opening it a deep blackness overtook my senses. I felt as if I'd fallen into a bottomless well." She added, "It must have been a powerful inhalant that caused me to faint; all I can remember is a sour sort of smell."

Annwynn sighed deeply and continued, "When I awoke, I was lying on a small bed in a tiny windowless room. My head ached and I was very thirsty. Just as I was about to move, I heard a key in the lock. I was terrified! Griffin entered the room and smiled at me triumphantly; it was a smile of victory and I was suddenly very frightened." Annwynn was silent for a moment and then continued, "He announced that within the hour Darvith was to become his Life-Mate and Bowdren was to be publicly executed for treason. He intended to have these two very important events take place simultaneously. As you can imagine, I was devastated."

She continued forlornly, "I could tell that Griffin had somehow learned of my love for Bowdren and was enjoying the pain he knew that I was experiencing from his terrible news."

Annwynn frowned and said, "Suddenly Griffin began to laugh; it was a horrible sound. He declared that he despised all weak people and as one of the weakest, I should have been drowned at birth. Then he raved on and on about how all Elgats are weak, sentimental and unproductive and therefore completely unfit to live, let alone run a country. Why if it weren't for his Elgans, Elgat would have fallen into ruin hundreds of years ago."

The remembrance of these recent events was becoming a very painful experience for Annwynn. Her bottom lip began to quiver but soon she was once again in control of her emotions. She continued, "Then once again he began to laugh his horrible laugh. As he turned to leave, he spun around and said there was one last bit of information I should be aware of, this would be his little gift to make my last minutes even 'more' unpleasant. He laughed malevolently and declared that there was no longer any need for me to worry about the Elgat Discs and wonder if they were still safely hidden. Then he held them up where I could see them and gloated, that as I could see, they were now in the best of hands."

Annwynn sighed deeply. "As you can imagine when I heard him lock the door I felt that all was lost. It was at that dark moment that I again heard a key in the lock. I prepared myself for another encounter with Griffin, but to my surprise it was Rowena who greeted me. She motioned that I should remain silent and then gave me a reassuring hug. This unexpected and kind treatment from one I thought of as an enemy, left me speechless."

Annwynn's body was rigid as she continued. "I silently followed her down a long corridor lined with doors, just like the one to my cell. We seemed to be in a kind of prison for I could hear moans and cries for help coming from behind some of the doors. Rowena pointed to a door marked 7 and whispered that she had spent a great deal of time in that particular cell when she was a child.

I continued to follow her when all at once a loud buzzing noise filled the air. It was the same noise that Darvith and I had heard in the Earthling meadow. Rowena quickly pushed me into a room to our left and explained that this was her private laboratory and that I would be safe until her return for she had the only key."

Annwynn's voice was now filled with urgency and panic as she continued. "Once I was alone I tried to imagine what Darvith would do under such circumstances. It was then that I decided to look for some type of weapon. I felt certain that Rowena would have something hidden away and sure enough I found a small, very sharp, knife and a sheath to hold it that could be attached to my lower arm. My sleeve easily concealed it. From time to time I heard voices in the hall just outside the door but no one tried to enter the room."

Annwynn's breathing had become irregular but she continued. "Finally Rowena returned. She locked and bolted her door from the inside and told me that we were going to escape through a body of water. There was no time to waste and I must follow her orders without any discussion. As you can imagine, discussion was the last thing on my mind. Rowena then pulled me through a wall panel at the end of the room that had only appeared to be solid, where a long dark corridor lay before us. We ran through the darkness at the end of the corridor. Suddenly we were in what appeared to be a large bubble; it projected outwardly from several exits. When I looked back to where we entered the bubble I could see that our exit was no longer visible. Rowena explained that it was her secret access."

Annwynn's body was becoming even more rigid and her breathing was shallow and quick as she continued. "The water that surrounded the bubble was a murky green. I guessed that we must be at the bottom of a pond like the one on Angela's property, for when I looked up I could see the Earth Realm's sun filtering down through the deep green depths. But then I remembered that Angela's pond was crystal clear, whereas this one had great amounts of vegetation growing up from its muddy bottom."

Annwynn's face grew pale as she continued, "There was no time for further speculation. Rowena threw some Toad skins that she had picked up from the floor in my direction and urged me to dress quickly! She hurriedly explained that all of the predators in and around this body of water avoided the toad, and there was the added benefit of the large webbed feet, which made swimming upward much easier and faster. We were about to dress when we heard voices and shouting, and the voices were becoming louder and louder. I had never been so frightened! Rowena shouted. 'The guards have seen us! Dive upward! Hurry! The bubble will not hinder you! Go! Quickly!! Dive! Dive!' Immediately four guards rushed in at us. Rowena began to fight them off, all of the time urging me to flee! I turned to make my escape through the bubble when one of the guards caught me and began choking me! Somehow the tiny knife was in my grasp and...and...I stabbed him."

Annwynn was now shivering uncontrollably. Bowdren put his arms around her but she gently pushed him away and continued. "Rowena had disabled two of the guards and was now struggling with the third. I was amazed at her bravery and strength. I could see that she was badly wounded; there was blood everywhere! The tiny knife was still in my hand and without hesitation I plunged it into her attacker's back. He fell to the ground, dead. I knelt over Rowena to help her up but it was too late, there was no pulse. I could hear the shouts of more guards on their way to us. There was no time to dress in the Toad skins. I dove up through the bubble."

Annwynn was calmer now as she continued. "I have no idea how I managed to make the long and agonizing swim upward. My lungs felt as if they were going to explode. Many strange creatures and plants surrounded me. At one point I felt like I was in someone's arms and he was helping me to reach the surface. I honestly don't remember pulling myself up onto the Lily Pad." She added, "However I do remember hearing familiar voices and trying to sit up and call out, but somehow being unable to move. I suppose the voices I heard were yours. I'm so grateful that you were there to find me."

Annwynn turned to Bowdren and asked hopefully, "Darvith is safe and here with you?"

Bowdren shook his head sadly. "No she isn't here. She is in Elgat with Stavro, where they are both searching for you." He quickly added, "I wasn't allowed to accompany them because the fact that Griffin can see my Aura might place them in danger as well. They insisted that I would be more useful here with Angela and her doll."

Annwynn looked puzzled and inquired, "Her doll...?"

Angela held the look-alike Darvith where Annwynn could see it and declared, "It looks just like her doesn't it!"

Annwynn was amazed at the resemblance but added, "Of course Darvith is much prettier. However there is certainly enough of a likeness to deceive someone at a distance, especially when the doll is wearing her clothing." She added approvingly, "I presume you are using it to fool the Trillan Elders and trick them into believing that Darvith is here with you. It should easily succeed."

Annwynn gazed up at Angela and smiled warmly. "I wonder if you realize just how helpful you have been to us. Your great kindness will not be forgotten, I promise you."

Then she turned to Bowdren and took his hand in hers. She pressed it lovingly to her cheek and murmured, "I'm so thankful that you are safe. Griffin is a very convincing liar. I really believed that I had lost you forever."

Angela tactfully decided that it was time for her to leave. After making arrangements for the daily visit to the stream with Bowdren, she said goodbye to her guests and left the room.

CHAPTER 22

Escape From Ilsted

In the Kingdom of Elgat a well rested and invisible Darvith and Stavro made their way to the Canyon and Ilsted.

Much to her delight, Darvith found that she and Stavro had exactly the same instincts as far as rescue plans and the collection of evidence to condemn their mutual enemy. It was just like having a mental twin. Darvith thought of Stavro as a dear and true friend, and a friend she would protect with her life if necessary. He was her chosen brother just as Annwynn was her chosen sister.

Earlier that morning on the roof of the Inn, Stavro had drawn a map of the layout of Ilsted and Darvith's quick brain memorized it instantly. He was very impressed and found that she was far more adept at seeing the whole picture and forming a correct strategy than his Generals, and that included his best, General Ulvang.

They had easily passed through the shielding into Ilsted and were now descending the wide steps that led to the sterile, white world that was Ilsted. All of the buildings, the ground, the furniture, were a brilliant white; even the workers wore white uniforms.

They quickly made their way to their first stop, the main conference area; it was there where they were most likely to hear news of Annwynn.

They were in luck! Griffin and some of his Elgan instructors were deep in conversation. Evidently there had been an escape and they were discussing the 'treacherous' Rowena and her part in it.

Griffin was very angry and shouted, "I shouldn't have listened to any of you! I should have terminated her, as I wanted to, right after the Bowdren incident!"

One of the Elgans, a young instructor by the name of Garth, interjected, "But how were any of us to know that she would help the Princess to escape? Rowena was the most extraordinary student I have had in my years as an instructor at Ilsted. She was brilliant and would have served the New Order well. It was such a waste to kill her!"

This last statement was given with far too much feeling. Griffin raised his chin and gave the speaker an icy stare and held his gaze for a long moment. He was not to be reproached by any mere instructor! He would have to teach Garth a lesson in respect, and soon, but not until he solved the puzzle of Annwynn's disappearance. He must have proof of her death. He must be certain!

All at once Griffin smiled and declared, "I am worrying needlessly. The fact that we don't have proof of Annwynn's demise doesn't matter. She's dead all right! She would never have been able to swim to the surface of the pond! Even our best swimmers are exhausted when they reach the top and they have the added push given by the Toad fins; and without the protection of the Toad skin covering, no doubt one of the many predators in the pond will have made a meal of her by now."

Griffin's face was alight with another of his enchanting and disarming smiles as he added, "I think it's safe to assume that the dear, dear Princess Annwynn has abdicated." Everyone in the room roared with laugher.

Darvith was overcome with rage and whispered, "I will kill him! I want to kill him with my bare hands. I want to feel the life leave his body!"

Stavro whispered, "Steady. He might yet serve us better alive."

Griffin and the others left the Conference room each entering different doorways spaced evenly down a long hall.

Darvith and Stavro followed the Ancient Trillan into another very well equipped laboratory. He began to hum a happy melody. He was obviously very pleased with himself. It had always amazed Darvith that Griffin's handsome face was never in any way altered by the evil intent that lay inside his brain; instead he had the appearance of one who was kind and benevolent.

Unexpectedly, Griffin turned on the Crystal on his desk and gave a series of orders. "The next time you see Darvith and Bowdren at the bank of the stream, I want you to capture them and take them to Trillan! Immediately, do you understand! That Earthling brat will be caught off-guard! I don't care how you do it, just make sure that the capture is a success! When I return to Trillan, I want my future Life-Mate to be there and waiting for me! Separate them immediately and guard them well! You know where to put them! Your punishment will be swift if you fail me!"

Griffin shut the Crystal off and was silent for a long moment. As always his thoughts were blocked to all.

He strode over to a wall cabinet and withdrew the five Elgat Discs.

Darvith and Stavro were shocked and dismayed to see that he now possessed all of them. Instantly the same thought occurred to them and they rushed toward him. They could not approach him. The Discs were shielding him in some way.

All at once a loud buzzing noise filled the air and there were excited voices everywhere. The pair followed Griffin as he rushed to greet the young men running down the corridor toward him. He demanded, "Well? Did you find any sign of the Princess?" They all shook their heads and smiled. Griffin's face shone as he asked, "And Rowena, was there any sign of her body?" Again they shook their heads, but this time no one smiled.

Griffin appeared not to notice and continued, "Dumping Rowena's body into the pond was a brilliant idea. The fresh blood would have attracted many more predators. Both of them will have been eaten by now." Once again a radiant smile graced his handsome face as he praised his group. "Good! I'm very pleased! Well done!" Then he turned and left.

Darvith and Stavro were desolate. In an instant their thoughts turned to rage and then to revenge. In unison, and as a single thought they both said aloud, "He will pay! He will pay with his life!" Once again, they were amazed to hear an identical thought spoken aloud.

Darvith reached for Stavro's unseen hand and held it tightly for a moment. Their bond was permanent now; they would be dearest friends forever.

Darvith was puzzled, she whispered, "What's down at the end of this corridor? I don't remember seeing this wing on your diagram?"

Stavro replied, "That's because it wasn't there. I had no idea that this area existed; Griffin keeps secrets from everyone. It would seem that each of us is given just a small piece of the puzzle." He added, "I think it must be an exit. Let's check it out!"

A few minutes later they were amazed to discover that the corridor led to an immense underwater bubble.

"Just as I expected! Stavro exclaimed. Griffin told us all about it in the Conference room. I'm sure both the skins and the fins are very useful." He explained further, "And the loud buzzing noise is the key that allows outsiders to enter through the bubble. Anything or anyone can pass through from this side, but in order to re-enter the area they had to devise a key that would both call and allow entry, hence the buzzing noise."

Darvith's eyes were drawn to the blood that still covered the floor. She sighed and murmured sadly, "Oh Stavro. Do you suppose this is Annwynn's Blood? She would never have been able to swim very far if she was wounded badly enough to have lost this much blood."

Stavro reached for the invisible Darvith and put his arms around her in comfort and replied sadly, "I'm afraid that this great amount of blood is more likely to belong to my very brave Rowena. She would have fought like a warrior."

Darvith was silent for a moment and then gently removed herself from Stavro's embrace. She had made a decision. She declared, "I must search the pond for Annwynn. I must see for myself that there is no sign of her. The thought of Annwynn, hurt and abandoned, would haunt me for the rest of my life! I must at least make an attempt at find her. We both know she would have hidden from the search party!"

Stavro could hear the anguish in Darvith's voice and longed to be able to say something that would comfort her. But her response was just as his would have been so he agreed that she should try. He advised her to wear the fins for swimming but Darvith stubbornly refused.

Stavro glanced upward and noticed the silver light from a full moon filtering down through the depths of the pond. He was worried and Darvith could hear it in his voice when he asked, "Will the Earth Realm's Moon give you enough light to see? I understand Trillans have difficulty with their sight in near darkness." Quickly adding, "And you will have no way of defending yourself once you're out of the pond. I must go with you!"

Darvith gently scolded, "I'm no mere Trillan! There is plenty of light for me and my invisibility will keep me safe from any predators. I'm not afraid!" Then she added, "Let's agree to meet in the Stone House in a weeks time, and with a bit of luck, Annwynn will be with me. You have important work to finish here. You must stay."

The invisible pair held each other one last time and whispered "Good luck!" in unison. Then Darvith took a deep breath and dove up through the bubble and was gone.

Unfortunately she found the water in the pond felt unexpectedly thick, just as if she were swimming in a creamy soup. She wished she'd taken Stavro's advice and used the Toad fins. Bits of weed pulled against her body and tugged at her invisible clothing like hundreds of tiny hands.

Enormous creatures swam by her, occasionally bumping against her; and then startled by the unseen obstacle they would swim swiftly away, pulling her for a distance in their wake.

Darvith's lungs were on fire and her head felt like it was about to explode when suddenly, what appeared to be a young man, placed a bubble over her mouth and nose and she could breath again. He held her in his arms and swam swiftly to the surface of the pond.

She was unconscious when he placed her gently on the soft grassy bed he'd been using at the edge of the pond. It had been his resting place for the last eventful nights. He gazed down at her, then knelt beside her and ran his fingers through her beautiful golden hair. The damp strands glistened in the moonlight. Darvith was still invisible but Arlen could see her and he was enchanted. Then to his surprise she suddenly became visible, as if by request. After removing most of her wet clothing, he covered her with a blanket then placed her outer clothing on the tall tufts of grasses that surrounded them. They were certain to dry by morning. It was then that Arlen decided to give her a special shielding to keep her safe while she remained in the Realm of the Earthlings. He watched over her until dawn when she began to regain consciousness. Only then did he move away.

Darvith sat up and tried to recall all that had taken place during her last minutes in the pond. She quickly dismissed the memory of someone helping her to swim to the surface and decided that it was an image brought about by an insufficient supply of air to her lungs.

She was alarmed when she realized that she was visible and quickly checked to make sure that her supply of pills was intact. They were safe and dry.

Then she noticed the bed of grass she had been sleeping on and her clothing now neatly hung in the grass and wondered if she would have had the presence of mind to do all that last night. She looked down at the blanket that covered her and murmured aloud, "Where did this come from? Someone 'must' have helped me! But where are they now?" She seemed to recall that it was a young man who held her in his arms and brought her to the surface of the pond. Could 'he' have done all of this for her? Good grief! Did he undress her?

Darvith was at first angry and then upon examining the clothing she now wore, decided that the stranger had allowed her some modesty, and it had been a very sensible thing to do. No one should sleep in wet clothing! Darvith smiled and called out, "Thank you! Whoever you are. Thank you very much!" She wondered why he didn't wait for her to wake up. She was filled with curiosity and decided that she would return later, but first she must search for Annwynn.

Arlen continued to watch as she carefully circled the pond. He had read her mind and knew that she, like the toad-creatures earlier, was searching for a young woman named Annwynn. But unlike the others, this beautiful golden creature was a dear friend of Annwynn's and carried great love and concern for her in her heart.

It was obvious to Arlen that the young woman they were all seeking had to be one of the lovely dark-haired creatures he had rescued only yesterday from the pond. He surmised that the toad-creatures must have been the ones to inflict the injuries to both. He now wondered 'which' of the young women was Annwynn.

Arlen had no time for memory scans yesterday. He could see that one was only exhausted and placed her on a Lily pad and surrounded her with an invisible shielding. He immediately took the other young woman, who was near death, to his community where he left her in the hands of the most gifted healers. There he was told to return to the pond in case there were others who needed help and to see if the other young woman had recovered.

Thus Arlen was at the pond and witnessed the rescue of Annwynn, although he was still unaware of her name. Her rescuers expressed great love and concern for her and obviously knew her, and that was all that mattered to Arlen. He released the shielding he had placed around her.

If no one had claimed her that day, he intended to take her to the Community where she would have been warmly welcomed. Once again Arlen found himself wondering if these beautiful creatures from the pond were related to each other or if they were related to the toad-creatures. He was also very curious about the Earthling child.

Diana and Adrian had left their home three years ago. The child's presence in the meadow must mean that the cottage has new occupants at last. Diana will be happy to hear that the home she loved so much would be taken care of once again. He murmured aloud, "I wonder how the Earthling child met the creatures from the pond? Could she be gifted with the same sight as the Hoptons?"

Arlen's thoughts were interrupted by Darvith's deep sigh. It was a sad, lonely sound that seemed to echo softly about the pond. It made him want to give her some words of comfort but he had been ordered to 'observe' only for the time being. No dialogue was to take place.

For her part, Darvith was very discouraged for there was not a single sign of Annwynn's presence. However, there were recent footprints in the mud; Angela sized footprints. There was a small chance that Annwynn could have been rescued. Darvith was once again filled with hope as she ran up the path toward the Stone House.

CHAPTER 23

Azoria

As she disappeared from Arlen's watchful gaze many thoughts flooded his mind. There were many questions still unanswered. Who were these creatures? Why had they suddenly begun to appear in the pond?

Finally Arlen turned and made his way back to his home. He was a tall and slender young man with bright green eyes. His hair was black, short and very curly and his skin tanned from the Earthling's Sun. Although he wasn't exactly handsome, his blunt and rugged features were attractive enough to win the hearts of many of the maidens in Azoria.

The Kingdom of Azoria had evolved slowly. It began with two exceptional Elgans named Azora and Doran, who had been Life-Mates for a thousand years. The Kingdom had been named Azoria in honor of Azora, for it was because of her that it came into being.

A thousand years ago Azora discovered that innocent babies were being terminated because their coloring was not pure Elgat, and therefore of no use to Griffin and his plan to infiltrate the Kingdom of Elgat. Griffin referred to all such babies as 'Rejects'.

Doran and Azora had no children of their own. When they heard of the disposals that were taking place they decided that something must be done; however many innocent lives were lost before they could implement a plan.

It was Griffin who gave them the opportunity they needed when he decided that further disposals would take place in the pond. And by a wonderful piece of luck, this horrific duty was assigned to Doran. The couple was jubilant! Griffin, the enemy to all, had made a rescue mission possible.

When the date arrived for the first of many thousands of disposals, Azora and Doran had all things in place; a safe way to get the babies to the surface of the pond, and a safe and shielded home for them in the lower meadow.

One day Azora ceased to work at Ilsted. Griffin never once questioned Doran as to her whereabouts. His workers had never been of any interest to him. Once they had their security check and began work at Ilsted, he never gave them another thought.

Thus Azora was able to stay permanently in the Earth realm, in the Kingdom of Azoria. Doran visited as often as possible. It was an agreement kept by this extraordinary couple that as long as Griffin was pursuing his present course of action in dealing with the unwanted babies, Doran would stay at his post.

The Kingdom of Azoria grew and flourished in the realm of the Earthlings, unseen and unknown to anyone venturing near, with the exception of the Hoptons.

The gifted children grew up in a society that worked for the good of all. They had no knowledge of Elgat, Trillan or Griffin because their Elgan guardians felt that it wasn't necessary to tell them about lands and people they would never see. But now they would have to be told.

CHAPTER 24

The Capture of Bowdren

Darvith continued to follow Angela's footprints. As she approached the Stone House she thought she could hear the child's laughter in the distance.

Immediately Griffin's plan sprang to her mind and she felt a sudden panic. She must reach the stream in time to warn them! She made her way to the upper meadow as quickly as she could calling out, even though she knew it would be impossible to hear her from the bank of the stream. The meadow was thick with new growth everywhere now blocking all of the familiar Trillan trails.

Unknown to Darvith, sly, malevolent eyes had been watching her progress, or rather watching with interest the movement of the plants as she pushed them aside in her haste to reach the bank of the stream.

The weasel was certain there was a meal to be had close by and he was very hungry. The creature pounced toward the movement only to bounce off something hard. It gave a little yelp of surprise and Darvith turned just in time to see it jump towards her again with the same result. She couldn't imagine why the creature turned away but was very grateful that it did. Her heart was still pounding! She had never seen such a frightening creature!

Darvith was out of breath when she reached the bank of the stream. She arrived just in time to witness Bowdren and her look-alike doll, disappear into the foaming water, and then watch as the doll floated to the surface and drifted away with the stream's current.

Darvith felt a rush of sympathy for the little Earthling, who now sat on the bank of the stream sobbing. She was such a pathetic sight.

The still invisible Darvith patted the slightly startled Angela on the arm and told her comfortingly that it wasn't her fault. "You mustn't blame yourself Angela. Bowdren was a fool! He should have been prepared for just such an event!"

Darvith then jumped up on Angela's lap and told her to listen to her without comment so the elders who were certain to be watching would continue to think she was alone. She explained, "Now I'm going to climb into the pocket of your dress. I want you to get up slowly and we'll go somewhere out of sight of the Crystal and the Elders."

Angela was still sobbing as she silently obeyed Darvith's orders and made her way to the path to the cottage.

As soon as they reached the path Darvith took one of the pills from the tiny waterproof pouch she wore around her waist and became visible. She then proceeded to tell Angela of all that had taken place in Elgat, including her ordeal in the pond. Then she asked hopefully, "Is Annwynn here with you?"

Angela was still sobbing but managed a weak smile, "We found Annwynn yesterday and aside from a few bruises, she seems okay. Rowena saved her life but died in the attempt."

Darvith nodded her head and replied sadly, "Yes, I know." She sighed deeply and continued, "We overheard

Griffin tell his Elgans at the Institute that he had Rowena's body dumped into the pond like garbage and felt certain that the turtles would make a meal of her."

She added darkly, "I know where I'd like to dump 'his' body, piece by piece!" Darvith looked up at the still sobbing child and demanded; "Now I want you to stop crying! I'm beginning to feel positively damp!"

Angela managed to smile through her tears and asked, "How will I be able to tell Annwynn? Will she ever be able to forgive me? I was supposed to take care of him?"

Darvith replied comfortingly, "Angela, you must stop punishing yourself. Bowdren was at fault not you. I know Annwynn will feel the same way. He is the adult you are the child. He should have known that an attempt would be made and have some sort of safety mechanism in place." She added softly, "Stavro would never have been so careless, but perhaps that's just the difference between a Commander and a Scientist."

Angela was comforted by Darvith's words and wiped her tear stained face with the bottom of her dress, almost dumping Darvith from the pocket.

"Angela! Do be careful! Do you want me to fall on my head?" Then she laughed and quickly added, "Don't answer that!"

She was suddenly serious and added, "I don't believe Griffin will hurt Bowdren until I'm safely in his clutches and you and I know 'that' will never happen! I don't want you to blame yourself for his capture in any way."

The cottage now stood before them and Darvith remarked on its great size. When she found out that Angela slept in an upstairs room she couldn't wait to see the view from its window.

As they entered the house Sarah called out. "Come here for a minute honey!"

Angela entered the study and Sarah looked up from her typewriter and smiled, "Lunch will be ready in about half an hour sweetheart. Would you set the table for me?" Then she asked, "Are you feeling okay? You look a little flushed."

Angela explained, "There's something in the meadow that's making my eyes water a little; some pollen I guess."

When she turned to leave the room Sarah called out, "Oh honey, could you take your kittens away with you? They are driving me crazy with their antics. Boris landed on my typewriter a few minutes ago and scared the hell out of me and almost pranged some of the keys." She pointed to the shelf above her and said, "He jumped down from up there. Can you believe it? Sometimes I swear he has more than a few watts shaved off his little light bulb!"

The kittens thrilled Darvith. She exclaimed, "Oh Angela! What magnificent creatures! Are they really yours? How fortunate you are!" Then she added, "You're mother is very pretty. Don't you think she looks like a Trillan?"

Angela nodded her head, 'Oh yes, I agree. Even Stavro thought so, and that was why he stabbed her in the foot and tried to drown her!" The incident seemed so long ago now.

As soon as they entered Angela's room she placed Darvith in the dollhouse. Annwynn immediately rushed to her and there was much kissing, hugging and laughter. Eventually Darvith informed Annwynn of Bowdren's capture and gave her all the details of Griffin's plan. She assured her that Griffin would not eliminate Bowdren as long as he could be useful.

Annwynn was very sad but did not blame Angela in any way. She knew Bowdren was at fault not the child.

Angela decided to leave the two friends to talk in private. It was time for lunch and she was very hungry.

CHAPTER 25

Stavro To The Rescue

In Trillan, Bowdren was in chains standing before an outraged Griffin who was issuing a screaming torrent of questions. "Where is Darvith? Is she with that Earthling brat Angela? Where is sheeeeeeee?" Griffin's voice was filled with venom. He pressed his hands around Bowdren's throat and he slowly began to squeeze. Unexpectedly he released his grip and smiled his most enchanting smile. "No. I must not harm a golden hair on that empty head of yours...at least not yet; in spite of the pleasure it would give me. You will be the new 'bait' for my trap. Darvith will be unable to resist the challenge, and this time she will not escape." He continued jubilantly, "Once she is here with me where she belongs, I will plan a wonderful farewell for you...wonderful for me that is."

Griffin was now smiling with pleasure at the thought of implementing his plan. He declared happily, "At the moment you are so hated in Elgat that whatever termination I devise for my Elgans to carry out, will seem too lenient.

Kidnapping and treason are the only crimes that are on your current record, but wait until the Citizens of Elgat learn of Annwynn's death by your hands." Griffin shook his head sadly in mock regret, "I'm afraid they will demand that your blood be spilled Bowdren; how very sad for you and how very nice for me."

Once again Griffin's face was devoid of expression as he said, "You have been very lucky until now Bowdren, undeservedly so, for you have made some unbelievably stupid mistakes. I shall now put you in a very special cell from which there will be no hope of escape."

Griffin then turned to his guards and ordered, "Take him away! He is to have no food or water and I want him to have four guards on duty at all times! If he escapes this time the guards on duty will pay with their lives!"

Luckily, Stavro was still in Ilsted, gathering material that might be useful in proving a case against Griffin, in Trillan and in Elgat. Bowdren's appearance was a shock until he remembered Griffin's plan. For the first time since Darvith left him he was grateful that she had convinced him to stay behind; soon he and Bowdren would be able to escape through the bubble exit.

Stavro followed Bowdren and the Guards down the hall. He didn't recognize any of them as they pushed, punched and jeered at his brother on the way to the cell. A deep anger rose in Stavro's heart. Rage filled his mind with violent thoughts of revenge against the man who was causing those he loved, so much pain. "I will cut off the dragon's head with my sword!" He murmured savagely under his breath. "I will kill Griffin slowly and with much pain so he will learn what it is to suffer! Then I will remove his head."

The four Guards locked Bowdren in his cell. Now confident that he could not escape they began to play a game of dice, and turned away from the cell door.

Stavro quickly and silently unlocked the door and let himself into the cell carefully closing the door behind him. "Brother…" he called out softly. "Take one of these pills and we'll make our escape."

Bowdren sat on the cot dejectedly, and without looking up, he whispered, "It would do no good. Griffin has given me a potion that blocks invisibility. He thinks Darvith will try to rescue me and wants to make it as impossible as he can. He has a view into this cell and is probably watching me at this very moment, which is why I'm not acknowledging your presence in any way. However, it is possible that he may have seen the door, open and close when you entered."

Stavro declared, "In that case brother dear, we'd better get out of here and fast!" With that said, he flung open the cell door and quickly dispatched the startled Guards. Stavro shouted to Bowdren, "Run down to the end of the corridor! I'll be right behind you and get rid of any unwanted interference!" The pair swiftly made their way to the bubble exit.

Bowdren was about to follow Stavro's orders and dive upward when a sharp, searing pain pierced his side. A dagger had been thrown from somewhere behind them and now impaled his body. He mistakenly pulled it out causing the wound to bleed heavily.

Stavro shouted as he put his arms around his brother, "Try to dive upward! I'll help you!" But luck deserted them when Bowdren suddenly collapsed. A blow to the side of his head had knocked him unconscious. There was blood everywhere. With no time to waste, the unseen Stavro held his wounded brother close to his body and jumped up through the bubble.

Bowdren was a dead weight in his arms. A trail of bright red blood followed their tortured ascent.

Stavro found the water thick just as Darvith had earlier and swimming upward an arduous task with Bowdren's added weight. He felt his lungs would burst. Thankfully he finally reached the surface of the pond and held on to a Bulrush until he had regained enough of his strength to swim to shore.

Once safely on the bank of the pond he turned Bowdren on his side and a great rush of water gushed from his open mouth. Bowdren was very pale and still, but Stavro could feel a faint pulse. As he packed and tied the horrific wound, he shouted Bowdren's name over and over in a voice filled with anguish. Stavro knew that if Bowdren were to be moved now the resultant bleeding would end his life.

Arlen had witnessed the arrival of the brothers from the shore and was touched by the great concern and love in Stavro's heart. He walked quickly to where they now rested.

Stavro, upon seeing a stranger, raised his sword to defend his brother. To his amazement his sword dropped to the ground when the young man drew near.

Arlen immediately explained that he meant the brothers no harm and that he would like to help, as he knew a great deal about healing.

Stavro was still suspicious and asked, "Who are you? Where are you from? You can't be a Trillan or an Elgat?"

Arlen smiled reassuringly and replied, "Surely none of that is important now. What do you have to lose? If you leave him as he is he will die."

Arlen knelt down beside Bowdren and put his hand on the wound, holding it there for several minutes. Then he looked up at Stavro and said comfortingly, "He'll be alright. I have stopped the bleeding and given him some medicine; the wound is serious but he will live."

Stavro felt Bowdren's pulse; it was stronger. Some color had returned to his cheeks and his breathing wasn't as labored. The young stranger had definitely brought about this amazing recovery.

Arlen smiled kindly and said, "Please don't worry about your brother. I'll take Bowdren with me. He'll be perfectly safe and well tended. I will return with him in two weeks time."

He added, "I know that you have important things to do and that one of them is to meet with Darvith. I'll give you a special shielding while you are here in the Earth Realm and it will protect you for as long as you stay here. You will certainly need protection from the many predators who are likely to be hunting at this time of night."

As if on cue, a fox pounced toward Stavro, only to bounce off from the unseen shield. Arlen began to stroke the startled animal and soon it was on its way. He smiled and explained, "All the animals know us by our scent and they leave us alone." He laughed and said, "You are just plain meat! However the shielding will protect you, enjoy the night!"

Stavro immediately took a pill and became visible. Arlen showed no surprise and Stavro was too distracted to think of it at the time. Instead he thanked the young man for his kindness and they set off on opposite paths.

It wasn't until after the stranger had disappeared with Bowdren that Stavro began to think about all that had taken place. He was still invisible when the young man approached and yet he wasn't invisible to him; and he knew Bowdren's name. And what about Darvith? Stavro wondered if the young man had read her name in his thoughts or if he had actually seen her. Why hadn't he thought of asking him? Why didn't he insist on learning more about his Kingdom or even the stranger's name? He was angry with himself until it occurred to him that the young man had obviously taken control of the situation in some magical way.

One thing was certain; if the stranger hadn't helped when he did, Bowdren would most certainly be dead by now. Suddenly another thought came to him. How could that tall slender young man lift and carry a man almost twice his weight? For a brief moment Stavro thought of turning back to follow him to the unknown Kingdom, but reason prevailed and his search for Darvith was once again his main concern. He must find her. Bowdren was safer where he was for the moment.

CHAPTER 26

The Healing Room

Arlen had reached Azoria. He took Bowdren to the healing room and then telepathically called Azora and Morgana. Bowdren needed immediate treatment.

Azora was the first to arrive. She gasped in surprise, "Why it's Bowdren, another of Elgat's greatest scientists."

She confided in a hushed tone, "All of Elgat thinks that he was executed last night for treason and the kidnapping and murder of Princess Annwynn. I imagine the wounds were sustained during his escape." She sighed with wonder and murmured, "How could he have reached the surface of the pond when he was so badly injured?"

Morgana was next to rush into the room where Bowdren was now suspended a few feet above the floor, seemingly held in place by a soft golden light. She quickly cleansed his wounds and then stood over his body and assessed his injuries. The head wound, she decided, might cause a temporary memory loss. The wound to his side was much more serious; and he had lost an enormous amount of blood. He was in fact just barely alive.

Morgana placed her hands on his chest; radiance emanated from them and before long Bowdren's pulse became stronger and his skin began to lose its ghastly pallor. She then ran her hands down to the terrible gash in his side and again the radiance emanated from the tips of her fingers. She held them there for a very long time then covered his wound with a transparent tie that she wound around his body several times.

Morgana gazed up into the anxious eyes of Azora and Arlen and said, "He must sleep now. I should think for at least three days." She smiled approvingly, "He's a very strong young man and wants desperately to live. He should soon recover."

Arlen began recounting the events he had witnessed. He turned to Azora and explained, "You asked how Bowdren reached the surface of the pond when he was so badly wounded; well he wouldn't have if his brother hadn't brought him. Commander Stavro possesses amazing strength and courage."

Azora was amazed, for only she knew of the great distance Stavro had to swim in order to reach the surface of the pond. She wondered what the Commander of the Elgat Guards involvement in the rescue might mean to the future of Elgat. Griffin would be furious!

Azora decided that for their own safety she should give Arlen and Morgana a brief history of Elgat and Trillan. She explained Griffin's plan to use the Elgans to infiltrate Elgat and gain control of both Kingdoms.

Finally, she told of Griffin's ruthless disposal of babies who didn't exhibit true Elgat coloring and were therefore of no use to him and his plans for Elgat.

They were horrified by this startling information but quickly recovered and soon asked many questions all of which were answered.

Azora was silent for a long moment and then said in a voice filled with concern, "If Griffin learns of Stavro's involvement with Bowdren's escape, Stavro will be finished in Elgat." She continued, "While it's true he's an Elgan, he has been a wonderful Commander, brave and just and much loved by the Citizens of Elgat. But his great popularity won't save him. I know Griffin well enough to be certain that he will never allow Stavro to live." She sighed deeply. "He must have known this when he saved his brother. It is just so sad."

All she was learning of Stavro touched Morgana. A man so brave and true that he would risk everything to save his brother's life; this would be a man worth loving.

Azora asked, "Why didn't Stavro return with you?"

Arlen smiled and replied, "He was looking for Darvith and believe me 'she' is worth looking for. He loves her but fears it is in vain. They were Oathed for a brief time until Griffin found an obscure Elgat Law that made it illegal and had his Elgans inform the Commander that the Oathing was annulled. Arlen added, "In spite of the failed Oathing, Stavro still wears the tiny case containing a lock of Darvith's hair on a chain around his neck. I have a feeling that he always will."

Arlen continued, "Both he and Darvith were wearing the cloak of invisibility when I found them. Stavro took a pill that made him visible, and I assume Darvith has her own supply. I shielded them both."

Azora was relieved by this news and declared hopefully, "Stavro has a chance then, as long as he has an excuse for being away from his Command, Griffin might not suspect that he had a hand in Bowdren's escape. That is very good news!"

Azora smiled at Arlen. "So you think Darvith is worth chasing do you?" She added, "Well you're not alone.

She is the young Trillan Princess that Griffin has become obsessed with. He wants her as his Life-Mate and apparently she has other ideas. I can't say that I blame her."

Azora looked puzzled for a moment and then added, "What I can't understand is how she came to be in Ilsted and have access to the pond? And you say she was looking for Princess Annwynn? Perhaps Rowena will be able to give us an explanation when she recovers."

Morgana had been studying the sleeping Bowdren and commented, "So this is what they call a 'Golden one'; a hybrid like the rest of us. I must admit he is very handsome and muscular. Are there many such as he in Elgat? Is Stavro a 'Golden one' as well?"

Azora smiled and replied to the second question first. "Stavro has the coloring of a typical Elgat, but he is an Elgan like the rest of us. Although he is very handsome he seems unaware of his good looks."

Azora smiled knowingly at Morgana and added, "He is adored by all the young women in the Kingdom." She continued, happy that at last she was able to talk about the kingdom where she grew up and fell in love.

She began, "There are many thousands of 'Golden Ones' in Elgat, but of course they are not all as attractive as Bowdren. However, they do all share the same coloring. It has long been considered a good Omen when a birthing presents one."

Azora's face clouded as she continued, "Sadly, this was not always the case. At the time of the restoration, all the Golden Ones that were presented were terminated. The Elgats wanted no reminders of Trillan treachery in their New Kingdom." She shook her head sadly and said, "It is a time in Elgat history that we all regret and remember with deep shame."

Azora added with a sad little smile, "Now a day in May is set aside for the lost children of Elgat. Each region has a Memorial in place where the Citizens gather and sing in remembrance. It is a beautiful Ceremony, filled with love." She continued with a hint of pride in her voice, "There were fifty 'Golden' babies lost to us and every Elgat, without exception, knows each of the birth names. They will never be forgotten and such an event could never take place in Elgat again. I'm certain of it!"

Morgana was puzzled and asked, "Golden ones are Elgans. Does Griffin control them as well?"

Azora shook her head. "He decided against it for several reasons but basically he found them to be too willful. They are bright and gifted in many ways but far less predictable than the rest of us."

She sighed sadly. "However his plan to infiltrate Elgat has been very successful even without the added numbers the Golden ones would have provided. I don't believe any Elgat knows of Griffin's plan, or even that he is still alive. They have no idea that their most hated enemy still lives in Trillan and has almost complete control of their Elgat Kingdom."

Morgana was intrigued, "I would love to visit Elgat one day. It must be an amazing place." She smiled at Azora. "I can tell by the way you speak of it that you miss your country and its people. You have given up a great deal for our sake. Perhaps one day you will be able to return. If you do, would you take me with you? Please say you will Azora?"

Morgana walked over to where Rowena lay suspended in the same golden light that bathed Bowdren; both patients were breathing evenly and were deeply asleep. She gazed down at the young woman and commented approvingly, "Isn't she lovely?"

Morgana glanced over at Azora and explained, "I proceeded with a memory scan yesterday. It seems she saved Princess Annwynn from certain death with the full knowledge that the Princess was Bowdren's intended Life-Mate. How could she do that when she loves him with such passion herself?" Morgana raised an eyebrow and observed aloud, "I'm not at all certain that I would have rescued the woman who had taken my place in the affections of the man I loved. I'm not certain at all."

Azora smiled and said, "Who can explain love and what it can make us do. It seems 'Bella' produces the most successful pairings. Doran and I felt it the first

Angela and the Enchanted Bell

time our eyes met." Azora's eyes misted and for a moment she was lost in her sweet remembrances.

Morgana teased, "A thousand years and you are still love-struck. It's unbelievable!"

Azora's eyes were filled with love as she replied, "I hope with all my heart that it will one day happen to you Morgana, for Doran and I have been truly happy."

Morgana placed her hand on Rowena's forehead and smiled. "She is so much better today. I like this young woman and I feel we will become good friends." Then she murmured inaudibly, "And who knows, Perhaps Bowdren will lose all memory of Annwynn and learn to love Rowena. It could happen."

Morgana's last comment had gone unnoticed. She turned to Azora and asked, "Are there any such as me in Elgat or Trillan?"

Azora shook her head and replied, "No. I'm certain that you are one of a kind and I'm sure that pleases you."

Morgana smiled. Azora was right. She was pleased. The fact that she was completely different from everyone else in Azoria had always made her happy and now to learn that she would also stand apart from the citizens in both Elgat and Trillan, her happiness was complete.

Morgana was very unusual. It wasn't just because of her ability to heal with her hands, a truly remarkable gift, but also because of her extraordinary appearance. Her long wavy hair was a deep rich red, her skin a pale ivory. Long black lashes framed eyes that were a startling mixture of blue and green. She was breathtakingly beautiful.

Unknown to the others, Morgana had another talent that only she possessed. She could instantly transport herself to any part of the meadow that she wished to visit.

She had discovered this particular gift when she was still very young. She was to be disciplined for disobeying Azora. Naturally she wanted to be somewhere out of sight and after 'imaging' a good hiding place, she had been instantly transported to the very spot.

From that day forward she kept this gift as her own and her secret. Morgana had never felt that she had to share her thoughts or her gifts with everyone else in the Kingdom. She was a loner and enjoyed her own company. She followed her own path.

The young women of Azoria found her to be too much competition and Morgana would frequently find that at parties she would either be surrounded by young men or left sitting on her own. None of the young women wanted to be compared unfavorably with her great beauty. Perhaps things would have been different if her personality had more warmth.

For the most part Morgana was untroubled by her solitary existence. She had her work, and whenever she wished for company Arlen was always to be found. They had arrived in Azoria on the same day and had spent their younger years together, much as Darvith, Annwynn and Planus had done in Trillan. He was her only real friend.

The young men in Azoria found her bewitching and she in turn found them dull and predictable, and none were as gifted as she, or in any way as remarkable. This was one of the reasons she was looking forward to many long conversations with Rowena and Bowdren, for unlike Arlen she was very interested in learning all that she could about Elgat and Trillan and its citizens, especially one very brave citizen.

CHAPTER 27

Stavro's Perilous Journey

In another part of the meadow, Stavro was making his way toward the path that led to the cottage. After checking the Stone House and finding it empty, he decided to see if Angela had company.

Amber eyes had followed his trek through the meadow with great interest, and now four large padded paws fell noiselessly on the path directly behind him.

An enormous black cat was stealthily tracking Stavro, waiting for the perfect opportunity to pounce on its unsuspecting prey. Stavro felt its presence and turned just in time to see the huge animal leap towards him!

The cat was a terrifying sight with its fangs and claws ready for the kill. Forgetting for the moment that he was shielded, Stavro raised his sword in what would have been a futile gesture just as the animal bounced backward, momentarily stunned. It shook its great shaggy head unable to comprehend what had just taken place.

Stavro laughed raucously, more as a response to the sheer terror he had felt than from high spirits; his laughter helped to release the tension of the moment.

The cat, all teeth and claws now, was unwilling to give up its meal and hissed as it once again jumped toward him, only to fall back in an angry heap.

The animal glared at Stavro with its huge amber eyes, and then with an angry growl and a gleaming flash of sharp pointed fangs, it slipped back into the darkness in search of easier prey.

As Stavro continued his journey to the cottage he became more and more relaxed. After all what had he to fear? He was invincible! The sights, sounds and sweet scents of the spring evening were exhilarating and filled him with a sense of expectation and joy.

Angela's cottage now loomed up before him. It seemed a gigantic structure. How was he going to gain entry? Just then he noticed that Rose vines traced their way up to and around an upstairs window. He remembered that Angela said she slept in an upper room that looked out towards the meadow. It was worth a try and it did seem the only option at the moment.

The climb was an arduous one. Luckily, he had never been bothered by heights and in this case, the cover of darkness certainly helped. He had never before been this far above the ground.

When he was very near the upstairs window a soft flutter of wings broke the stillness of the night. He turned his head and was amazed to see a large owl bounce off his shielding, with wings askew and feathers flying.

Unfortunately, in turning he lost his footing and the thorn that had been supporting him gave away. He fell into the darkness, crashing against branches, blossoms and thorns on his downward flight!

Somehow he managed to catch hold of a rose and held on to it for dear life while it swung back and forth in the darkness. His heart was pounding as he maneuvered his way slowly back to the main part of the vine and once again began his ascent.

Sadly, the fall forced him to re-climb at least half the distance that he'd already covered, with the added burden of having to deal with some painful, though superficial, injuries.

His progress was agonizingly slow and he found that he had to make frequent stops in order to rest. The events of the day were beginning to take their toll. It was only through sheer determination that a desperately tired Stavro reached the outer shelf of the window.

He was in luck for it was a wide space. When he pressed his face against the glass he was relieved to see Angela's sleeping form on a bed close by. He began to pound against the window as hard as he could, but it was no use, she couldn't hear him.

Stavro sighed resignedly and decided that he'd make his bed on the wide windowsill for the night. He was exhausted and every muscle ached from the exertion of the last few hours. After gathering some rose petals and leaves, he made a reasonably comfortable bed for himself, wrapped himself in his cloak and fell into a deep sleep.

Stavro awoke at dawn and watched for any sign of movement in the room. At last he saw Angela move to the side of her bed and sit up. She yawned and stretched. He began to pound on the window and jump up and down.

A very surprised and happy Angela grinned broadly and rushed to the window to let him in.

Darvith and Annwynn were still sound asleep in the dollhouse. Angela gently shook their beds and then placed the very hungry Stavro at the kitchen table. All of the food that Angela served him was quickly eaten.

Darvith was the first to wake and looked adorably disheveled when she peeked through the doorway into the kitchen. She immediately ran to Stavro and gave him an enormous hug. He lifted her up and swung her around.

Darvith laughed happily and asked, "But how did you get here?" She hugged him again. "You have no idea of just how happy I am to see you dear friend." She took his hands and held them tight. Then she noticed his scratches and bruises and whispered softly, "Oh Stavro what has happened to you? Have they tortured you?"

Stavro laughed and muttered something about a little accident and that there was nothing to be worried about.

Now Annwynn joined them and there were still more hugs and kisses. There was so much to talk over.

Angela left discretely but returned an hour later with more food and some steaming sweetened tea.

Once all of their important information had been exchanged they began to make plans. For three days they discussed the termination of Griffin and his followers.

On the morning of the fourth day, Stavro and Darvith had decided to return to Elgat until it was time to meet Bowdren at the pond.

The three friends were standing on the windowsill in Angela's room, gazing out at the meadow, when suddenly a flame haired young woman appeared before them. They were startled into silence.

As usual it was Darvith who was the first to speak. She demanded! "Who are you? And how in the blazes did you get here?"

Morgana smiled and replied, "You must be Darvith. I've heard 'so much' about you." She hadn't the slightest intention of deferring to Darvith in any way and continued without answering the questions. "I came to give you good news of Rowena and Bowdren. You'll be glad to hear they are both recovering nicely." She quickly added, "However, I'm sorry to have to tell you that Bowdren's head injury has caused memory loss, in spite of the fact that Rowena has been working with him every day. She is wonderful with him. They must have been very close." Morgana was reading Annwynn's Aura and knew the effect her words were having.

Stavro was overjoyed by the news and asked, "Are you telling us that Rowena is alive? But everyone thought she was dead, even Griffin! How did you manage to bring her back to life?"

Darvith interrupted, "How do we know she is telling the truth? She could be working for Griffin. Don't be so gullible Stavro!" Darvith did not like this young woman. She did not like her manner or the fact that she was deliberately trying to hurt Annwynn.

Morgana decided to try a different approach. She smiled and ignoring Darvith's accusations, she turned instead to Stavro. "You are obviously very fond of Rowena. I like her very much as well. She has a good heart and a brilliant mind. She was terribly injured, when she saved Annwynn's life, but I have healing techniques that can deal with the most difficult of cases." She then glanced over at Annwynn and said somewhat derisively, "I see you managed to escape unscathed."

Darvith interrupted in defense of Annwynn, "I'm sure Rowena is very brave but she was trained as a warrior. Annwynn had never held a knife in her hand before and yet managed to kill two of the guards herself. Now that's what I call bravery! One does not have to be bloodied to be brave." This was a direct reference to Morgana's last statement, which still rankled Darvith.

Stavro had been watching Morgana closely. He found her great beauty disturbing, although he couldn't imagine why he should. He had seen many beautiful young women. Perhaps it had something to do with her height for she could look directly into his eyes and her eyes were magnificent, they were almost hypnotic. No, it wasn't her eyes, there was something else about her that was very unsettling and unattractively so.

Stavro's glance then rested on his beloved Darvith's lovely face. He noticed that she too was studying Morgana but he could read nothing in her thoughts. It was obvious that Darvith didn't like her and that there was something about the young woman that bothered her as well.

In his mind he tried to make some sense of the way he felt about Darvith. His love for her became stronger with every passing day. She took his breath away. What was he to do? Every time he looked at her he felt an ache in his heart. She meant more to him than anyone he had ever known, even his family; and when he found her here and safe, he thought his heart would burst with happiness.

Morgana was thinking too; she was not overly impressed with Darvith or Annwynn. They were both very attractive in their own way but they were not beautiful. 'She' was beautiful and she knew it.

Morgana continued to study the group as they discussed Rowena and Bowdren and what they should do.

Arlen had wanted to wait for the agreed time and see Stavro at the pond. However, she had been able to convince him that the sooner Bowdren met with all of them, the sooner his memory would return.

Morgana had cleverly arranged her schedule so that nothing could prevent her from making this visit. She wanted to see Stavro for herself; she was not disappointed in any way by what she saw. He was just as she had imagined, tall and handsome.

Morgana turned her wondrous eyes toward Stavro and smiled. "I see you have made a decision and now have a suggestion."

Stavro returned her smile and replied, "We have decided that we should all go to Azoria. Once Annwynn has been made comfortable and we have had a chance to visit with Bowdren, Darvith and I will go on to Elgat where there is much to be done."

Morgana was very pleased. She would have been much less so, had she been reading Stavro's thoughts earlier, when he had been thinking of Darvith and of his great love for her. For as it stood now, Morgana didn't feel that Darvith would be serious competition.

She smiled winningly at the group and asked, "When would you like to leave, perhaps under the cover of darkness would be best. You are all shielded so it will be quite safe."

At just that moment the door opened and Angela entered the room. Morgana was momentarily caught off guard, as was Angela.

Angela blurted, "Who is she? Where did she come from? How did she get here?"

Darvith laughed lovingly at the child's obvious distress and offered teasingly, "She's not a fairy and that's for certain!" Thus referring to Darvith's first encounter with Angela, so long ago it now seemed.

Everyone laughed but Morgana, who failed to see any humor in the remark and was certain that they must all be laughing at 'her'. She was annoyed and instantly projected herself to the shelf that stood next to the open door where Angela was now standing.

Angela's eyes widened in startled surprise and she stammered, "How...how did you do that?"

The others too were amazed and began to question the clever and beautiful Azorite. She ignored them. They had been rude when they laughed at her. She would not acknowledge such disrespect.

Morgana ran her hand through Angela's silver hair and commented, "You have a very young face and body for one so old."

Once again everyone laughed and now Morgana was furious. She decided to erase her little trick and their disrespectful laughter from the memories of all those present and once more stood with the others.

Eventually it was decided that they would leave at dusk, when Stavro no longer had to worry about the rays of the sun damaging his skin. Angela would take them as far as the stone house and they would manage the rest of the distance on foot. The shielding would protect them.

Darvith, Annwynn and Stavro were very eager to have a closer look at the meadow and pond and excited about visiting an unknown Kingdom.

Angela was delighted to learn that there was a Kingdom called Azoria existing in the Earth realm and asked if she could visit with them one day.

Morgana replied somewhat coolly that she would have to discuss it with the others but it seemed most unlikely. Then she unexpectedly smiled. She had read Angela's mind and knew that the child planned to begin a search the very next day. She chided, "There is no use of your trying to find us. We are not visible to Earthlings unless we choose to be."

Morgana smiled and added, "It was different with the Hoptons. They were the couple that lived in the cottage before you. They weren't as other Earthlings. They could always see us when we were near and have been very helpful to Doran and Azora. We often visited the cottage when they lived here; I've been in this room many times."

She explained, "They would read to us here in their huge library. The stories were wonderful. They had hundreds and hundreds of leather bound books; there were many great masterpieces of literature. The days we spent here with them were unforgettable."

Angela wanted to hear more about the mysterious Hoptons but was distracted by a knock at the door. She ordered with urgency, "Quickly! Jump into the doll house and pretend you're dolls!"

Morgana was puzzled but behaved as the others and sat as still as she could on one of the kitchen chairs.

Sarah entered the room and smiled as she said, "Hi sweetheart! I'm going to town! Is there anything you need or would you like to come with me? You could visit with Eric?"

Her attention was drawn to the dollhouse and she exclaimed, "My word but your dolls are life-like! They are so much more attractive than anything I had to play with as a child! When did you buy the red-haired one? She is breathtaking!"

Sarah moved toward the dollhouse in an effort to look more closely at Morgana, but Angela cleverly blocked her way and said with some urgency, "Don't pick her up mom! She's broken!" Quickly adding, "Mugsy gave her to me. Don't you remember?"

It was a little white lie that Sarah easily believed. Angela felt very guilty. This was the first time she had ever lied to her mother and it had been so unnecessary because each of her visitors could have disappeared. Oh well! It was too late to change things now. She wouldn't do it again. She gave her mother a huge love-filled hug and said that she wanted to stay home. Sarah was soon on her way to town.

Morgana was very pleased that she had been singled out and thought of as being 'breathtaking'. She hoped Stavro heard the remark.

In actual fact, Stavro was completely unimpressed. He had used Angela's order to the occupants of the Dollhouse as an excuse to pull Darvith onto his lap on the chesterfield in the living room. A fact that Morgana was unaware of for Darvith had jumped up as soon as Sarah left the room.

At last dusk approached and it was nearing the time for them to leave for Azoria.

Sarah had returned from her visit to town and by the sound of the familiar tap tap of the typewriter keys; she was now back at work on her latest novel.

Angela carried her visitors downstairs in a small open box, but once out of sight of the house, the occupants requested that they be allowed to walk the rest of the way.

Darvith, Annwynn and Stavro were very grateful that the shielding allowed them to experience the Earthling's Realm in this new and thrilling way. This trek to the Stone House in daylight was a very exciting experience for them.

Once they reached the Stone House they thanked the little Earthling for all her help and Angela sadly watched as her visitors walked away and soon disappeared from her sight. She had no way of knowing that because of events that were soon to take place, several years would pass before she would see them again.

CHAPTER 28

The Grand Ball

The four walked around the pond and then turned off to the lower meadow. Morgana was leading the way and as she walked she sang. It was a wonderful haunting song. She was very happy. This was her Realm and the playground of her childhood and now she was sharing it with Stavro; he would soon fall in love with her and they would be very happy together. There was not a doubt in her mind.

Darvith too loved the Realm of the Earthlings and vowed to spend more time enjoying its beauty once Griffin and his followers had been taken care of. Griffin! Why had she allowed that evil creature to enter her mind? Darvith immediately dismissed him and once again allowed her thoughts to drift with the beautiful song Morgana was singing.

They were now approaching a huge pile of rocks interspersed with weeds and stinging nettles.

Morgana turned to them and smiled. She declared mischievously, "Well here we are! Azoria! Home!" Then she laughed uproariously. Now 'they' would learn how it felt to be left out of a joke.

Darvith, Annwynn and Stavro all stared at her, then at the uninviting pile of rocks and then back at her again. There faces filled with bewilderment.

As usual, Darvith was the first to speak. "Are you telling us that you live within those rocks; or are they some kind of shield?"

Stavro was now scowling and she didn't want him to be angry with her so she immediately explained, "Yes it is a shield of course." Then with a wave of her hand a beautiful village presented itself.

She turned to them and smiled charmingly at Stavro. "Please forgive my little joke. I couldn't resist showing you how our village appears to any outsider who might happen to visit this part of the meadow." She added, "Doran and Azora devised the shield and I can assure you that it presents an insurmountable barrier on many levels"

Again Morgana smiled and directed her conversation to Stavro. "I've no idea how they managed to find a land that was so beautiful and yet uninhabited. Mind you there apparently were some temples and houses standing when they first arrived but not a sign of life, as we know it. Doran and Azora can tell you more about the ancient structures. They used the stone from them for some of the buildings in our village."

She continued, "Of course there are many lovely creatures here, even some tiny duplicates of those that live with the Earthlings; and there are many similar plants."

The foursome walked up one of the charming cobbled streets as Morgana continued. "The village itself is modeled after the Hamlet where Adrian and Diana once lived, a far off village in a far off land. Thanks to them we had many photographs to use as reference so everything is authentic looking.

In fact Adrian supervised most of the construction. He is an engineer and Diana specializes in Interior

Design. They have been marvelous assets to our Kingdom and its development."

The group continued to follow Morgana up the village streets that were lined with shops containing everything from items of clothing, to dishes, to anything else a family might need, and all were charmingly displayed.

Darvith was delighted to see so many interesting looking young people everywhere. She was looking forward to both meeting them and engaging them in conversation.

They reached their destination and now stood before a cottage that was very like Angela's home. The garden was filled with blossoming trees that swayed in the gentle breeze. It was a lovely setting.

Morgana smiled and explained, "This is our guest house and your home for as long as you wish to stay with us." She was looking directly into Stavro's eyes as she spoke and then as an afterthought she quickly included the two young women.

Darvith failed to notice Morgana's interest in Stavro or the blush on her cheek whenever she spoke to him. She was too distracted by her new surroundings.

They were all very eager to visit with Bowdren and Rowena and asked if they might visit them now. Morgana agreed and immediately took them to the resting area where the pair had been staying the last few days. When they entered the room they were amazed to see Bowdren and Rowena seated at a table laughing and talking. They both looked fit and well.

As always, Bowdren's eyes danced with mischief. He called out, "Morgana! Well it's about time! Rowena and I were beginning to think that you'd lost interest in us, and just when we were running out of reading material."

Bowdren failed to notice Rowena run to Stavro's waiting arms. He had already turned to Annwynn and Darvith, "Oh good! You've brought some people for us to talk with. Are they your patients too?" There wasn't a hint of recognition in his eyes; but his heart raced when his eyes met Annwynn's. She was so lovely he couldn't take his eyes from her face.

Annwynn rushed over to him and put her arms around him; huge tears were welling up in her beautiful eyes.

Bowdren gazed down at her and murmured softly, "Please don't cry. I guess this means that I know all of you. Perhaps if we talk for a while I'll begin to remember something." He added, "Rowena has been trying to bring some of my memory back but there is nothing there." He added impatiently, "It's just so frustrating!"

Stavro was still in an animated conversation with Rowena and every once in a while he would give her an enormous hug. He was so glad to see that she had recovered from her terrible wounds; it was obvious to all who were present that they cared deeply for each other.

Annwynn joined them and held Rowena closely for a long moment. She said with great sincerity, "I can never hope to repay you for saving my life, but I want you to know if there is ever anything I can do for you, your wish is my command."

Rowena had wanted to dislike Annwynn but found it impossible. All of the resentment that had once filled her heart magically vanished as she warmly embraced her new friend.

Morgana had been studying them and reading their thoughts. She knew they would become good friends and this fact for some reason angered her.

However the deep resentment was quickly replaced by a calm acceptance and a realization that a 'best friend' would just get in her way and worse, rob her of her precious freedom. Friends require maintenance and she really didn't have the time, or to be perfectly honest, the inclination to furnish it.

Morgana continued to study the group as they engaged in conversations about what did, could, and would happen. She was trying to perfect her memory-scan technique as it related to groups of people. She found that she could easily break through the rather primitive blocks that this particular group had in place.

When she turned to scan Stavro thoughts it infuriated her to learn that he was thinking of Darvith in spite of the fact that he was deep in conversation with Rowena. Morgana momentarily lost her concentration and she felt her cheeks burn with rage.

As a distraction she forced herself to watch Annwynn with Bowdren. They were very in love. It was just a matter of time until Bowdren's memory returned. Their Aura's were perfectly melded when they stood together. Just like Doran with Azora.

Morgana was impatient for this meeting to end and suggested that it might be for the best if the patients were allowed to rest now. The group could visit with them again tomorrow.

Annwynn kissed Bowdren on the cheek before she left the room and their eyes held contact for a long moment, again his heart raced. She whispered tenderly, "Until tomorrow." And then left the room with the others.

Morgana accompanied them to the guesthouse and informed the group that there was to be a gathering held that evening to introduce the visitors to the Citizens of Azoria. Everyone was anxious to meet the strangers who were from Kingdoms previously unknown to the young Azorians.

Darvith could hardly contain her excitement; she felt like celebrating and there might be dancing!

Morgana informed the group that there would be suitable clothing for them to choose from in the upstairs closets.

As had been promised, Darvith and Annwynn were greeted with a lovely selection of Ball Gowns when they opened their closets. There were small containers attached to each clothes hanger and these containers held suitable jewelry, dancing slippers and purses to match each dress. The problem was that there were so many beautiful designs that Darvith and Annwynn found it difficult to make their choice. However, after much deliberation, each young woman made a final decision.

Annwynn chose a full-skirted dress with a dropped waist that was fashioned from a shimmering pink fabric overlaid with a silver design. A deep ruffle of the same fabric encircled the bottom of the gown. A large stand up lace collar and long sleeves completed the dress. Her beautiful jet-black hair was swept up and held in place by an exquisite Tiara. She looked enchanting and every inch, a Princess.

Darvith finally decided on a dress of sheer fabric with a floral overlay in silken thread. It was lined with a white shiny material beneath which lay enormous amounts of delicate netting. The sleeves of the dress were exquisitely puffed.

Both dresses had very full skirts, but where Annwynn's skirt was ruffled at the bottom, Darvith's was full and plain until it reached the floor then caught up at regular intervals by clusters of tiny flowers made from crystal and pearls. The tight fitting bodice of her dress was delicately trimmed with the same tiny crystal flowers Darvith's unruly hair was causing them some difficulty until Annwynn decided to sweep it up and fasten it at the crown with a clasp decorated with the same Crystal flowers that decorated her gown. This allowed the great masses of her golden curls to fall freely down her back.

The effect was charming and completely misleading. Darvith looked wonderfully sweet and vulnerable. They turned to each other and laughed uproariously!

Annwynn was still laughing as she wagged her finger at Darvith. "Now I want you to behave! Let's see if the girl can match the image even if it's just for tonight. Remember, you are among innocents."

Still smiling, Darvith walked over to the window. She could see the "Great Hall' where Morgana had said the celebration was to take place; soft golden light was already shining from its high-arched windows.

The Guesthouse where they were now staying rested at the very edge of the enormous tree-filled garden surrounding the massive structure. It was twice the size of the "Great Hall' in Trillan.

Darvith continued to watch as young men and women made their way along the many paths throughout the lovely gardens, perhaps they too should be on their way. She was about to mention this to Annwynn when there was a knock at the door.

Stavro called out to them and they bid him enter. He looked very handsome in a deep blue tunic trimmed with gold. His leggings and boots were in a deeper shade of the same blue.

Stavro found the sight of Darvith in the beautiful white dress returned a flood of bittersweet memories of their Oathing in the Stone House. But he knew in his heart that Darvith hadn't given the similarity a second thought when she dressed. She would have just considered it a perfect dress for the evening. He knew that for the moment she thought of him as a dear friend so he behaved accordingly and smiled warmly at the Princess' and told them of how lovely they looked.

Annwynn gazed lovingly at Stavro and Darvith. What a handsome couple they were, if only wishing could make it a real pairing.

Just then there was a light knock on their door. Stavro opened it and found Morgana to be on the other side. Again he felt the same strange uneasiness as their eyes met.

Morgana was the most beautiful, in the purely physical sense, of the three young women. And when she entered the room Darvith and Annwynn exclaimed an almost involuntary 'how lovely' for she presented an image of perfection.

Her gown was full and made from a sheer blue fabric splashed with an intricate design in silver. Her long hair was curled in a most becoming fashion and she wore jewels around her neck and in her hair that mirrored the startling color of her magnificent eyes. The effect was stunning.

Darvith and Annwynn both complimented her but Stavro remained silent. She was so obviously aware of her beauty that he saw no need to add to her confidence with a compliment.

They followed Morgana as she led the way out of the cottage and took one of the many paths to the hall.

The warm evening air was filled with the sweet combined scents emanating from the hundreds of flowering plants now blooming in the formal gardens.

A light breeze fluttered the leaves of the trees and caused the gaily-colored lanterns hanging from their lower branches to gently sway. It was a magical evening that they would never forget.

As the group drew closer to the hall, the sound of music and laughter filled the air. Darvith was alive with expectation and she wasn't to be disappointed, for the scene that greeted them once they passed through the front entrance, was one of great beauty and elegance.

The main ballroom was immense. A huge dance floor was at its center and surrounding it on three sides was a slightly higher floor where many tables glistening with china, were arranged.

The orchestra stood on a still slightly higher level at the very end of the huge room, and much to Darvith's delight, dance music was being played.

Balconies ran the full length of each of the side walls where still more guests sat. There were garlands of flowers looped all around the balcony area and these were combined at various sites with softly glowing crystal lights. The whole atmosphere was one of warmth and gaiety.

Morgana had entered the room first and introduced Darvith, Annwynn and Stavro to all who were present. She had taken hold of Stavro's hand, somewhat possessively he thought, when they first entered the room and he had shaken it off. He did not like clinging females! Nor did he want Darvith to get the wrong impression. He was in no way interested in Morgana.

As it happened Darvith hadn't noticed and it wouldn't have mattered to her if she had. She was caught up in the excitement of the evening and was already under its spell. The music thrilled her. It made her heart sing and her toes tap. She smiled inwardly and murmured softly, "These may be Elgans but they are playing Elgat music and performing Elgat Dances. I can join in! Oh please! Please! Please! Someone ask me to dance!"

Stavro was just about to do so when a young man he hadn't seen in time to cut off, asked her and swept her away.

They spun gracefully across the floor and when Darvith gazed up into the eyes of this young man she had the uncanny feeling that they had met before. But where she wondered? She quickly dismissed the idea. After all how could she possibly know him, all that mattered to her now was that he was a wonderful dancer; nothing else was of any importance to Darvith at this moment.

They were in each other's arms for ten consecutive dances, but neither seemed to notice the time. It wasn't until the music stopped and they could see that refreshments were being served that they realized how much time had passed. Darvith was enjoying the company of this young man and didn't feel the weight of Stavro's eyes as he watched them.

During the meal, Darvith and Arlen discussed everything that was of interest to them, jumping from one topic to another. Their conversation was frequently interrupted by gales of laughter. They were completely oblivious to anyone else. Darvith liked this young man. He was very interesting and best of all he made her laugh. She loved his wicked sense of humor. Her lovely laughter had frequently drifted over to where Annwynn, Morgana and Stavro were seated in the area just opposite.

Annwynn glanced at Stavro many times during the intermission and observed the sadness in his eyes as he watched the animated conversation taking place directly across from him. She noted that Morgana was watching Stavro with the same sadness in her eyes.

All evening Morgana had been refusing dances with the handsome young men who were continually asking her. She hadn't wanted to be unavailable on the chance that Stavro might ask her. She couldn't understand why he wasn't paying more attention to her? She was more beautiful, more intelligent and more gifted than any young woman in the hall! Why then was he ignoring her? Morgana was filled with frustration and anger. She followed his glance across the hall and saw Arlen with Darvith. For some reason Stavro's thoughts were blocked to her but there was no mistaking where they were focused. Darvith! What did he see in her?

Just as the dancing was to begin again, Azora walked over to where Darvith and Arlen were still deep in conversation. "Well Darvith." She confided happily, "I see you've finally met Arlen, the young man who rescued you and the others from the dangers of the pond."

Darvith clasped his hands with hers and exclaimed, "I knew I'd seen you somewhere before! She flushed a little when she remembered that he had seen a great deal more of her than she might have liked, but quickly recovered and asked, "Why didn't you stay and help me look for Annwynn?"

Arlen smiled as he replied, "But I did stay until dawn and when you decided to leave the pond area I gave you a shielding to protect you from the predators in the meadow. The truth is, Azora requested that I not make contact with any of you."

Then he looked up at Azora and held his hands over his head as if to deflect a blow and teased, "And we are all very frightened of Azora."

Azora laughed and hugged him. He was obviously a great favorite of hers.

Darvith smiled at both of them and said with great sincerity, "How wonderful it must have been to spend your childhood here, surrounded by so much love and warmth.

Impulsively she leant toward Arlen and tenderly kissed him on the lips. Then she gave him one of her most enchanting smiles and murmured, "Thank you Arlen, from the bottom of my heart. I hope one day I can come to your aid. I like to repay my debts."

Arlen was momentarily at a loss for words. The unexpected and very exciting reward had taken his breath away.

Stavro had seen enough. He left the table abruptly, strode over to where Darvith stood and asked her for a dance. It was not so much a request, as a command.

Darvith was very annoyed by his manner, but not wishing to make a scene, held her temper and allowed him to sweep her away in his arms. They did not speak for a long moment and when Darvith finally gazed up into his eyes, she could see anger and something else smoldering there. Jealousy! Stavro was jealous of Arlen and of his attention to her!

Now it was Darvith's turn to become angry. She declared sharply, "This simply will not do Stavro! It is not my wish to hurt you, but I will not have you behave as if you have some sort of hold on me! I am free! I do as I please and answer to no one, not even you!" Her anger was quickly spent and she smiled at him winningly.

Stavro answered it with a wry smile accompanied by a heartfelt apology. He knew in his heart that of course she was right. She did not and probably never would belong to him. He had behaved like an idiot and felt like a complete fool.

Within minutes they were deeply engrossed in a conversation about their departure the following morning.

While at any other time Darvith would have been more than happy to continue with talk of plans to overthrow Griffin, at this very moment all she wanted to do was dance and let the wonderful music fill her senses. She longed to be in Arlen's arms again and be free of everything but the sensation of dancing to beautiful music. She wanted to once again become lost in the hypnotic rhythms; it was just like escaping to another world, a wondrous world.

Annwynn was still sitting next to Morgana. She too had been refusing dances all evening, preferring to watch the magnificent spectacle. When Annwynn saw Darvith and Stavro dance across the floor, she said aloud, "Ah! That's better."

Morgana turned to Annwynn and demanded with an angry edge to her voice, "Why? Why is it better that she dances with Stavro than with Arlen? Is Arlen not good enough for her? Who is 'she' after all?" Morgana continued with her tirade, "She's just a Trillan and not a very pretty one at that! What is it that you think is so special about her? Why does anyone think she's special?"

Annwynn could hear the anguish in Morgana's voice, anguish and frustration. This was probably the first time in her life that she was unable to attract the young man she wanted, and it was obviously a very painful experience for her.

The Princess took Morgana's hand in hers and explained, "It's not that he's not good enough. I'm sure that Arlen is a wonderful young man, but many men find Darvith attractive and I can assure you that none of them mean anything to her. I doubt if they ever will."

Annwynn continued in a kindly tone, "You see she values her freedom above all else. I just don't want Arlen to be hurt. I doubt if he's ever met anyone like Darvith before and might very well lose his heart to her as so many have done before." She added, "Whereas Stavro knows that he hasn't a chance to win her, or at least he should know by now."

Morgana remained silent as Annwynn continued. "Do you know, I think that it's Darvith's attitude toward them that most men find so attractive. She doesn't bother to hide her contempt for men in general and they find it challenging. She thinks that men are quite capable of looking out for their own interests and have far too many advantages already, so why should she worry about their feelings."

Annwynn smiled reassuringly at Morgana and said, "I love Darvith very much. No one could ask for a better or more loyal friend. It's because I love her and know her so well that I can honestly say that she is not interested in Stavro as anything but a friend and would be very happy to learn of your love for him. She thinks of him as a brother. In fact she considers us the brother and sister she never had." Annwynn declared with great sincerity, "I know Darvith would not stand in your way if you should wish to pursue Stavro. She would be very happy for both of you."

Morgana was not convinced. It was easier to blame Darvith than to believe that 'she' was unattractive to Stavro. No! It was Darvith who was at fault! She was deliberately leading Stavro on and flirting with him at every opportunity.

Darvith was in heaven! It was magic! She had been rescued! Just as the music came to an end Arlen asked her to dance and quickly swept her away to the far end of the dance floor. Once again Stavro was taken by surprise.

Unknown to Darvith and Stavro, Arlen had been watching them very closely and had calculated every little swirl and spin. He waited at the very spot where they were sure to be when the music came to an end.

As so many others before him, Arlen found Darvith enchanting. She was an exotic little 'Golden' creature so unlike the maidens of Azoria. He could still feel the soft pressure of her lips on his, and his heart raced unreasonably with the memory of it. And now she was once again in his arms.

Arlen had a romantic, poetic nature and had kissed many lovely young women but never before had he felt such excitement or momentary loss of self. When she looked up into his eyes he longed to kiss her again and duplicate that delicious sensation.

Darvith had read his thoughts and smiled at him innocently while ticking off his name on her conquest list. Men were such fools to lose their objectivity to a pretty face. She smiled again as she began to tell him about her return to Elgat with Stavro. In other words warn him that she would not be staying in Azoria and not to become too attached to her.

Arlen felt an inexplicable ache in his heart when he realized that she would probably be lost to him forever in just a matter of hours. There and then he decided that he would accompany her party to Elgat whether they wanted him to or not. He must somehow make himself indispensable. Although just how he was going to accomplish this task was still a bit of a problem.

Arlen glanced over to where Morgana had been sitting all night waiting for Stavro to ask her to dance. Poor Morgana. What a pair they were! At just that moment he noticed the handsome Elgan walk toward her.

Morgana looked up to see Stavro standing before her and she flushed a beautiful pink and felt once again that her heart might stop beating. She silently scolded herself. And then as if by magic she was in his arms, exactly where she had longed to be all evening. Her heart soared!

They danced the rest of the night together. Stavro found that Morgana could be quite charming company and was surprised to discover that they had a great many interests in common. Not quite as many as he was led to believe however, for Morgana had the advantage of the information she had gleaned from his brother Bowdren's memory. She had made a point of learning everything she could about Stavro right from Bowdren's earliest memory of him. The more she learned of him the more she loved him. She thought Darvith was a fool not to return the love of such a man.

The celebration of welcome ended at midnight and soon everyone began to leave for home and bed.

Arlen and Darvith had danced the remainder of the evening together and were deep in conversation when Stavro and Morgana joined them.

Arlen decided to seize the moment to ask if Darvith and Stavro would consider taking the two of them on their trek back to Elgat, stressing their obvious usefulness to the pair in the Earth Realm.

Darvith and Stavro looked at each other for a moment and as usual their thoughts were identical. They agreed that that the young Azorites could accompany them to the entrance of Elgat but that it was far too dangerous to take them into the Kingdom.

Morgana and Arlen were each convinced that there would be enough time during the journey to Elgat's border to change the minds of the Elgan and Trillan. They were both determined to visit Elgat.

Darvith thanked Arlen for all the dances then yawned sleepily and said it was time she went to her bed. Everyone agreed that they would all rest for a few hours and then meet at the Guesthouse.

Stavro offered to walk Morgana to her door. It was a lovely evening for a walk but most of it was spent in silence for their conversation had been exhausted. After a gentle kiss Stavro was soon on his way. It had meant nothing to him.

The kiss was far more meaningful to Morgana. It had caused her heart to pound and her knees to feel weak; it was everything she had hoped for, the perfect ending to a perfect evening. She was confident that he would soon be hers.

CHAPTER 29

Vanished from Sight

A few hours later at the Guesthouse Darvith was awakened by Stavro's knock at her door. Although the sky was barely light, it was time to begin their journey to Elgat. He informed her that Arlen and Morgana were already waiting for them downstairs. Stavro laughed wickedly and said, "I Think they were afraid we were going to leave without them." Then as one thought they added in unison, "And we did give it some serious thought!" They both laughed uproariously!

Darvith was sitting in bed with her golden hair loose and tumbling all about her bare shoulders. She looked adorable.

Stavro felt the same ache in his heart that he always felt at the mere sight of her. He silently chastised himself. I'd better get out of here before I make a fool of myself! With that thought in mind, he grabbed Darvith's travel clothing from the chair where it lay scattered, threw it at her, and advised her to hurry.

Just as he joined the others, Doran and Azora rushed in. Doran was the first to speak and declared, "I'm so glad that we've caught you in time. Your mother and her followers have overthrown Griffin! Both Trillan and Elgat are calling for his immediate execution for treason." Doran paused then continued, "Unfortunately one of Theda's followers proved to be an informant and warned Griffin so he was able to escape. No one knows where he is or of how many of his followers are still with him and worse, he still has the Discs"

Stavro asked, "Is my mother safe?"

Doran nodded his head. "She received a minor wound in the struggle but is recovering. All of the wounded have been taken to the Institute."

Azora interrupted, "She has no idea that her sons are still alive. All of Elgat thinks that Bowdren was executed for treason and kidnapping and that you were lost in a mysterious hunting accident. We were unable to get the news of your safety to her."

Darvith now joined them. She had heard most of the news and asked, "Are you not frightened that Griffin will find a way into Azoria?" She added, "He will be twice as dangerous now that he has all of the discs. Indeed he may have followed you, Doran to where you are standing this very minute." She felt an icy chill invade her body.

Doran smiled at her reassuringly and shook his head. "It would be impossible for Griffin to enter our land. It was built to repel all intruders who haven't the key. I can assure you that no Trillan, Elgat or Elgan can enter Azoria without the aid of an Azorite, and we have no traitors here."

The others continued to discuss the uprising in Elgat while Darvith found herself wondering if Griffin had ever visited this land. A sudden thought entered her mind from out of nowhere. What if this was a Kingdom once, a Kingdom called Aleesha? Griffin had said she was a daughter of Aleesha. What if she was taken from 'this' land when she was still a baby? He visited the Kingdom of Elgat freely, might he not also have visited other Kingdoms?

Morgana said the land was empty when Azora and Doran found it except for some temples. She decided to ask about them." She turned to Azora and Doran; "Morgana mentioned that there were some temples on this land when you discovered it. Could you tell me something...anything about them?"

Stavro frowned and said impatiently, "What are you getting at Darvith? We have much more important things to worry about than temples!"

Darvith put her hand on his shoulder and explained, "This will just take a minute Stavro. Be patient!"

Doran offered, "Well as a matter of fact there were some stone structures, but they weren't suitable for our needs, so we dismantled them and used the stone for many of our present day buildings." He continued, "Our 'Great Hall' now sits where the largest group of them stood. I thought it must be a sort of temple complex."

Azora added, "Most of the structures that surrounded the main building consisted of pillars with domes and all of them were studded with brilliant blue stones. It was a beautiful sight to behold and covered an immense area. We've kept all of the blue stones but haven't been able to find where they were mined." She added, Years ago I made some sketches of the temple and surrounding complex. I'll search for them and show them to you when you return."

Darvith smiled and said, "That would be wonderful. Thank you. I'll explain why I'm so interested when we return."

Azora looked at Darvith and then turned to Doran and said, "Doesn't she look like the young women in the murals?" He agreed.

She turned back to Darvith and explained. "The interior walls of all the buildings were decorated with beautiful murals some of which depicted what we imagined were fair-haired goddesses. Most of them were dancing, some were playing stringed instruments and others had their mouths open as if they were singing. They were enchanting to look at and it's unfortunate that we were unable to save them all."

Doran broke in, "The oddest thing, as far as I'm concerned was the complete absence of any males, not 'one' was shown in any of the murals." Azora has done some beautiful sketches of the murals that we couldn't save." Then he smiled at Darvith and commented, "You know, Azora's right. You do look very like the golden women in the murals."

Morgana had heard enough. So now they want to make Darvith a Goddess! From her earliest memory Morgana had called the beautiful golden creatures in the murals Goddesses. In her mind Darvith looked nothing like her 'Golden Goddesses', nothing at all like them! She took hold of Stavro's hand and said with some impatience, "Hadn't we better leave!"

Stavro unceremoniously shook his hand free and motioned to Darvith and Arlen that it was time to be on their way.

During the trek it had been decided that as Griffin was no longer in Elgat, Morgana and Arlen should visit the beautiful Kingdom.

When they arrived they could see signs of battle everywhere. Darvith and Stavro were saddened by all the destruction about them but at the same time they were grateful that Elgat still had its wondrous light and thankful that Griffin was no longer in control.

Arlen and Morgana were both enchanted by all that they saw; it was such a beautiful Kingdom! Both of the Azorites attracted attention, but Morgana drew most of the interest. The Elgats had never seen anyone like her and she enjoyed every moment of the attention she was being given.

Stavro's first duty was to stop at the Command Center to receive a briefing and take charge of the situation.

General Ulvang had been doing a splendid job in his absence but was nonetheless very happy to see Stavro once again and quickly allowed him to take charge. There was something in his manner that disturbed Stavro. They had been good friends for many years and Stavro could sense that something was in the air, something was not quite right.

Ulvang was also an Elgan who had infiltrated and worked his way up through the guards. This shared secret had formed a strong bond between them. He was a ruggedly handsome young man who was a good deal taller than Stavro. In fact he was one of the tallest men in Elgat and had a regal bearing.

Like Stavro, Ulvang had never Oathed and now he was very grateful that he hadn't for he had just met the young woman of his dreams. He found that she filled his thoughts since their first meeting. He thought she was stunning; he even loved her name. "Morgana." He said softly and tenderly as if she were in his arms.

At just that moment Stavro entered the room. He smiled at Ulvang knowingly and thought, better you than me, but said nothing. Stavro was now satisfied that all the affairs of Elgat had been taken care of successfully and all regions were stabilized.

It was time to visit with his mother at the Institute. The fact that she was recuperating there and not in a proper facility with all of the other wounded troubled him. He intended to move her just as soon as possible. It had been Ulvang who had placed her there supposedly for her own safety. This surprised him for there were many institutes of medicine in Elgat that would have been more appropriate and just as safe. The whole set-up was strange.

Darvith, Morgana and Arlen now joined him. They had just returned from the Palace. Morgana and Arlen were very impressed with the structure and Darvith had enjoyed showing it to them.

Arlen had just told the girls a funny story and they were all laughing as Ulvang entered the room. He strode over and greeted them all but it was obvious that Morgana was the one he wanted to talk to, and he immediately engaged her in conversation.

Arlen was grateful for he wanted to have a private moment with Darvith. There was to be a gathering that evening and he intended to ask her to attend it with him. There would be music and dancing so he felt certain that she would agree. Ulvang was extending the same invitation to Morgana and both young women accepted.

Soon they were on their way to the Institute.

Theda was overjoyed to see Stavro and learn that Bowdren too was safe and well. She hugged Stavro, kissed him and then hugged him again. It was as if she wanted to make certain that she wasn't just dreaming.

Finally Stavro gently pulled away and asked, "Does anyone have any current information as to Griffin's whereabouts? Was he wounded or hurt in any way?"

Theda shook her head sadly. "No, unfortunately he wasn't wounded." She added, "Of course he will be executed if he is ever found now that his terrible plan is known to all. As a matter of fact, the Trillan and Elgat Elders are meeting on this very day to discuss the manner of his execution."

She added ruefully, "Only one of the Elgan Elders was a follower of Griffin while pretending to be with us. She was the one who warned him and took the Discs from the palace where Annwynn had hidden them."

Stavro lifted his chin and said, "Arella?"

Theda nodded her head and echoed, "Arella."

Stavro introduced the others to his mother and she greeted them all warmly and told them that she hoped they would enjoy their stay in Elgat.

She then turned to Darvith and smiled approvingly. "I've looked forward to meeting you my dear. Both of my sons think that you are very special, and as I've never known them to agree on anything before, I suspect that you must be very special indeed."

Once again Morgana felt anger and resentment well up inside of her but managed a smile. Soon it would be she who would gain praise from Stavro's mother. It was just a matter of time.

Darvith smiled and said a simple thank you, then added, "Both of your sons are very special to me; I suppose they are the brothers I've always longed for."

Theda was touched by the sincerity of Darvith's last words and reached out to take her hand when, just as she moved forward, Darvith vanished!

Everyone in the room gasped in shock!

Stavro shouted an agonized, heart rending, "DARVITH!" But there was no reply. Darvith was gone.

CHAPTER 30

Darvith's Worst Nightmare

It had been easy...so very easy. Now at last Darvith was where she belonged. Griffin had plucked her out of that room as easily as if she had been a tiny flower in a Trillan meadow.

Trillan and Elgat were lost to him but it didn't matter. There was time, endless time on his side. He and his followers would build a new Kingdom in the meadow near the pond. Now his power was almost absolute and Darvith was here with him. This would be a wonderful new beginning for both of them.

Darvith had no idea as to where she was or how she had arrived for that matter. The last thing she remembered was visiting with Stavro's mother in the Institute. What could have happened? Then the obvious answer, she was Griffin's prisoner. She should have realized that the Institute wasn't a safe place for her to enter! What had she been thinking? She had been a fool and now she must pay the price!

Darvith took a deep breath and murmured softly, "For every great problem there is usually a solution. I will find one. I must find one!" She began to explore her surroundings. It seemed she was in a spacious and exquisitely decorated room. There were no doors and instead of windows, vast areas of the walls were covered with beautiful scenes that were slowly yet constantly changing. She was in an elaborate prison. Her heart sank and she sighed deeply.

Griffin had been studying her actions from the next room and decided that she was ready to see him. He suddenly appeared before her.

Darvith was startled but rather than call out or even speak she decided to remain silent and see if his new powers had changed his personality in any way.

Griffin smiled as he took her hands in his, and said softly, "My darling Darvith, today you will become my Life-Mate."

Darvith was horrified but felt powerless to say or do anything but stand motionless before him. It was her worst nightmare! Then still holding her hands in his, he looked deeply into her eyes as she answered an involuntary, "Yes."

It was as if someone else had said it. Tears began to form in her beautiful eyes and one of them traced its way down her cheek. Griffin gently brushed it away and then kissed her tenderly. It was as if she had no will at all. Now others began to enter the room. Stavro would have recognized four of his guards and the Elder Arella. They were all complete strangers to Darvith.

Arella was holding a beautiful dress in her arms and led Darvith into an area hidden from the others by a screen. Darvith was filled with a terrible panic. I must wake up! This is just a terrible nightmare! I must wake up! But even as her brain screamed out commands, she allowed herself to be dressed by Arella, just as if she were in a trance.

Then Arella took her by the hand and led her to Griffin. He smiled lovingly at her as he held her hand.

They repeated the Ancient Oaths in front of the witnesses and Elder Arella performed the beautiful Ceremony. To any outsider, the event would have seemed a joyous one between two very attractive young people. Indeed they might have believed that the tears tracing their way down Darvith's cheeks were tears of joy.

Meanwhile, in Elgat, an inconsolable Stavro was carrying on with the last of his responsibilities. Now that daily life was more or less back to normal in the Elgat Kingdoms, he planned to take an extended leave in order to search the Earth Realm for Griffin and Darvith. The searches in Elgat and Trillan had been extensive and provided no clues as to where Griffin was now living therefore the Earth Realm was the next logical place to look.

General Ulvang would be in charge during his absence. He had proven his worth during a time of great crisis. Stavro had great confidence in his ability to handle things well.

Stavro had hoped to carry out the search on his own or with Bowdren but Morgana and Arlen convinced him that they would be of enormous help to him and he finally agreed.

Morgana had been seeing a great deal of Ulvang and had to admit to herself that she did enjoy his company. She also enjoyed the power she seemed to have over this very influential General. She knew he would do anything for her. While his kiss did not thrill her as Stavro's had, he was pleasant to kiss, and it was a nice change to be with a man so much taller than she was. Everyone noticed them wherever they went and she loved the attention.

In spite of Ulvang's obvious infatuation, she was still determined to win the love of Stavro and this was why she insisted on aiding him in his search for Griffin and Darvith. She didn't believe for one minute that they would find them but she wanted to be there to console

Stavro when he finally accepted the fact that he would never see Darvith again.

It had been decided that they should visit Azoria before they began the search and give everyone the latest news on all that had taken place in Elgat. Stavro was also hoping that Bowdren would be well enough to help.

The Group did not speak during their trek from Elgat to Azoria. All were lost in their own private thoughts. When they entered the Kingdom three anxious friends who were full of questions greeted them.

Bowdren was the first to speak, "How's mother? Tell us all that has taken place in Elgat?" He gave Stavro an enormous hug and continued, "We have had no news at all and it has been driving us crazy!"

Stavro smiled sadly as he replied, "Well brother, I'm glad to see that your memory has returned. At least we have something to be thankful for." Stavro then told them of Darvith disappearance.

There was a shocked silence. Then Rowena asked, "Where were you when this happened?"

Stavro answered, "With the wounded in the Institute. Why?"

Rowena was silent for a moment then shook her head in disbelief. "I'm afraid that Griffin may have used a devise that I had only begun to experiment with. It was a type of transporter." She added in a hushed tone, "I only used inanimate objects like tables and chairs, and I could more or less move them from room to room but I would never have dared to use a living creature!" Rowena sighed deeply, "If Darvith was able to make the transfer she may be altered in some way."

Stavro's face grew red with rage! He shouted angrily, "Altered? Altered? What do you mean by altered?"

Bowdren put his hand on his brother's shoulder, "Stavro, your anger will not help Darvith. We must try to be calm and logical." Then he added with a wry smile, "Take it from one who knows from first hand experience,

Darvith is at her very best during a crisis. The more desperate the situation the more intelligent and shrewd she becomes. If anyone can outsmart Griffin it will be Darvith."

Stavro reluctantly agreed then he put his hand on his brother's shoulder and said, "Arlen and Morgana are going to help me with the search. I would like you to join us if you feel up to it."

Bowdren nodded his head and then explained to the two young women who were to stay behind that the group would return to Azoria as soon as possible.

After a tearful farewell, the group left for the meadow early the next morning. The weather was perfect and thanks to Arlen they were all shielded.

It had been agreed that they would remain visible in the hope that Darvith might see them and somehow be able to make contact. Griffin would have been able to see them anyway so nothing was lost.

CHAPTER 31

The Search

Many long weeks were spent in their search. The quest seemed more hopeless with each passing day and all but Morgana were filled with a sense of utter frustration.

Morgana tried to hide her growing elation. She had never been so happy for she was exactly where she wanted to be. With each passing day she grew to love Stavro more. It didn't matter that he rarely spoke to her and seemed indifferent to her presence. One day soon he would love her and her alone. She was certain that Darvith would never be found, not if Griffin was as clever as everyone seemed to think. Yes, One day soon, Stavro would belong to her and she could wait; he was worth waiting for.

Morgana continued with her daydreams. She smiled when she reflected on all the attention she had received in Elgat, far more than Darvith. It was she, Morgana who was the most beautiful and the most talented. She would move to Elgat and join their Institute and thrill them with her genius. She would become so famous that Stavro could no longer resist her. She smiled dreamily and sighed.

A troubled Arlen had been watching Morgana these last weeks. He approached her and sat down, pulling her toward him in a brotherly hug he murmured softly, "Wishing will not make it happen dear friend and in the end it might do you a great deal of harm. Please give up these unproductive thoughts before they injure you. Stavro will never love you and in your deepest heart you know that I am speaking the truth."

Morgana blushed red with rage and stood up. "How dare you invade my private thoughts! Don't you dare to do it again or I promise, my thoughts will injure you! Stavro will fall in love with me! He will! We belong together!" With that said, she angrily strode away.

Endless weeks had now passed into months. It was near to the end June and they were running out of time.

Stavro must return to Elgat by July.

Today they had decided to search the area between the pond and the Stone House. As they moved into a thicket of tall grasses, Arlen murmured, softly, "Ahhhhhh…We have found the 'Evil One's' lair."

The others saw nothing and turned to Arlen in disbelief then Stavro scowled and demanded impatiently, "Tell us what you see!"

Arlen shook his head in bewilderment. "It's gone! It was there a moment ago but now it's gone!" He quickly explained while stepping forward, "It's not invisible; it's just no longer there! Amazing!"

All at once Darvith stood before them. She walked over to where Stavro stood and held him close for a long moment. When she gazed up at him, her eyes were filled with great tenderness and she murmured, "My dear, dear friend. You have no idea of just how wonderful it is to see you again." She kissed him tenderly on the lips then once again held him close.

Morgana felt her heart contract with excruciating pain and her eyes flooded with tears when she saw the love that showed in Stavro's Aura when Darvith held him and kissed him. It was a love she now knew would never be directed toward her. At that moment she began to hate Darvith.

Arlen had been watching Morgana and now walked over and took her by the hand. It broke his heart to see his friend suffer this way and put an arm around her shoulders in comfort.

Stavro and Bowdren were now telling Darvith of how long they had been searching for her and how wonderful it was to see her again. There were still more hugs and kisses.

From the first breathtaking sight of Darvith, Stavro noticed an added dimension to her appearance. She was lovely before but now she had a special quality; it was an exquisite beauty that was beyond compare.

Morgana had noticed it too and it filled her with despair. Now she was no longer the most beautiful of them all.

Darvith knelt down in the tall grasses and lifted two adorable babies from the safety of their covered resting place. She smiled enchantingly and said softly, "I am not alone." She held one in each arm. They both had curly golden hair and bright green eyes. Darvith read the thoughts of the group before her and declared lovingly, "Yes. They are mine."

An amazed Stavro and Bowdren uttered, "Two?" at exactly the same moment.

Darvith laughed softly and nodded. She explained, "It seems that the 'Daughters of Aleesha' frequently present twins." Her eyes were soft and filled with love as she gazed down at the tiny creatures in her arms. Then she looked up at the group and announced, "I'd like to introduce you to my twins, a girl that I have named Angela in honor of our little Earthling friend who has been such a help to us; and a boy I have named Rowan simply because it's a name that I've always liked."

Darvith's face shone with happiness as she continued. "I have always loved children, but because of my resolve to remain free, I had given no thought to having any of my own. I consider my twins to be a wondrous gift in spite of Griffin's involvement with their presentation."

Darvith's voice was filled with conviction and power as she continued, "I will teach them to be strong and brave, to seek truth and justice for all and to have great compassion for their fellow creatures."

Darvith's lovely face reflected deeper thoughts that she would not share, at least not yet. She continued, "You would have been amazed to have seen the love and great tenderness that Griffin lavished on his children. I would never have believed he was capable of such genuine, heartfelt emotions if I hadn't seen them displayed with my own eyes." She added with a chilling smile, "Losing his children forever will be an appropriate and just punishment; he did after all 'steal' them from me. They will have no memory of him. I will explain that their father died in battle." Darvith had walked through fire; she had survived and she was stronger than before.

Stavro rushed over to where Darvith stood and took the babies into his strong arms. They smiled up at him as he pressed them gently to his chest and kissed each twin on the forehead.

Once again Morgana's heart contracted in pain and her beautiful eyes stung with still more bitter tears. The tenderness Stavro was showing the children of an enemy, just because Darvith was the mother, filled her with rage. She began to tremble uncontrollably and felt that she must get away! Then a second thought occurred to her; all was not yet lost. After all, this was just Stavro's first reaction to Darvith and the babies. Morgana was certain that he would see things differently tomorrow. He must!

Surely he would not want Darvith when she brought with her, Griffin's Children.

As the group made their way to Azoria, Stavro turned to Darvith and asked, "If you're up to it, why don't you tell us more about what has taken place since we last saw you?"

Darvith laughed her lovely laugh and declared, "How very tactful of you Stavro!" Then she flashed a triumphant smiled and exclaimed, "Of course I feel up to it! Why ever wouldn't I! I am free! I have my beautiful babies! I have beaten my enemy and given him an excruciatingly painful punishment that he must live with daily!"

She laughed again, this time exultantly. Then she began to relate all that had taken place. "Within minutes of my disappearance from Elgat, I was Griffin's Life-Mate. An Elder named Arella officiated and there were Elgan guards as witnesses. At that time Griffin had a strange and absolute power over me. It was my worst nightmare."

She shivered at the remembrance and then continued, "Griffin was unexpectedly kind to me, even loving and tender but I found this new behavior in a strange way even more menacing. It's hard to explain because I seemed to have no will of my own; I felt like I was watching all that was taking place from a distance. Escape would have been easy but I was somehow compelled to stay. I might just as well have been in chains."

Again her countenance became unreadable as she continued, "When the twins were presented, they became his life. He absolutely adored them and played with them endlessly. The more he loved 'them' the stronger I became, until finally his power over me ceased to be, and all of my strength of will returned."

Darvith frowned and quickly added, "Of course I didn't allow him to learn of this in any way, not in thought or deed. I made good use of my time and managed to locate all of the exits and obtain copies of important keys. And of course I was always on a continual search for the Elgat Discs; those oh so very elusive Discs!" She sighed deeply and continued. "Eventually I discovered that they were built into the structure where we now lived; we were in a kind of travel machine. Griffin referred to it as his 'Ship' and I suppose it was in a way; he was certainly the only one who could direct and control the energy the Discs produced."

Darvith smiled and added, "I believe the reason my sense of self returned was because at least half of his energy was now directed toward his children." She lifted an eyebrow and remarked, "A nice touch of irony don't you think? An emotion he seemed incapable of liberated that which he most desired."

Darvith's eyes shone with victory as she continued, "When you entered the range of his detection system, he decided to accelerate to a different position in the meadow. As he proceeded in his work, I swiftly made my way to an exit with Angela and Rowan safely in my arms. Then thankfully, Griffin and the others vanished and my babies and I remained here with you."

As if on cue, the twins looked up at Stavro and smiled. He gazed down at them and laughed softly, "Yes! It was a good joke on Griffin wasn't it?" He laughed again and this time Darvith joyfully joined in.

As he gazed down at her his eyes were filled with wonder. Any other young woman he knew would have been devastated by what had taken place, but not Darvith. She had escaped intact and if possible, stronger than ever.

The Oathing Ceremony she had experienced with Griffin could not bind her in Elgat, or in Trillan. And now with children to care for, might she not consider becoming his Life-Mate?

When they entered the safety of Azoria, Stavro's heart was full. All his old hopes and dreams once again filled his thoughts.

CHAPTER 32

Griffin's Just Reward

Weeks had passed and Griffin had spent this particular morning watching two young Earthlings playing in the meadow.

Angela was very happy! The summer holidays had arrived and the weather was perfect but best of all Mugsy was with her now and would be staying for the whole month of July. They had been playing in the meadow all morning quite unaware that green malevolent eyes were observing their every move.

Angela gazed at her friend with great affection. How she had missed her! They had first met in Kindergarten.

Their teacher Miss Plum had decided to group the whole class into pairs. On that first day Angela's vivid imagination had transformed Mugsy, with her beautiful tawny skin and enormous up tilted dark eyes, into a young Royal from an exotic land. And before Miss Plum had a chance to pair her with someone else, Angela quickly reached for the hand of the Princess. From that day onward they were almost inseparable.

Mugsy had been spellbound on this warm summer day as Angela told her of all of the adventures she had experienced in this very meadow. From her first meeting with Darvith to their last goodbye when Darvith, Stavro, Annwynn and Morgana had left for the Kingdom of Azoria.

Mugsy wanted to hear more and so did Griffin. He had never heard of the Kingdom of Azoria or of any creature named Morgana. He listened intently to every detail.

Griffin was alone and for the first time in his long life, he felt lonely. This angered him and filled him with a dreadful, all consuming rage. Darvith had tricked him and soon she would pay with her life. But the thought of ending her life did not bring him pleasure. Instead it made him feel even lonelier. He knew her death would not ease this terrible loneliness; it would only add to it. For in truth had grown to enjoy her companionship, and to appreciate her brilliance during their many long discussions. He had even confided in her and told her of things that were important to him; he had shared his most private thoughts. Each day had brought her closer to his heart.

Griffin sighed deeply as his thoughts drifted to a remembrance of Darvith lovingly playing with their twins. It was an image that burned into his brain. He shouted in anger, "Even then she was planning her betrayal!" But his heart still felt the pain. Nothing seemed to ease the pain; it was a new and terrible experience for him. He murmured softly but with great conviction, "I will learn more of this new Kingdom. Tomorrow I will send some of my Elgans on a search of the meadow."

Griffin again sighed deeply as he slumped into his chair. All of his accomplishments seemed meaningless to him now. He must have them back! He will have them back!

Sheilah Rogers

ABOUT THE AUTHOR

Sheilah Rogers was born in a mountain village in British Columbia. Her early childhood was a solitary one, where she relied on her imagination for much of her entertainment. All of this changed when her family moved to the city where she pursued degrees in Archaeology. Married, she has traveled extensively, living at one time, for 5 years in Africa. Her interest in folklore and ancient civilizations has given keen insight into the beliefs and superstitions of all races. This insight, together with her imagination from earlier years, has given her a wealth of material to draw upon for her stories. Sheilah is also a successful commercial artist, with works in private collections, throughout the world.

Printed in the United States
39701LVS00003B/62